A LIFE WITH NO REGRETS

Fairhope, Book 5

SARRA CANNON

Dead River Books

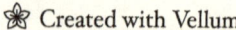

For Paul

*One of the greatest men I have ever known. Even in the face of ALS,
your light continues to shine. It is a light that will live on long after
you have passed from this earth and into God's loving arms.
We will know it by the lasting work of your hands, and we will
recognize it in the hearts of all those whose lives you have touched.
I hope you know how much you've touched mine.
With love for you and Linda. Always.*

CHAPTER 1
JO

I wipe the back of my hand across my forehead and take a deep breath. I've been lost in the bar's rhythm for the past couple hours, but now that I take a second to step back and really look around, I realize just how packed the place is tonight. We're already out of glasses and have resorted to using an old stash of plastic cups from the storeroom. I've had to send Knox to the back twice to grab more longnecks.

"Hey, can I get three Coronas and a vodka cranberry?"

A young, blond guy who looks like he just stepped off the beach leans forward and flashes a smile. I double-check that he's wearing a wrist-band and nod.

I reach into the cooler and grab three Coronas, pop them open with record speed, and shove a slice of lime into the top. I sink a plastic cup into the ice and tilt the vodka bottle up for a three-count.

"Twenty-two," I say as I top it off with cranberry juice from the gun and another slice of lime. Damn, we're about to run out of those two, and I don't have time to slice more. We seriously underestimated the crowd tonight.

Blondie holds out a credit card, but when I go to take it he won't let go. I pull again, confused, but when I look up, I see that familiar look in his eyes. He wants to flirt.

I sigh. I so do not have time for this.

"Want to start a tab?" I ask.

"What I really want is to find out what time you get off work tonight," he says.

I raise an eyebrow in warning, and he finally lets go of the card. I slip it into the cardholder under B for Blondie.

I look to the woman next in line, hoping he'll just let it go at that.

"Two BudLight Limes," she says.

"I'm serious," Blondie says as I reach into the cooler again. Apparently not getting the message. "Let's hang out. We could have some fun."

"Is that right?" I ask, not stopping for a second. I hand the girl her beers. "Ten bucks."

She hands me a ten and tosses three dollars into the tip jar.

"Thanks," I say and flash her a smile.

I try to remember who was next in line and turn to an older guy standing at the end of the bar.

"What can I get for you?"

Before the guy can answer, Blondie slides in front of him. "Hey, listen baby, there's no need to play hard to get," he says. "I'm already interested."

I take a deep breath. Why do guys think this is attractive?

"I hate to crush your school-boy dreams, but I'm not

playing hard to get," I say. I look him straight in the eye and lean over the top of the bar, making sure he hears me. "I'm the one who's not interested. Not today. Not ever."

A few people standing around us make rude noises and begin to cheer. Blondie narrows his eyes at me and gathers his drinks from the top of the bar.

"Bitch," he mutters under his breath. He turns away so fast he bumps into an even bigger guy behind him and nearly spills the cranberry. I try to hide my laugh, but it sneaks out anyway.

"Didn't your daddy ever teach you not to scare the customers?"

Behind me, Colton's warm breath sails across my cheek and his body presses against my back as he reaches around me to grab a fresh stack of cups. Goosebumps break out all over my arms, and I shiver.

We've been working together behind the bar for a few months now, but from day one he's always known just how to get under my skin. It makes me want to punch him in the face.

Or jump his bones.

I'm not sure which one just yet.

"Didn't your momma ever teach you how to actually work for a living?" I turn around to face him, which is a big mistake. He doesn't back away and now I'm close enough to smell his cologne. "Because last time I checked, you were stationed at the other end of the bar."

He lifts his hands in mock-surrender and takes a tiny step backward. "Whatever you say, Boss," he says. "I just needed some more cups, and I couldn't help but overhear you berating the customers. Hey, if you don't feel like serving

3

people tonight, send 'em my way. I could always use the extra money."

Our eyes meet for a brief instant and my stomach flips in this way I haven't felt in years. My gaze drops to his lips and something inside me ignites. Colton has this way of smiling with only one side of his mouth that absolutely destroys my concentration.

"You're not going to be serving many customers while you're standing here bothering me, so maybe you should get back to your side of the bar," I say.

"What? Are my disarming good looks distracting you?"

He winks and saunters away, leaving me a little weak in the knees. I blow out a breath and steady myself against the bar.

I want to hate him, but there's something about him that turns me completely upside down. He's the exact opposite of the kind of guy I need in my life, but there's no way to get around the fact that we work together four or five nights a week.

He's hot, but he's dangerous. I, of all people, should know better than to start something with a guy like him.

My father comes in from the back office and works his way behind the bar, mercifully giving me something else to think about. He puts his hand on my arm, his eyes widening at the size of the crowd already gathered in his bar.

"Did you expect it to be this busy tonight?" he asks.

"I was hoping, but didn't dream it would be this big," I say. I don't stop taking orders and working. From the looks of it, we've almost gotten control of this crowd. At least until everyone gets thirsty again.

"What time does the band go on?" he asks, glancing at the gold watch he's worn ever since I can remember.

"Nine," I say.

"That's still half an hour away."

He smiles like a kid in a candy store, making him look about twenty years younger in an instant. Pride shines in his eyes, and it sends a warm sense of satisfaction through me.

We did it, I want to tell him. *We turned this place around.*

A couple years ago, my dad was worried the whole place was going to go belly-up. He'd taken out a second mortgage on the house just to keep this place running, but we'd been scared, even if we didn't like to say it out loud. When my cousin Knox had come home, that had changed everything.

He'd loaned us enough money to get back on our feet, agreed to work here at the bar for next to nothing, and helped me start brainstorming ways to promote new business. The way things were looking now, we might actually be able to pay him back soon.

I glance over at Knox working the middle section of the bar, and he winks. I remind myself to tell him again how much I appreciate everything he's done for Daddy and me over the past couple years.

But now is not the time. After the night is over, I'll pour us a couple shots and celebrate a job well done, but right now, the name of the game is churn and burn. Get drinks in hands and make sure everyone's having a good time. Business has been growing steadily for a while now, but this is the biggest night yet. From the looks of it, half the town of Fairhope is heading this way, and I want to make sure when they leave, all they can talk about is what a great time they had at Rob's tonight.

Someone pushes through the crowd and taps a hand on the bar to get my attention. I'm about to tell him to wait his turn when I look up and see that it's Mason Trent. I smile and lean forward, trying to get closer so I can hear him over the noise.

"What's up?" I ask.

"Just wanted to let you know we're all set up on the stage and we're just going to take a quick break out back to get our heads on straight." He looks around, a smile in his eyes. "Can you believe this? I never dreamed we'd have this kind of crowd. I hope we're ready for this."

"You are. You guys rock." I smile and pull back to fill a few fresh cups with ice and water. "Here. Take these to the guys."

"Thanks," he says. "We'll be back in a few. Let Colton know we're almost ready."

I lift my chin in acknowledgement and go back to pouring drinks. We have margaritas and Bud Light on special tonight, and I'm starting to worry we're going to run out before we close at two in the morning. It's getting wild in here. And hot. Sweat trickles down the back of my neck and spine as I move from one customer to the next, slinging drinks and counting cash.

I glance toward the front door and see that my friend Slim is waving to get my attention.

"Hey, Daddy? Can you take over for a sec?" I shout. "I'm gonna go see what Slim needs."

"Sure thing, Jojo," he says. My dad steps forward and motions for the next in line to order.

I walk the length of the bar, knowing my chances of getting to the door are much greater if I hop the bar than if I try to push through the crowd. At five foot three, I'm not exactly the tallest girl in the world. I could get lost in a crowd like this.

As I pass behind Colton, every inch of my body is aware of just how close I am to him. I try not to stare at the way he's smiling at the girls who just ordered or the way his cheek gets that dimple on one side that just wrecks me every time I see it. I try to ignore the muscles that stretch his black t-shirt to its limits, his arms flexing as he pops open a couple longnecks.

He turns his head to give me a smile, but I avoid his gaze as I slide behind him and hop onto the top of the bar at the very end. There's a group of guys parked down here with their drinks, and they offer their hands to help me across. I wave them away and twist my body around, not needing any help. I've done this a billion times in my twenty-two years.

Hell, I grew up in this bar and there is no place in the world I'd rather be than right here, right now.

I wade through the crowd near the entrance and finally tap on Slim's shoulder. "Everything going okay?"

He nods and holds his hand out to the next couple girls in line. They fish their ID's from their purses and hand them over, along with a five-dollar bill each to pay the cover charge.

"We're getting close to max capacity," he says. "I estimate we can bring in another five or six people, and then we need to put a lock-down on this place until people start leaving."

A surprised smile spreads across my face, and I lift both fists into the air.

"Hell yes," I shout. "Are you kidding me? A sold out show on our first night?"

I take pride in being a hardass sometimes, but tonight I can't even pretend to contain my excitement. A packed house at max capacity nearly an hour before the band even plays? And on a night with a five-dollar cover?

The cover was my friend Penny's idea. Lately, she's been making a name for herself around Fairhope, helping people set up their own small businesses. Taking a risk, I hired her to come in and take a look at our books. She suggested we think about doing some special events, and it was Colton's idea to offer live music on Saturday nights. It seemed like a perfect idea to invite Penny's husband, Mason, and his band to play our first night.

Penny was the one who suggested a cover charge and an ID bracelet so we wouldn't have to keep checking ID's all night. I had protested at first, saying that if we really wanted to bring in the drinking crowd, we should make it free to enter like every other dang night we'd been open for the past twenty years.

But Penny had insisted, saying the cover would make it feel more exclusive and would bring in the kinds of customers who would be willing to pay for the drinks and stay awhile.

Hell if she hadn't been right. When I find her in the crowd, I'm going to kiss her square on the lips. My brain can't even process the kinds of numbers we're bringing in right now, and the night has just begun.

I slap Slim on the back. "Let the next few in and shut it down," I say, and he nods. He's a big guy, of course. All dudes called Slim usually are, right? It's like guys named Tiny being six feet tall. Slim is about two hundred pounds of pure muscle, and at six-foot-two, no one is going to mess with him.

I take a quick look past the girls standing in the door and am surprised to see there's a line of almost twenty or so more people just waiting to get in. Unbelievable.

Practically humming with excitement, I leave Slim at the door and push through the crowd to hop back over the bar. I nearly trip over a box of cups on the other side, and Colton reaches out to steady me. His arms go around my waist, and on instinct, I put my hand on his shoulder to steady myself. Our eyes meet as he sets me down gently, and I curse the warm feeling that shoots through me.

Damn, has it just been a long time since I felt a set of strong arms around me, or is this a Colton-specific phenomenon?

Because if this is really about Colton, I need to get myself in check. Fast. I don't date bartenders, and I certainly don't date employees. I learned that lesson a long time ago. One bad apple was enough to spoil the bunch, so to speak.

"Thanks," I say, pulling away as fast as I can.

"Anytime, short stuff."

I glare at the cocky smile that seems to reach all the way to his eyes. Why does he have to be so ridiculously charming and happy all the damn time?

"How are things looking at the door?" he asks.

"Amazing," I say, unable to contain my own smile now. "This is going to be our best night ever."

"Told you so," he says.

Several women are standing impatiently at the counter, cash in hand. I nod to them. "Are you planning to stand here making chit-chat with me all night, or are you planning to serve some drinks in your spare time?"

He laughs again and grabs a couple beers from the cooler. "Guess you better stop flirting with me, then," he says. "I have work to do."

I shake my head and watch as he glides over to hand the ladies their drinks. All frustration melts from their faces and they lean over the top of the bar, smiling.

It's a scene I've watched a thousand times since he started working here a few months back. There's no doubt hiring him was the right move, and I have my friend Jenna to thank for that. I may have poached him from Brantley's, but the guy definitely has a way about him. One flash of that smile of his and the ladies are ready to sit at the bar all night just to get another glimpse.

Realizing I'm still staring instead of helping get these people their drinks, I tear my gaze away and start back toward my side of the bar.

But I stop short, frowning. Daddy is struggling with a credit card at the machine, his hands curled awkwardly around the plastic and his eyebrows cinched together. He tries to run the card and drops it to the floor. He's kind of a big guy after years of drinking his own wares, and he struggles to bend down to retrieve it. After a couple attempts, he can't seem to get his fingers to work around the small card.

I rush over, my heart racing. "I'll get it, Daddy."

I grab the card and run it through the machine.

"Thanks, Jojo," he says. He shakes his hand and curls his fingers into a fist a few times, letting them open and close. "My hands aren't working right tonight for some reason. This crowd has me all nervous."

He says it with a laugh, but the hint of concern in his eyes sends an uncomfortable zing through my stomach. He's been having a lot of problems with his hands the past week or so. Just last night he dropped a couple brand new pint glasses on the floor when he was trying to fill them from the tap. I thought maybe he wasn't paying attention to what he was doing, but this is something else.

I place a hand on his arm and lean close. "Everything okay?"

He shrugs and touches my hand. "I'm fine," he says. "Maybe my age is just catching up with me."

"Not getting enough sleep is what's catching up with you," I say. I hear those late-night infomercials at two in the morning. He's had a problem with insomnia ever since Mom left us back in the day, but I thought it was getting better for a while. Maybe he's just tired and overworked.

"I thought I was supposed to be the parent in this relationship," he says.

"Someone's got to look out for you," I say. I grab his shoulder and go up on my toes to plant a kiss on his cheek. "We've got it covered back here for the night, now," I say. "Why don't you help Slim manage the huge line outside the door for a while?"

He raises his eyebrows. "There's a line?"

I smile. "Yep," I say. "And we're almost at max, so he's having to make people wait until someone else leaves. Go see for yourself."

A proud smile creeps over his face, and he nods. "I think I will," he says. "It's been a long time since we had a line at the old bar. Things are looking up."

I laugh and watch as he makes his way through the

crowd, shaking hands with old friends and beaming with pride. He's earned this after years of hard work to keep this place going, and I have to hold back tears as I think about everything he's been through.

I roll my eyes and run a finger under my eye. This is not a night for silly tears. It's a night for celebration and making money. It's a night for breathing new life into a place that means more to my father than just about anything in this world.

I turn to the next customer in line. "What'll it be?" I ask.

And just like that, I'm lost again in the rhythm of this place. The constant push and pull, the give and take. The dance that keeps the bar spinning all night long.

It's my favorite place to be on a Saturday night. I'm safe and happy here, and I don't want anything to change.

Colton catches my eye and smiles, one eyebrow raised.

I suck in a breath and force my gaze away, trying to ignore the way he makes my cheeks flush and my heart race. He's the kind of guy who acts like he wants to turn my whole life upside-down.

Well, no thank you.

I had my life turned upside-down once before, and I barely survived it. Things are finally back on track, and I am not about to let someone like Colton Tucker mess that up for me.

And yet, I can't resist risking one more glance his way.

CHAPTER 2
COLTON

"How y'all doing tonight?" I say into the microphone.

The crowd screams, holding their drinks up. We spent all morning moving the tables out of the bar so that we'd have more room, and every inch of floor space is packed. The place is electric with energy and excitement.

"We here at Rob's want to thank you all for coming out tonight and supporting us. Where is old Rob?" I ask, lifting my hand to cover my eyes so I can see through the crowd.

Over by the door Rob gives a salute, a huge smile plastered across his face. I've never seen him so happy.

"There he is," I say. "Let's give it up for Rob."

I hold my mic out to the crowd and they eat it up, screaming at the top of their lungs.

"Just to let you guys know, we'll be having live music here at Rob's every Saturday night, so I hope to see y'all right back here next week," I say. "But I'm sure you didn't come

SARRA CANNON

here to hear me yap my trap all night, so let's get down to the music."

More screams, and I'm loving every minute of it. I laugh and for some reason, find myself searching for Jo behind the bar. Our eyes meet across the crowd, and she smiles and shakes her head. She holds up her index finger and swirls it around, motioning for me to wrap it up. I laugh and nod.

"Without further ado, let's give it up for one of our newest and best local bands, The Mason Dixon Line."

I settle the mic back in its stand and step back to give Mason room to take over. "Knock 'em dead, man," I say, patting him on the back.

"Here goes nothing," Mason says.

He strums the first few chords of a popular country song and the crowd goes completely nuts.

I jump off the edge of the stage and weave back toward the bar, saying hello to friends on my way through. Someone grabs hold of my belt loop and pulls me backward. I stumble and nearly bump into the kind of guy you just don't mess with, but I manage to avoid him and turn toward the mystery girl.

"Colton Tucker, you sexy thing. Where do you think you're going?" Missy Cartwright has her hands around my waist before I even realize what's going on.

"Hey, darlin', you having a good time?" I say. Missy's a sweet girl. We went out a few times last year, but it never turned into anything serious.

Story of my life.

"I am now that I found you," she says.

She's obviously had a few drinks and is feeling good. I

14

glance toward the bar and when I catch sight of Jo, she looks away a bit too fast.

My mouth goes dry. "It's good to see you, too," I say, but I'm already pushing her away. "I need to get back to work, though, so I'll catch up with you later, okay?"

"I'm going to come find you," she says in a sing-song voice. She lifts up on her toes and kisses my cheek.

I laugh and pull her hand away from my hip so that I can make my escape. Another girl I used to know tries to stop me, but I just say hello and push on. This place is a total madhouse tonight.

I head back to the bar as fast as I can and when I climb over the top and pass behind Jo, she stops and turns around.

"Good job on stage," she says.

"Thanks."

"For a minute there I wasn't sure you were going to make it back to the bar," she says. "Was that your girlfriend?"

"Who, Missy?" I ask. "Nah, she's just a girl I used to know."

"Of course she is," Jo mumbles. She turns back around to start taking orders, but her shoulders are tense and so is her jaw.

I just shake my head. Is she jealous?

Jo is a hard nut to crack. I can't seem to figure her out.

Sometimes I could swear she's flirting with me, but then the next thing I know, she's shutting down so fast it makes my head spin.

Which is probably for the best, considering that she's basically my boss here at Rob's. I like this job, and I don't want to mess it up.

Back when I left Brantley's I wasn't sure it was the right

move. Maria—my manager over at the restaurant—was good to me, always giving me great hours and letting me pretty much run things the way I wanted. It was a quiet gig where I got to talk to people and take things slow, but there were too many nights where I walked out the door with nothing more than a couple of twenties for an eight-hour shift.

That doesn't happen here at Rob's. We're not usually this packed, but business is good and I've never left with less than a hundred bucks. I can't afford to lose this job, so the worst possible thing I can do is start flirting with the woman who signs my paychecks, but damn. Some days it's just hard to resist her.

I've never met a girl who could take my teasing and turn it right back around on me. It's fun, but I don't dare try to take it any further than that. I'm half afraid she'd bite my head off if I actually tried to get anything started with her.

I've never actually seen her go out with anyone, come to think of it. No girlfriends. No boyfriends. She mostly just works and hangs out with her dad. I've heard her talk about going out to the lake house with Knox and Leigh Anne, but other than that, I have no idea what she does to have fun. Does she ever just let her hair down and let loose?

Mmm, there's something about the mental image that conjures in my head that makes me want to grab her and loosen her braids until her hair rolls down her back. Dangerous thoughts, but hard ones to get rid of.

I head back to my station and get back to work, pouring drinks and opening bottles as fast as I can. I have to go into the storeroom to get more beer and cups twice and there's still a crowd waiting for drinks. The way the tip jar is filling up, this looks like it's going to be the best night I've ever had tending bar.

God knows I can use the money, too. It'll be fun to do some counting once the place is empty.

Thank goodness for Penny's suggestion to bring on a waitress tonight, or we'd be even more slammed up here than we are. Suzanne comes up to the drinks station at the end of the bar and plunks down a long list of orders.

"Have you ever seen anything like this?" she asks, using her notebook to fan herself. Her blonde hair is up in a pony-tail and there's sweat trickling down the side of her face.

"Good times," I say, having to shout over the music. I pick up her list of orders and start setting up cups and filling them with ice.

"What are you doing after?" she asks, leaning over the top of the bar so that her ample cleavage is practically in my face. There's a sly smile on her pretty face, and I'm surprised at the blatant flirtation. We hardly know each other except for hanging out a few times here at the bar.

Is she asking me out?

I measure out shots of vodka and pour them into the cups, daring a quick glance at Jo down at the other end. What is she doing after? That's what I really want to know. Maybe I could convince her to hang around the bar for a while once it's empty.

I shake my head. Wasn't I just telling myself to stop thinking about that girl? I'm off my game. She's got me all turned around.

Normally, I wouldn't hesitate to tell a girl like Suzanne hell yes, let's hang out as long as she wants after, but tonight I can't even force interest. What the heck is wrong with me?

"After this, I'll probably want to spread my cash on the bed and pass out for about twelve hours," I say with a laugh. "I'm exhausted and we've still got hours to go."

"I could come over and we could lay low. We could rent a movie or something," she offers as she arranges the drinks on her tray. "If you want, I mean. I've got a couple of those free Redbox codes. Might be something good left by the time we knock off."

"Catch me on the flipside," I say, even though I'm not really interested. "But I have a feeling I'm not going to want to do anything but sleep once we close this place down."

Disappointment flickers across her features. "Oh, me too, I'm sure," she says. "Maybe some other night."

"Sounds good," I say. "Get back out there and make some money."

"You know it," she says with a giggle.

She lifts the heavy tray over her head like a pro and wades through the dense crowd. I keep an eye on her for a while, even as I take a few more drink orders and fill them up. Suzanne is definitely easy on the eyes with her curvy body and baby blues. A few weeks ago, I would have been eager to accept a movie invitation from a girl like that, with every intention to skip the movie. Hell, I've never been one to shy away from a good time with a pretty girl. But ever since coming to work at Rob's, I haven't been able to get Jo off my mind. There is just something about that girl that drives me crazy.

She's feisty. Smart with a quick wit that makes it fun just be around her. She makes me nervous in a good way, like I'm always wanting to impress her. I'm not sure a girl has ever made me feel quite like that, and I'm not sure what to make of it.

She's not my usual type. She's closed off and makes it obvious at every turn that she's not interested in a relationship. I've heard plenty of guys hit on her during her shifts, but she shoots them down every time without blinking an eye.

She's exactly the kind of girl I should stay away from.

I glance her way and whistle softly. She looks good tonight, though. Her long black hair hangs down her back in a braid and she's wearing tight jeans, doc martens, and a tight little black tank top that hugs her curves in all the right places. There's a grace in her movements that does something to my insides every time I look at her.

Yeah, there's definitely something about that girl I can't resist.

It may be a mistake to flirt with my boss, but something tells me it's a mistake I won't regret making.

CHAPTER 3
JO

The bar is trashed, and I've never been happier to clean the dang place in my life.

When the last of our customers walks out the door, I lock it and throw my hands up in triumph. "We did it!"

Colton is standing by the tip jar digging out dollar bills and smiling like a kid on Christmas morning. "I've never been so happy to be so tired," he says. "This place was packed. Could you believe that crowd?"

"I was hoping it would be a good turnout, but I never dreamed it would be so huge," I say. "I just feel like flying. Damn, that was fun."

I sit down on a barstool across from Colton. He's staring at me like I've gone crazy.

"What? I'm not allowed to be happy?" I ask.

He laughs. "It's not that. It's just that I don't think I've ever heard you say the word fun," he says. "I wasn't sure you knew the meaning of the word."

I frown. "I know how to have fun."

"Okay, so when was the last time you had a really crazy, let-loose kind of good time?" he asks.

I open my mouth to answer, but he holds up a hand.

"And it doesn't count if it happened here at the bar," he says.

I pout. "That's not fair. I'm always here."

"Exactly," he says, one eyebrow raised.

I roll my eyes and help him count the tips. "I know how to have a good time," I say again. "I've just been working a lot lately."

"We both have, but I still know how to go out after with my friends and live it up."

"Don't kill my joy, Colton," I say. "I want to enjoy this."

He smiles and our eyes meet over the counter. There's something brewing in his mind, I just know it, but I can't even let myself go there. He's an employee and besides, it would never work between us.

Knox comes out of the storeroom and slaps his hands together. "Finished," he says. "I'm exhausted."

"Me, too," I say. "I can't wait to get home and put my feet up for the next twenty years. Thank God we're closed on Sundays. I don't want to put shoes on again until Monday."

"If y'all are good, I'm going to head on home."

"You don't want to wait for your tips?" I ask. "We're almost done and then we'll see what Daddy has on the receipts."

"Nah, Leigh Anne's been waiting up," Knox says, giving me a kiss on the cheek. "Don't forget about the barbeque at the lake next weekend. Colton, you're welcome to join us if you want."

I suck in a breath and glance sideways at Knox. Why did he have to invite Colton? I've been looking forward to some quiet time with just the family for weeks. Maybe he'll be busy.

"Sure, when is it?" Colton asks.

I bite my lip. Damn.

"Next Sunday around lunch time," Knox says. "You remember how to get out there, right?"

"I think so," Colton says.

Knox says goodnight, leaving Colton and I alone in the bar again. Daddy's in the office going through receipts.

It's strangely quiet after the deafening noise of the music and the crowd.

"Thanks for staying to help clean up," I say, just trying to break up the silence. "I heard you and Suzanne might be going out, so if you need to go, I can finish up on my own."

I don't even know why I mentioned Suzanne, but she cornered me earlier to tell me she was going to ask him out, and it bothered me. Like, really bothered me.

Which only upset me even more.

I watch his expression to see how he'll react, half-expecting him to run a rag over the counter and call it a night. Instead, he shrugs.

"I don't mind cleaning up," he says. "Besides, I don't feel like partying tonight. I just want to stretch out in front of the TV for a while."

"All those late-night infomercials are really gaining traction among the male gender these days," I mumble.

He raises an eyebrow in question.

I laugh. "Sorry. My dad hasn't been sleeping much these days. Any time I wake up in the middle of the night, he's lying in his recliner watching people get stains out of their carpet or talk about how to get your beach body ready for summer."

"I can't stand those things," he says. "Everybody trying to sell you on some product that you know isn't going to work worth a damn. You guys seriously need to get Netflix or something."

I stand and roll my eyes. "We have Netflix. I don't even know why he's up watching those things," I say. "Maybe he's hoping they'll bore him to sleep. All I know is they're driving me crazy."

"Have you ever thought about getting your own place?"

I clean off the booth tables and pick up all the empty cups and bottles that got dropped on the floor. "I guess I thought about it a few times, but it seems silly. It's just easier to stay home since we live right behind the bar," I say. "Besides, it's just been the two of us for as long as I can remember. I don't like to think about him living there by himself with no one to look after him."

"He's a grown man. I think he could probably handle it," he says. He's done counting the money and a large stack of bills sits on the counter as he washes out glasses.

"How much?" I ask, nodding to the cash.

That crooked smile breaks out on his face, and I have to look away.

"Five hundred sixty-two smackeroos," he says.

My jaw drops. "Are you sure?"

"Counted it twice."

I smile and shake my head. I can't believe it. If that's what we brought in from cash tips alone, I can't wait to see what the bar tabs look like.

"Do you live by yourself?" I ask, going back to the previous subject. I know surprisingly little about Colton other than what nights of the week he works here. Is he going to college? Does he have a girlfriend? I never realized just how little he actually talks about himself.

"In a way," he says. When I stare at him, he continues. "My family's what you would call close, I guess."

"Care to elaborate on that? Or are you just going to let my imagination run wild? Because I'm picturing you in a big barn with one giant family bed right now."

He laughs so hard he has to lower his head and stop cleaning for a second. "It's nothing like that," he says. "Some people think we're a bit strange, though, I'll put it that way."

"Aww, come on, you've got to give me more than that," I say, honestly interested now in figuring out what he seems so hesitant to explain to me.

He pulls a couple fresh shot glasses from the pile and sets them out. "Come take a break for a minute and have a celebratory shot," he says. "And I'll tell you all about my crazy family."

I was hoping to get this done and crawl into bed for the rest of my life, but my interest is piqued and I can't resist. Besides, tonight's success calls for a little celebration.

"Why not?" I say. I drop the mop and sit down across from him.

He looks shocked, but recovers quickly.

"Scotch," I tell him, but he's already got my favorite brand in his hand and is pouring it before I finish the word.

Someone's been paying attention.

He pours a whiskey for himself and leans his forearms against the wood of the bartop.

"To the best night Rob's has ever seen," he says, holding his glass toward me.

I nod and clink mine against his before taking a long drink. I slam it down on the counter, enjoying the warmth as it trickles down my throat. My shoulders immediately relax, and I nod for him to fill it up one more time. "If I'm going to take a break, let's make it worth my while," I say.

"Hell yeah," he says and fills my glass again.

"Okay, so tell me about this crazy family of yours," I say. "You guys all live together?"

"Are you really interested?" he asks.

"Yes," I say. "We've been working together for months, and I really don't know that much about you."

"Okay," he says with a sigh. "My great-grandfather bought a nice piece of wooded land on the other side of the county line about a hundred years ago," he says. "He had a lot of ideas about government control and wanting to stay as private and as off-the-grid as he could, so he set up what he called a sanctuary for all his kinfolk."

I narrow my eyes. "So you live on a commune?"

"No, nothing like that," he says with a laugh. "More like a trailer park owned and operated by my daddy."

My eyebrows shoot up and I nearly spit out the scotch I've just sucked down. I cough and wipe my mouth. "Wait, what?"

"I know it's a bit unorthodox, but my dad and his brothers still own the land and they let all of us live there," he says, tossing back another shot. "If you're family, all you have to do is pick out a lot and set up camp. No questions asked. No money exchanged."

"So everyone just buys a trailer and finds a place to park it?" I've never heard of anything like this in my life.

"I guess you could put it that way," he says.

"How many people are we talking about?" I ask.

He looks up toward the ceiling as if the answer's written in the air. "Let's see. Ten trailers at the moment," he says. "Each one with between one and seven people living inside. Don't ask me to do math at this time of night, though. I'm guessing about what? Forty people?"

"Wow, so forty people all living on one plot of land as one big happy family?" I simply can't imagine it. "This is something I have got to see for myself."

The words are out of my mouth before I even realize it. Colton studies me.

"I can't tell if you're making fun of me or if you're genuinely interested."

"Interested," I say. "It sounds about as opposite from how I grew up as you can possibly get."

"I know it sounds weird—"

"You keep saying that like you feel you need to apologize," I say.

He shrugs, but I can see the embarrassment in his eyes. It's the first time I think I've ever seen him look uncomfortable. "A lot of people don't understand it," he says. "They think we're crazy or some kind of redneck cult or whatever just because we all settle down on the family land. But it's not like that at all. I mean, yes, my great-grandparents had some ideas about conspiracies and the government being up in everyone's business, but it's not like we hold anti-government rallies in the backyard."

I try to imagine what it would be like to live that close to forty of my own family members and come up empty. Other than Knox coming back to town, it's been me and my daddy alone for years. I don't even know where my mom is, and I haven't seen her since I was five years old. For all I know, I have sisters and brothers out there I've never met.

Truth be told, Knox and my dad are the only family I have in this world, so trying to imagine forty or more is next to impossible for me.

"So where do you fit into the Tucker family trailer park situation?"

"I've been living in one of the smaller trailers on the property the past year or so," he says. "It's not mine, though. It belongs to my cousin Tammy, passed down to her from my Aunt Carla when she moved to Kentucky a few years back. But then Tammy met some guy on the internet and took off to Texas, so I moved in."

"What happens if Tammy decides to come home?"

"That's a very timely question," he says. "Because she'll be back in about two weeks, newly engaged to the Texan, who is coming with her."

"Ooh, you're going to have to move out, I'm guessing," I say.

"Yes I am," he says. "And the thought of moving back in with my parents gives me nightmares."

"Why don't you get your own place?" I say. "And I'm not talking about a trailer. Why don't you get an apartment here in town so you can be closer to the bar? You're here almost every night anyway?"

"I guess I never really thought about it," he says. "It might be nice to have a little privacy once in a while. I wonder how expensive those apartments near campus are?"

"I think Leigh Anne said they were about six hundred a month," I say.

Colton whistles and shakes his head. "No can do. Not without a few more nights like this," he says.

Daddy comes out of the back room smiling like a loon. "What a night," he says. "I think we should turn on some music, because I feel like dancing."

He grabs my hand and pulls me out of my chair, spinning me around like a ballerina. I laugh and wrap my arms around him.

"I see you two started the celebration without me," Dad says. "Pour me one and then let's call it a night. I'm exhausted."

"Me, too," I say. "One more to toast the best night Rob's has ever had."

Colton grabs another glass and pours three more shots. "To Rob's," he says.

"To Rob's," Daddy and I say in unison as we all clink our glasses together and throw them back.

It's one too many for me, and by the time the liquor has reached my brain, I've apparently lost all sense because I turn to Colton and say the dumbest thing I've said in a long time.

"You should move into the apartment over our garage."

I know it's a dangerous thing to offer, because the thought of him living just a few steps away from me gives me hives, but I can't help myself.

"What's going on?" Daddy asks.

"Colton was just talking about how he's about to be homeless, so I was thinking about how Knox just moved out of our apartment over the garage." I turn to Colton, the booze completely clouding my judgment. "It's nothing fancy, just a small one-bedroom place with a full bathroom and a kitchenette, but it's furnished and we could rent it to you cheap."

He raises and eyebrow and something about the way he looks into my eyes sends a shiver of excitement down my spine. "How cheap?"

I look to Dad and he shrugs. "How does two-fifty a month sound?"

My heart skips a beat, and I have a feeling I'm going to regret this. We already spend way too much time together, and now he's going to be living just a few feet away? I'm playing with fire, and we all know what that leads to.

But it's too late. The damage has been done.

"Two-fifty would be amazing," Colton says. He holds up the stack of tips and smiles. "Do you take cash?"

CHAPTER 4
JO

Colton says goodnight and heads home, so Daddy and I finish up and lock the doors before making our way out back to the house.

He puts his arm around me and hugs me close. "You did an amazing job tonight, Jojo," he says. "I'm so proud of you. You've really stepped up this year. I honestly don't know what I'd do without you."

"Thanks, Daddy." My heart swells with pride. I've been working so hard lately, but it's finally starting to pay off. "It was a good night."

"I like that Colton boy," he says as he unlocks the door to our small two-bedroom house and pushes it open. "It was nice to see you two having a good time together. You don't take enough time for yourself."

I take a deep breath and step inside. Not this again.

"I don't need time for myself, Daddy. I like working at the bar with you," I say. "I'm happy."

"I know you say that, but no girl your age should be hanging out with an old guy like me all the time," he says. "You need to get out more. Hang out with your friends and have some fun. You've earned it."

"You're my friend," I say.

"Josephine, you know that's not what I mean," he says.

I hate it when he calls me Josephine. It's like he thinks using my full name is going to make his words mean more or something.

"I know what you mean, but I'm telling you that I'm fine," I say. "Let's not spoil a perfect night by talking about it, okay?"

He pulls me closer and kisses the top of my head. "I just love you so much. I don't want to see you work so hard that you forget to have fun," he says. "It can be a really lonely life when you refuse to let other people in."

I wrap my arms around him and close my eyes as I sink into his chest. I know he means well, but sometimes he sounds like a broken record, always pushing me to make more friends or go out on more dates. He just doesn't understand. I like my life just the way it is. It's safe like this. Simple.

"I'm not lonely, Daddy," I say. "I have you."

"I won't be around forever, Jojo," he says.

I pull away and shake my head. "Don't talk like that. You're going to live forever," I say. "I'm tired. I'm going to bed, and I better not wake up in an hour and find you out here watching TV, you hear me?"

"Yes, ma'am," he says with a laugh. "Goodnight, sweet girl. Get some rest. I love you."

"I love you, too."

I brush my teeth and strip down to my tank top and underwear before crawling under the covers. I expect to fall asleep in an instant, but instead I toss and turn half the night thinking about risk and regret and what it might feel like to finally let someone else in for a change.

CHAPTER 5
COLTON

My sister's newborn baby opens her mouth in a wide stretch of a yawn, her tiny hands curling around her face. I smile and snuggle her closer, wrapping the soft pink blanket tighter around her little body.

"She's really beautiful, Cammie. You did good," I say.

Cammie smiles and leans back in the big tattered recliner that used to belong to my dad. He moved it over here a few weeks ago before they brought the baby home from the hospital. We don't have a lot in the way of material possessions in this family—never have—but it's a sign of love for Dad to have moved his favorite recliner over here to make the new mom more comfortable. After watching most of my older siblings go through this with their first babies, I know Cammie is in for a lot of sleepless nights sitting up in that chair, nursing and rocking this little thing back to sleep.

"How are you feeling?" I ask.

"Still a little sore, I guess, but mostly good," she says. "More than anything I'm just exhausted. You would think I would have figured out how this works after watching so many babies being born in this family, but damn. I wasn't prepared for just how tired I would be all the time."

"It won't last forever," I say. The baby—Emma—opens her eyelids a tiny bit and shows off her dark blue eyes. I smile down at her. She's so tiny and fragile in my arms. "I'm taking a lot of shifts at the bar, but if you ever need an extra set of hands during the day, just let me know. I can come sit with her a while so you can rest, if you need me."

Cammie closes her eyes and rocks the chair back and forth. "That would be heaven," she says. "Honestly, even just an hour of uninterrupted sleep right now would feel like a year."

I look over at my sister. She's the closest to me in age of all my siblings and we've always been close. I'm happy for her, but there's a part of me that had hoped she'd wait just a little longer to start a family. It feels strange to be the only one now not married with a family of my own.

Sometimes I think maybe I'm just supposed to be the fun uncle who comes over to babysit every once in a while but never has a wife and kids. It's hard to imagine settling down like this, but I'm happy to help when I can.

"Why don't you go to the bedroom and take a nap, then?" I say. "I've got her for a little while."

Cammie opens one eye and stares at me. "Are you sure?" she asks. "Aren't you working tonight?"

I shake my head. "We're closed on Sundays," I say. I need to think about packing up my stuff so I can move into the new apartment, but it can wait a couple hours. "I've got this. She just ate and she'll probably fall asleep here in a few minutes. You may as well take advantage of the peace and quiet while you can."

She stands and crosses over to us, planting a kiss on my forehead. "Thank you, Colton, this means a lot," she says. "You'll come get me if you need anything?"

I raise an eyebrow. "You're wasting precious sleeping minutes here," I say, teasing. "We'll be fine."

My sister smiles and runs her hand along Emma's fuzzy head of blonde hair, so fine it makes her look like a baby chick.

"You're so good with her," she says softly. "When are you going to find the right girl and settle down with a family of your own, baby brother?"

"Not you, too," I say, shaking my head.

Ever since she first announced she was expecting, that's all I've heard from everyone around here. I'm the last to settle down and get married, so I guess that means no one is going to leave me alone until I do.

Well, they're just going to have to wait.

"Sorry," she says with a giggle. "You know we just want you to be happy."

"I am happy," I say. "You know me. I don't think I'm really the settling-down-type. After all, someone has to be the family screw-up around here. Might as well be me."

"Don't say stuff like that," Cammie says. "No one thinks you're a screw-up."

I laugh and shake my head. "Maybe someone ought to tell that to Dad."

Cammie touches my hand. "I know he's hard on you, but he means well," she says. "You're the only son he has, and he wants you to be just like him. Don't let it get to you. I love you just the way you are."

"Thanks," I say. "Just don't expect me to be bringing home a baby any time soon, okay?"

"You just haven't found the right girl yet," she says. "But when you do, man, you'll know it."

My stomach flips and I adjust my position on the couch, propping a pillow under my arm and carefully avoiding my sister's eyes. For some reason I'm afraid she'll see something there I don't want anyone to see.

So what if there's been one particular woman on my mind a lot lately? It's just because we're working together so much. It doesn't mean anything.

"It really is worth it, you know?" Cammie says, a dreamy expression in her eyes as she stares down at the baby.

"You better get to sleep or I'm going to take back my offer and go play some video games instead," I say.

Cammie laughs and shakes her head. She knows I'm bluffing, but I like to see her smile, anyway.

"Thank you," she whispers again, and disappears to one of the trailer's back bedrooms.

I sigh and settle deeper into the couch. The baby is fast asleep now, her pink face peaceful and still. I don't dare turn on the TV or make any noise. I don't want to wake her up, because I know the second she begins to cry, Cammie will be right back out here fussing over her.

Instead, I find a comfortable position and stare into that sweet baby's face as she sleeps.

"Your mommy's wrong," I whisper. "I'm never going to settle down like this."

Emma yawns again and wraps her tiny finger around mine, as if to say that no matter how hard I try to resist, someday someone is going to wrap her life around mine and never let go.

"Well played, baby," I say with a laugh. "Well played."

৯৯

AFTER CAMMIE WAKES UP, I HEAD OVER TO MY PLACE AND start clearing things out and cleaning up. All of the furniture and things are my cousin Tammy's, so there isn't much in here that's actually mine. I grab a big duffel bag out of the closet and start stuffing all my clothes inside.

Other than that, all I have is a few pictures and CD's and things here and there. My laptop. Not much else. I don't need too many things.

Thank goodness Jo's apartment is already furnished, or I'd be sleeping on a sleeping bag for the next few weeks.

I load my bag and a couple boxes into the back of my truck and am just about to leave when I hear footsteps behind me. My chest tightens, and I turn around and cram my hands into my pockets. I was hoping to avoid a confrontation, but here we go.

"Hey, Dad," I say.

"Going somewhere?" he asks.

"Since Tammy's coming home soon, I thought maybe it was time I found a place of my own," I say. In this family, a place of your own means staying right here on our land.

My dad frowns and takes a pack of cigarettes from the front pocket of his t-shirt. "Now, I told you you're welcome to come stay with us," he says. "There's no need to go wasting money on a place in town. Just go on and move those things up to our place."

I shake my head and kick at the dirt with my boots. "I appreciate it, Dad, but I got a really good deal on a place right behind the bar. It'll be convenient to work and it's already furnished and everything."

"That's what I was coming to talk to you about, anyway," he says. "You've been doing real good for yourself working bars, but don't you think it's time you got a real job, son? You need to be thinking about setting down roots, getting a steady paying job that will help you support your family when the time comes. No more of this bartending business."

"I like working at the bar, Dad," I say. "I'm doing just fine."

"Fine for a guy who's got no one to support, but what happens when you decide you want to settle down?" he asks. "It's your job to be the man of the family, Colton. You can't spend your whole life partying and being irresponsible. Now I've been talking to my old boss. You remember Neal, right? He says all you have to do is come in and fill out a few forms, sit through an interview, and he'll make sure you get a spot in training with the company. The interview and stuff is just a formality, but the job's yours."

I swallow the anger in my throat and inhale slowly. "Being a trucker is not really at the top of my list of life's ambitions, Dad. But thank you."

"Dammit, Colton, I'm tired of hearing this mess from you." He throws his cigarette to the ground and stomps it out, a long stream of smoke coming from his lips. "You think you're too good to be a trucker like your old man?"

"I didn't say that."

"You're always acting like you're a hotshot with your Fairhope job catering to all those rich college kids, but slinging drinks is something any fool could do," he says. "It's not a real career, and I want to see you make the best of yourself."

"And you think driving trucks is the best I can be?" I ask, knowing I'm pushing my luck here.

"See, there you go again, thinking you're too good." He lights another cigarette. "It's time to grow up, Colton. Take some responsibility for your life."

He steps toward me, takes a long drag on his cigarette, and then points it at me with two fingers.

"I set up an appointment for a week from Monday at nine sharp," he says. "Move out to your own place if you want, but if you leave, don't expect to come crawling back when you're late on rent or things fall apart, because with you, they always do. I expect you to be at that interview next week, Colton. Show me what kind of a man you plan on being."

He walks away, and I have to stop myself from punching a hole straight through the side of my truck.

Nothing I do is ever good enough for him. He wants me to follow in his footsteps, but as I watch him disappear into his house, I hope that someday I can work up the nerve to tell him that his footsteps are not ones I care to follow.

CHAPTER 6
JO

Colton moves into the small apartment above our garage on Sunday afternoon. I meet him out front with a set of keys and a cup of coffee.

"Is that all you've got?"

I expected him to show up with a truck full of stuff, but he's only got a duffle bag and two boxes in the back of his truck.

"I pack light," he says, slinging the bag over his shoulder and picking up one of the boxes.

"I'll get the door." I unlock the garage and show him up the stairs to the apartment. "There are two different keys. One for the outside door, and one for this inner door. They're each marked with a different color."

"What about cable and internet?" he asks. "Do I need to call and set that up?"

"Nope," I say, opening the door and scooting to the side so he can get past me. "We've got it all setup to use the cable and internet from the house, so you don't have to do anything. Utilities, too, all included."

"Are you trying to seduce me?" he asks. "Because this sounds a little too good to be true."

I ignore the twisting in my stomach at the word seduce.

"Knox was living here rent-free since he helped us so much with the bar, and before that it was empty for a long time. He did a lot to fix this place up in his spare time, so it'll be nice just to see a little income from it," I say. "We don't need much, and if it'll help you out, we're happy to do it."

Colton sets his things down on the kitchen table. "I really appreciate this," he says. "I wasn't sure I'd be able to afford one of those big places by the campus, so you just saved me the horror of living with my parents for the next year or however long it would take for me to save up for a place of my own."

"No problem," I say. I hand him the extra cup of coffee, feeling awkward for just standing around. I thought it might take an hour or so to get all his things moved in, but one more box and he's done. Not that I was looking forward to spending time with him or anything. "Want a tour?"

"Sure," he says, glancing around. "Doesn't look like it'll take long."

I laugh. "I told you it was small."

I show him around the kitchen, pointing out the small collection of basic pots and pans, plates, silverware, and all that. I walk past the table where he set his belongings and he runs a hand over the smooth wood.

"This is gorgeous," he says. "Knox?"

"Yeah, he made that after he moved in," I say.

"That guy's got some real talent," Colton says.

"If you think that's good, you should see what he's done out at his house on the lake. It's absolutely gorgeous," I say. Then, just like the other night, words start tumbling out of my mouth before I realize it. "I hope you'll think about coming out with us next weekend for the barbeque. The weather should be perfect."

"That sounds great," he says. "I haven't had a chance to see the place in a while. Who all will be out there?"

"The usual suspects," I say. "Knox and Leigh Anne, of course. Daddy. Me. Penny and Mason, probably. Preston and Jenna said they'd come out if they got home in time."

"Where are they?"

"They went to some craft festival down in Savannah for the week," I say. "Jenna's been building up her art business and is trying her hand at selling at some of these craft fairs. I think she's doing pretty well with it."

"I'm sure she is," he says. "Have you seen some of the work that's on display in her store downtown? It's gorgeous. I never even knew you could do so much with paper."

"I've been down there a few times," I say. "That won't be awkward for you at all, will it?"

"What?"

"Hanging out with Preston and Jenna. I know you and Jenna used to date."

I hold my breath waiting for an answer. I saw the way he used to look at her. Does he still have feelings for her? I've never really known him to be in a serious relationship, and I don't know why I even care, but my heartbeat quickens just thinking about it.

"Oh, no, not at all," he says, and I can tell from the look

in his eyes he's being sincere. "I love Jenna, but we never had what she has with Preston. I'm happy for her."

"That's good," I say, exhaling. "Are you, uh, seeing anyone these days?"

My little tour of the apartment seems to have stopped before we got a hundred feet in, but this is a question that's been on my mind for a while, whether I want to admit it or not.

"Why so interested?" he says, causing my heart to rise into my throat. "You thinking of asking me out?"

Warmth creeps up my neck, and I just know my cheeks are probably bright red. Shit.

"No, I just was wondering if I should be expecting there to be a lot of late night visitors to the apartment," I say, trying to cover my tracks.

"Uh huh," he says, a knowing smile crossing his lips. "Well, don't you worry your pretty little head about that. I may have my eye on a girl but until I work up the nerve to ask her out, it'll probably be quiet up here."

I try not to react, but the thought of him interested in another girl makes my heart fall right to the bottom of my stomach like a stone.

I will not ask him who it is. It's none of my business.

"That's good," I say, clearing my throat and avoiding his eyes. "Let me show you around the rest of the place real quick and then I need to get going. There's a new shipment coming in this afternoon and I need to make sure the store-room is cleaned out."

"You need help?"

"I can handle it," I say. My voice comes out sharper than I intended.

I take him through the living room with its loveseat and recliner, a simple coffee table also made by Knox, and a nice-sized TV with a Blu-ray player. The second I step into the bedroom, my awkwardness is back in full force. If the thought of him having another girl over here bothers me, the thought of him bringing another girl into this bedroom nearly makes me want to jump out a window.

The bedroom is sparse and simple, with nothing more than a bed, a nightstand, and a chest of drawers. There's a bathroom attached, but it's small.

"Sorry it's so tiny in here," I say. "I hope this will be good enough."

"This is a mansion compared to what I'm used to, trust me," he says. "This is more than enough, and I really want you to know how much I appreciate this, Jo."

He sounds so sincere and heartfelt, it catches me a bit off guard. Colton is always sweet, but he's usually more of a surface kind of guy. Always happy and smiling and joking around, but not one for getting into deep conversations or sharing his innermost thoughts about life.

"You're welcome," I say. "You can stay as long as you like."

"Thanks."

We're standing in the doorway to the bedroom, and I'm aware just how close he is to me. It's getting hotter in here by the second, which means it's time for me to go.

I don't need this kind of complication in my life, especially with him moving in next door.

"I should go," I say, ducking back into the living room and heading straight for the exit. "Let me know if you need anything."

I don't wait for him to say a word in response. I shut the door behind me and race down the stairs.

I don't dare look back, practically running all the way back to my house and into my bedroom. I close the door and place a hand over my heart. What in the world have I gotten myself into?

It feels as if there's a boulder rolling down a hill and it's too late to stop it now.

I sit on my bed and close my eyes, listening to a tiny little voice deep down inside that says maybe I don't want it to stop. Maybe I've been waiting for something like this to happen for a very long time.

CHAPTER 7
COLTON

I stroll into work Monday afternoon with a smile on my face. I'm still on a high from Saturday night's crowd, and I'm looking forward to another great night.

At least that what I've been telling myself.

Okay, so there might be a small part of me that's looking forward to spending some more time with Jo. It'll be just the two of us tonight, and those are my favorite kinds of nights here at the bar. Mondays are usually pretty slow, and it gives us a chance to fool around and talk.

I couldn't believe it when she actually sat down and had a shot with me after work on Saturday night. I think that was the most we've actually talked since I started working here over the summer, and gosh, I don't think I've talked about my family that much to anyone in as long as I can remember.

It felt good to really connect with her, and no matter how much I tell myself it's a long shot that a girl like that would ever want to go out with me, I've been thinking about asking her anyway.

There's a fifty-fifty shot she'll slap me across the face, but I'm willing to take the risk.

"Hey," she says when I walk through the door. She's wearing her hair in two separate braids that hang over her shoulders, and she's got my favorite pair of jeans on tonight. "You're early."

"Easy commute," I say, and she laughs. "I thought you could maybe use my help getting the tables and chairs back on the floor, but I see you guys already took care of that."

The place looks back to normal.

"Knox came over earlier and helped me set it up," she says. "It's going to be a pain to keep pulling those tables and chairs out every weekend, but I don't see any way around it right now."

"We could always expand," I say, half-teasing.

She takes in a breath and puts her hands on her hips, looking around the place. "In a dream world, maybe," she says. "It would be nice to have a bigger stage and more bar space, but there's no way we could afford that right now. Maybe after a year of great nights like we had this weekend. We ended up taking in over a grand on the covers alone, if you can believe it."

"Considering it took me most of the weekend before I started to feel my feet again, I believe it."

She laughs, and the sound reaches into my heart and speeds it up like a drug.

"It was worth it, though, huh?"

"You bet your ass it was worth it," I say. "I'm already looking forward to this weekend."

For more reasons than I want to admit. I haven't been able to stop thinking about Knox's invitation to the lake next

Sunday. I'm looking forward to spending some time with Jo outside work to see if this little spark I'm feeling is something more than just a work thing.

"We've got that band coming from Alabama this weekend," she says. "I need to get some flyers printed out and start posting them around town tomorrow. I'll see if Leigh Anne can pass some out around campus for us, too."

"I can help if you need it," I say. "What can I do to help you get things ready for tonight?"

"Would you mind restocking the coolers? I haven't had a chance to do it yet."

"On it, Boss," I say, and she rolls her eyes. Man, I love getting under that girl's skin.

I wonder if she has any idea just how much she's getting under mine.

☙

THE BAR IS BUSIER THAN NORMAL FOR A MONDAY, AND AS much as I need the money, I'm disappointed I haven't had more time to talk to Jo. We've been slammed for the past few hours, and there just hasn't been a chance to hang out. It's finally starting to clear out, though, and there are only a few tables left and a few regulars sitting at the bar.

I've been trying to work up the nerve to ask her out, but so far, I can't think of anything clever enough to say. I can't even think of where I should take her if she actually happens to say yes. Nothing seems good enough for a girl like her.

My normal dinner and a movie or a walk on the beach won't cut it. I need something really spectacular. Something totally wild and fun that will pull her completely out of work-mode. I want her to have the time of her life.

She deserves something like that.

"Earth to Colton," she says, and I clear my throat.

"Sorry, what happened?" The back of my neck grows warm. Totally busted.

She laughs. "I asked you if you wanted to head home early tonight," she says. "I know we were all exhausted after Saturday and it looks like it's really slowing down now."

My heart sinks. She's sending me home?

"I don't mind sticking around a little longer."

She shrugs. "It's your call," she says. "I just thought you might have something else you wanted to do tonight."

Normally, yes, but right now all I want to do is be with her. Does she have any idea how I'm feeling? I'm worried that it's written all over my face. I'm not used to being nervous about asking someone out. It's awkward, and I feel like I'm fifteen years old all over again.

"What did you end up doing yesterday?" she asks me.

"I slept like the dead," I say with a laugh. "Didn't get up until about noon, and then I went over to my sister Cammie's house for a little while. She just had a new baby a few weeks ago, so I watched Emma while my sister got a little bit of sleep."

Jo raises an eyebrow. "You were babysitting on your day off?"

I keep my hands busy washing glasses. Why am I so nervous around her tonight?

"When you have as many nieces and nephews as I do, you get used to babysitting here and there," I say. "Don't look so shocked."

"I guess I just never pictured you as the babysitting type," she says.

"What did you do?"

"I spent most of the day here at the bar doing inventory," she says, twisting one of her braids around her finger and driving me out of my mind. "Dad put in a huge order this morning just to restock what we sold over the weekend. It was insane."

"I bet," I say. I cannot take my eyes off that finger. I suddenly want to pull her close and take those braids out of her hair. I want to kiss her and show her what it could be like to give in every once in a while.

Man, what is wrong with me?

I force my eyes away, glancing briefly at the door to the bar as it opens. Two guys walk in, laughing and leaning on each other. It's obvious they had a few before they got here.

"Shit," Jo mutters.

I assume she's referring to their inebriated state, but when I look up, her entire face has gone sheet white.

"What?" I ask.

"Joey, long time, huh baby?" The taller of the two guys slaps his hand against the bar and Jo visibly jumps.

My hand tightens around a glass.

"Don't call me that," she says. "What are you doing here?"

"What? No welcome home?" the guy says, placing a hand on his chest and flashing a shocked look at his companion. "A guy can't come back to his old stomping grounds and get a drink these days? Jesus, Joey, you don't have to be so uptight. From what I remember, you used to know how to have a good time."

At her sides, her hands are fists, and her jaw is so tight I'm afraid she's going to break it. Are those tears welling up in her eyes?

Oh, hell no. I'm not going to let some jerk rattle her up like this.

"Jo, weren't you about to go check in the back to see if we had more of that thing we needed?" I ask, touching her hand. Her skin is freezing cold.

She sucks in a breath and tears her eyes away from the guy standing on the other side of the bar. She shakes her head as if she didn't even hear me. "What?"

"You know, that thing you were going to check for in the back?" I ask. I lean close to her ear. "Let me handle this."

"I can handle myself," she says through clenched teeth.

I have no idea what's going on, but I've never seen her this upset. Who the hell is this guy? And what kind of history do they have together?

"Bryan, what are you doing here?" she asks. "I told you never to step foot in this bar again, and I meant it."

"What are you going to do? Throw me out?" He laughs and slaps the shoulder of the guy standing next to him. They both laugh like it's the funniest thing anyone's ever said.

Yeah, they've both had way too much to drink, and I'm losing my patience with this whole situation.

"You heard the lady," I say, unable to just stand back and watch this go down. "Why don't you guys find another place to get yourself a drink? We were just about to close things down for the night."

"Bullshit," Bryan says. "Rob's doesn't close until Eleven on Monday nights."

"Our schedule just changed," I say.

"What's your problem, man? Who the hell are you, anyway?"

"I'm the guy who's giving you one last chance to get the hell out of here before you regret ever walking through that door," I say. My muscles are tensed, ready to throw the first punch if that's what it comes to. I've been through my fair share of bar fights over the years, and no matter how big they are, drunk guys are always slow.

Bryan stares at me and a slow smile spreads across his face. There's something about the look in his eyes that turns my stomach to knots. I know guys like this. They live for causing trouble.

I may have underestimated him. Shit.

"You got another thing coming if you think you could lay a hand on me and not regret it for months to come," he says. "Now go back to minding your own business so I can talk to an old friend."

He sits down at the bar stool across from Jo and leans forward. "Come on, Joey. Let's put the past behind us, what do you say?" He reaches for her hand, but she pulls back. "After all, I'm going to be hanging around town for a while."

"What happened? You get kicked out of whatever hole you crawled into last time?" she says. "I told you, Bryan, you're not welcome here. Get the hell out of my bar."

There's an edge to her voice that scares me. I'm afraid she's going to reach across the counter and try to beat the crap out of him before I have the chance to do it for her.

Bryan stares her down, but just when I think something's about to come to a head, he laughs and lifts his hands up in surrender.

"I was just teasing you, Joey," he says. "I missed you, that's all. But if you want me to go, we'll go."

"I want you to go," she says through clenched teeth.

"Okay, but you know where to find me if you change your mind," he says. "Come on, Jeff, let's get the hell out of this dump. It's dead in here, anyway."

The two guys get up and stagger to the door. I practically hold my breath until they are out of sight and the door is safely closed behind them.

I touch Jo's hand, but she pulls away so fast it makes my stomach hurt.

"Are you okay?" I ask, although it's obvious she's not.

"I'm fine," she says. She swallows hard and takes a deep breath that hitches in her chest. "I just need a minute."

She heads toward the other end of the bar, and as much as I want to follow her, I decide to leave it alone. She's obviously upset, and I don't want to make it worse. Besides, I need to make sure those assholes don't try to come back in and start something. I'm tempted to lock the door for a while and just tell people we're closing early.

Jo disappears into the storeroom, and I lean against the top of the bar, finally letting go of the tense breath I've been holding onto since those guys walked through the door.

What the hell was that all about? Was that guy one of her ex-boyfriends?

I've never once heard her talk about an ex or any other guy that she's dated, but there surely have been some along the way. And apparently this guy is a memory she was hoping to forget.

I wish he'd never walked through those doors. And I wish

I could go find her and comfort her and make sure she's okay.

"Colton, can we get another round over here?" One of our regular couples is sitting at a table in the center of the room, and I give them a nod.

I pour two more glasses of Jack and Coke for the couple and bring them out to the table, but my mind isn't on the bar right now. It's on the woman in the back room going through something I can't even imagine, and how I wish more than anything that, whatever it is, she would let me help her through it.

CHAPTER 8

JO

I let the door to the cooler close behind me and lean against it, my hands shaking violently.

The cold air rushes over my skin as tears pour down my cheeks. I swipe at them, hating that I let that asshole get to me the way he did.

What is he doing back in town? The day he left I prayed he would run as far away from here as possible and never come back. I honestly thought he'd never be stupid enough to come home. At least not for any prolonged period of time.

But from what he said, it sounds like he's back for good.

What am I going to do?

I can't deal with him coming into the bar and giving me hell every night. I don't think I could survive it.

And I hate that Colton had to see me so worked up.

I've gotten really good at not letting that kind of emotion show through in front of anyone. I spent a lot of time back then learning how to shove those feelings into a tiny little box in the pit of my stomach and throw away the key.

Of course there are times when I think about what happened all those years ago, but I was not prepared to see Bryan again. Why did he even come here?

I shake my head and wipe more tears off my face. He and his brother had obviously been drinking, so somewhere in his hardhead, he must have conjured the idea that it would be fun to come and mess with me a little bit.

Thank God he left when he did. I was seriously about to smash a bottle of beer on the counter and send the jagged edge of it through his eye. And, even if I had somehow managed to hold onto my cool, I'm pretty sure Colton would have done it for me if things had progressed any further.

I slide down the door until my butt hits the floor. I wrap my arms around my body and lay my head against them.

Of course this is when he'd choose to come back to Fairhope. Just when things have been going so well for us here at the bar. Life is good, so of course something has to go terribly wrong. Story of my life, it seems like.

He looks terrible, too. Worn out, somehow, even for twenty-eight. I have no idea what he's been up to all these years, and frankly I don't really care. I just wish he'd stayed there.

I'm glad my dad wasn't here tonight, at least. I may have had a hard time keeping it together, but there's no way Daddy would have been as calm. He's going to freak out when he hears about this.

I take deep breaths and wait for my hands to stop trembling. I wait for my heart to stop racing and the tears to stop flowing.

Everything is going to be okay. He was just drunk and being stupid. I told him I don't want him coming into the bar, so that's the last time I'm going to see him in here.

I tell myself these lies to try to feel better, but deep down I know this isn't the end of it. Suddenly I'm fifteen-years-old again and scared out of my mind.

I'm going to have to get an alarm installed at the house. Maybe even one here at the bar. It's the only way I'll be able to sleep at night with that guy back in town. He nearly destroyed my life once, and I'll be damned if I let him do it again.

I slowly stand up and take a few more deep breaths before I open the door to the cooler and step back into the hallway. I take a few minutes in the bathroom to make sure my eyes don't look too red from crying, and I head back into the bar.

Colton looks up from the book he's reading, and I can tell he wants to talk about it. But this is one secret I'd rather take to the grave. Daddy and I worked so hard to make sure no one knew about my stupid mistake all those years ago, and I'd rather not start talking about it now.

I'd much rather go on pretending it never happened.

He starts to walk over, but I shake my head. He stops short and frowns. I know he just wants to help, but I'm beyond help right now. I need time to clear my head and come up with a plan. I need to talk to my dad and figure out how we're going to handle this.

Bryan-Freaking-Thompson is back in town to stay.

I suddenly realize that pretending it never happened is no longer going to be an option.

CHAPTER 9
JO

I have been looking forward to Sunday all week, and as I pull up to the lake house, I feel every muscle in my body relax. Last night was another killer night for the bar, and I'm looking forward to a day of rest and fun at the lake.

Daddy thinks I've been working too hard, but I don't want anything to mess up this streak of good business we've been having lately. He suggested I hire a few more people to work the bar, but ever since he gave me more responsibility in running the place, it's been hard to let go of my control and let someone else run it for the night. Even when Knox is there on my night off, I still stress out that something will go wrong. I usually end up making the short walk from our house to check on things, anyway.

We don't usually open up until six on Saturdays, which is nice, but we're open at five on the weekdays. On my evenings off, I often have some kind of catering event planned, so it's never really a night off. I cherish my Sundays more than anything these days.

The weather has been brutal this summer with temperatures in the hundreds, so the fact that the forecast said to expect a high of seventy-eight today makes me almost giddy with excitement.

Knox and Leigh Anne are setting things up in the kitchen when I arrive, my hands full of groceries.

"Am I the first one here?" I ask. I'm surprised because Daddy left the house at least half an hour before I did. He said he needed to get gas and pick up a few things, but I still thought he'd beat me out here.

Knox gives me a brief hug and helps me unpack the bags of food. "I cannot wait to taste your new recipe," he says.

"I spent most of the summer perfecting it, so I really think you'll like it," I say.

"What is it?" Leigh Anne asks.

"A new coleslaw recipe," I say. "I made a huge batch yesterday morning. If you like it, I'll leave some here for you."

"Mmmm. This is freaking amazing." I turn and see that Knox has already located the coleslaw and dipped his spoon into it.

"Hey, that's supposed to be for lunch," I say. "Get your grubby hands out of my slaw."

I grab the container from him and cover it back up, sticking it in the fridge.

"I was eating that," he protests.

"Which is why I took it from you." I grab the spoon from his hand and wave it at him. "No sampling the food before everyone is here and the whole meal is ready to go."

I set a pan on the stove, and when I turn around again, I see that Knox has opened another container and is sniffing the contents.

"Knox!" I sigh. "Leigh Anne, can you control your boyfriend for me, please? He's going to ruin his appetite."

Leigh Anne laughs and throws her hands up. "I can never control him around your food," she says. "It's your own fault for making everything so delicious."

"Is this the sauce for the ribs?" he asks. "I've been dying for this recipe. When are you going to share it with me?"

"No way." I pull the container out of his hands and he frowns. "Secret family recipe."

"I am your family," he says. He quickly dips his spoon into the sauce and sneaks a taste before I can pull it away. "Is that cinnamon? I can't quite put my finger on it."

Leigh Anne swats him with the back of her hand. "Leave Joey's food alone," she says. "Be good."

"I absolutely will not," he says, his eyes narrowed, but playful. "I've been looking forward to this for weeks."

I shake my head. "You're completely hopeless."

He smiles. "I just love good food. What's wrong with that?"

"Come on, help me get the ribs in the oven," I say. "They're going to need a good hour in here and then we'll take them out to the grill."

"Sounds good," he says.

I look out the window and frown. "You haven't heard anything from Dad yet?"

"No. Want me to call him?" Knox asks as he loads the ribs into the oven.

"I guess not," I say. "I don't want to call when he's driving. I'm sure he'll be here in a few minutes."

"He probably just saw someone he knows in town and is talking their ear off," Knox says.

"What else can we do to help?" Leigh Anne asks.

I put her to work chopping vegetables while Knox goes out to load some beer into his cooler. We talk about how things have been going with school and how she's feeling now that her trial is finally over.

If someone had told me two years ago that I'd be hanging out here at the abandoned lake house with Leigh Anne Davis. I never would have believed them. We'd been friends for a while back in elementary and middle school, but we drifted off once high school started and all the little cliques separated into rich and not rich. Popular and not popular. I was definitely in the not popular crowd, and Leigh Anne was queen of the richies.

I thought she was such a stuck-up snob back then, but she had either changed or I had completely misjudged her. These days, I wasn't sure I had a closer friend.

"Oh, I almost forgot. I have something for you guys. I'll be right back," I say, remembering the belated birthday present I'd bought for Leigh Anne.

I run out the back door to retrieve it from my car and see the familiar sideways smile of Colton Tucker as he pulls up in his truck, country music blasting. He parks next to me and leans his arm out the window.

"Hello, gorgeous," he says. "I hope I'm not too early."

"Not at all. Leigh Anne and Knox are inside," I say. "I just came out to grab a gift I brought for Leigh Anne."

"Were we supposed to bring something?" he asks. He

smiles and holds up his left hand. "All I brought was a six pack of beer."

I shake my head. "No, I've had this for a while and just haven't had a chance to get out here and give it to her," I say. "Come on, let's get inside. I'll put you to work in the kitchen."

I glance down the red clay drive that leads out to the main road.

"You didn't happen to see my daddy anywhere did you? He left before me and he's not here yet."

"No, I didn't see him," he says. "Did you try calling him?"

I shrug. "I'm sure he's fine," I say, and reach in the car to grab the wrapped gift on the passenger seat. When I straighten, I notice Colton's been studying my backside. I give him a look to let him know I've caught him ogling, but he just tilts his head to the side and raises an eyebrow. He gives me that half-smile of his that gets my heart racing every time.

Why does my body insist on betraying me every time he's around? Most of the time, he aggravates the mess out of me, but for some reason, when he gives me that certain look, my insides catch fire.

I spin on my heel and head toward the house, determined to give him absolutely no encouragement.

Inside, the smell of ribs and baked beans fills the house, and I inhale deeply.

"It smells amazing in here," Colton says, coming in right behind me.

He's uncomfortably close, so I move deeper into the kitchen and place my gift on the table.

"Hey, Leigh Anne," he says, pulling her into a hug. "What are you guys cooking?"

"Not us," Leigh Anne says, hugging him back. "Joey. She's the cook around here. Trust me when I say that no one wants to eat my cooking. Not until I can convince Joey to give me a few lessons."

"Wow, Joey, I had no idea," Colton says, my high school nickname rolling off his tongue with a sly smile.

"Jo, okay? Leigh Anne gets a pass because she actually knew me as Joey growing up," I say, putting a finger against his chest. "But to you, I'm Jo."

"Okay, Boss, whatever you say."

I narrow my eyes at him, and press my hand harder into his chest, backing him up toward the counter until he hits it and stops abruptly.

He's laughing so hard, I'm having a hard time holding onto my serious I-mean-business face.

"I am not going to let you get under my skin today, do you hear me?"

His lips stretch up into that familiar smile. "I get under your skin?" he asks.

Crap. I did not just admit that out loud.

I groan. "No, that's not what I meant," I say, fumbling my words and walking away. "I just mean you're not going to start today."

"Mmm-hmm," he says, grabbing a carrot from the cutting board.

I turn back to stir the sauce, hoping he can't tell that I'm blushing. My entire face is flushed and warm.

"Why don't you head out back with Knox and do manly

SARRA CANNON

things together?" I say. "Make him take you out to his shop and show you what he's working on or something."

"You're the boss," he says.

I turn around, my eyes widening. He just isn't going to let up, is he?

He meets my eyes and winks, and I swear I just want to jump over the island and wring his neck.

Which of course brings to mind an image of us jumping on the island together and making out. What the heck is wrong with my brain?

I shake my head and try to push these images from my head. I don't know what is wrong with me lately. After my run-in with Bryan the other night, I made a specific effort to avoid Colton most of the week. I just didn't want to deal with all the questions I know he wanted to ask. I switched a couple shifts with Knox and didn't really have to spend much time with Colton until last night.

Luckily we were so busy that we didn't do anything more than work our butts off for most of the night, and when it was all over, I left the guys to do all the cleaning while I went home to get some rest.

I was exhausted from watching the door all night to make sure Bryan didn't try to sneak inside. Slim was under strict orders to send him away if he showed up, but when I asked at the end of the night, Slim said he hadn't seen any sign of the guy.

Dad had been pissed to hear that Bryan came into the bar. He agreed with me about putting in an alarm system at the house, and it's scheduled to go in next week sometime. It might end up being overkill, but I don't want to take any chances of

64

repeating what happened when I was in high school. Bryan just isn't the type of guy that can be trusted to act like a civilized human being. Especially when he's been drinking.

"What are you thinking about?" Leigh Anne asks. "You look so angry all of a sudden. Is Colton really getting to you that much?"

I shake my head. "No, gosh, no. Colton's fine," I say. I pause and set down my spoon. I didn't want to mention what happened to anyone, but Leigh Anne has more experience with this stuff than I do. Maybe she could really help. "Can I ask you a personal question?"

She picks up the knife and gets back to work cutting carrots. "Of course."

"When you were still living on campus after what happened to you, how did you handle it when you ran into him?" I ask, hoping I'm not going to upset her by talking about this. "I mean, did he ever threaten you or try to talk to you again?"

Leigh Anne studies me. "Has something happened to you?" she asks.

I close my eyes and sigh. I should have known better than to start a conversation about this when I know I'm not ready to talk about it.

"I wasn't raped, if that's what you mean," I say. "I just went through some hard times with a guy back in high school, and he showed up again at the bar the other night. It was really tough seeing him again. I'm just not sure how to handle it. Emotionally."

She takes a deep breath. "It's a difficult thing to handle, when you've been through something traumatic because of someone else," she says. "When they've hurt you, but they refuse to really take responsibility for it."

Her words echo deep inside that locked chamber in my heart, and I have to turn away so she won't see the tears in my eyes.

"To be honest, I didn't handle it very well," she says. "Not at first. He acted like he couldn't imagine he did anything wrong. Like hey, maybe we could go out again sometime and didn't we have such a great night together? It made me sick to my stomach. Most of the time I tried to avoid him. If I saw him somewhere, I'd turn and go a different way. But when I did run into him, I just made sure to never let him see that he'd won, you know? I kept my head up, and I held it together. I didn't want him to know he still had any power over me."

I nod and wipe the back of my hand across my cheek.

"Hey, are you crying?" she asks. I hear the knife hit the cutting board, and seconds later she has her hands on my shoulders, spinning me around. "What's going on, Joey? Are you alright?"

She pulls me closer and wraps her arms around me.

I can't help but sob into her shoulder and hold tightly to her. "I'm going to be okay," I say through my tears. "I know I probably sound crazy, but I really appreciate you talking to me about it."

"You don't sound crazy," she says. "You sound scared. You can always come to me if you want to talk about it."

I pull away and sniff, wiping the tears from my face.

"Thank you, Leigh Anne. I can't believe I just cried all over your shirt," I say with a choked laugh.

"It's okay, really," she says. "And I understand if you're not ready to talk about what happened yet. I've so been there. But just know that I'm here, okay?"

I nod and take a deep breath. "Thank you."

Outside, the sound of tires crunching on gravel catch my attention. I stand on my toes to see out the window above the sink, grateful when my father smiles and waves.

CHAPTER 10
COLTON

The food looks so amazing, it's making my mouth water.

"You really cooked all this?" I say to Jo, amazed. "I had no idea you were such a chef."

"Jo is the best cook in the state, I swear to God," Leigh Anne says. "Just wait 'til you taste these ribs."

"Yeah, if she doesn't give up the recipe to this homemade bbq sauce soon, I'm just going to ransack her house and come find it for myself," Knox said.

"Come on now, you don't think I'd be dumb enough to actually write it down, do you?" Jo lifts an eyebrow and stares Knox down as she sets a basket of bread on the table.

It's a gorgeous day out and the leaves are all just starting to change colors, so the forest is lit up with bright reds and oranges. Penny and Mason arrived with Penny's twin brother Preston and his girlfriend Jenna, so we have a full, happy group. We all sit down at the large picnic table Knox made and Rob offers to say a quick prayer.

"Dear Lord, thank you so much for this delicious food that my daughter has prepared for us. Thank you for the gift of such beautiful weather," he says. "And most of all, we thank you for this time spent with friends and family. Amen."

"Amen."

"Colton, pass me your plate, and I'll get you started with a slab of ribs," Knox says.

"Thank you, sir." I hand my plate over and Knox loads it up with ribs that are dripping with bbq sauce.

Jo is sitting across from me, and she takes a heaping spoonful of coleslaw and then passes the bowl over. I cannot wait to taste all this food. There's corn on the cob fresh from the grill, homemade bread, baked beans, and I heard a rumor there was a chocolate cake for dessert.

"How come you've never talked about how much you like to cook?" I ask as we pass the food around the table.

Jo shrugs. "It's never come up."

I take my first bite of the ribs and my mouth explodes with flavor. The meat is so tender it falls off the bone.

I literally moan, it's so good. "Oh, my Lord, that's the best thing I've ever tasted in my life."

Jo giggles and tries to hide her face behind her hands.

"You're going to be hooked for life," Mason says.

"I can't believe this," I say between bites. "Why aren't you serving this in the bar?"

"We don't have a license to serve food," Jo says. "We don't even have a proper kitchen."

"Build one," I say.

"Hush," Jo says, shaking her head.

"Now, wait a second, that's not a bad idea," Penny says.

She leans forward against the table.

"Things are going so well at the bar lately, we could really use this momentum and make plans to build an addition," Knox says.

"Hold on, this is crazy," Jo says. "We just barely got back on our feet. We can't afford to build an addition right now. And do you know how much is involved with starting a restaurant? There are all kinds of codes to meet, inspections, permits."

"I'm not saying it would be easy, I'm just saying you could make a fortune selling food like this," I say. "It would be worth it. People would drive a hundred miles to get a taste of these ribs."

Jo's face flushes a dark crimson and she lowers her head to her hand. "Seriously, you guys, don't be ridiculous." She looks up and holds her palm out toward Rob. "Tell 'em, Daddy. This is crazy, right?"

Rob's eyes are sparkling, and I smile. He's on board, I can tell.

"It's not a bad idea, pumpkin," he says. "Think about it. We could put together a whole menu of your favorite recipes. Heck, we could even open up for lunch."

"That would take an entire renovation," she says. "We'd have to close the whole place down, get permits from the city, hire a contractor, go through inspections just to make sure the kitchen's clean. We'd also have to hire more employees like an extra cook and some servers. I couldn't be in there cooking all day by myself."

"Oh, I see what the problem is," Knox says, threading his fingers together and narrowing his eyes at her. "You just don't want to have to share your recipes with someone else."

She smiles and tosses a fresh piece of bread toward his head. She aims too high and it goes sailing off into the dirt several feet behind him.

"You guys are just ganging up on me now," she says. Then she turns to me, her eyes focused in on mine. "This is all your fault Colton Tucker."

I smile. "I'll gladly take the blame if it means you actually take this under consideration."

"You can't really think this food is good enough to open a restaurant," she says.

"I do," I say, completely serious. "It's some of the best food I've ever tasted in my life. You could really have something here."

"I agree," Preston says. "This is amazing."

She takes in a breath and runs a hand over her hair. It's pulled back in a loose ponytail today.

"You did try to start a catering company," Leigh Anne says. "So it's not totally out of the ballpark, right?"

"I tried, but it was just too much to keep up with," she says. "Too much to do on my own and work the bar at nights, too. I couldn't manage it all. All I'm doing is a few small jobs a month, nothing significant."

"If you open a restaurant right at the bar, it would be so much easier to manage than trying to advertise and drum up business. Much less having to cart everything off to different locations for catering jobs," I say. "This could really be something special, Jo. I'm not joking around. You should really think about it."

"I don't even know where we'd get the money," she says.

"I'll invest," Knox says. "I can even agree to be your contractor, if you want. I can bring in a few of the guys who have been working for me lately, and we could build the addition ourselves. Make sure everything is done just right."

"I bet my dad would be interested in investing in a new restaurant here in town," Preston says. "Just say the word. We could probably help swing all those permits you were talking about."

Jo meets my eyes again and shakes her head. She's trying to hide it, but a smile breaks out on her lips. She ducks her head again and laughs.

"This is a crazy idea," she says.

I clean the rest of my plate and watch her. I've never seen her look so happy and vulnerable, as if this is something risky but worthwhile.

"Maria's going to kill you for suggesting this," Leigh Anne says, joking about our old boss at Brantley's. "More competition in town for a good bar and grille is the last thing she needs."

"I won't tell if you don't," I say.

Everyone laughs, but it's Jo who has my attention. She looks up, her face half-hidden behind her hands with her elbows propped up on the table. She shakes her head again, but I can see the smile in her eyes.

"Just promise me you'll think about it," I say. "The world needs this kind of food."

She giggles again and picks up a piece of bread, aiming for my head. "Let's change the subject, before I run out of bread to throw."

But I can see the pride in her eyes. I can see just how important something like this would be to her. And more than anything, I realize just how exciting it is to see her be truly happy.

CHAPTER 11

JO

After lunch, the guys offer to clean while Leigh Anne and I relax by the lake. I look around. I'm not sure where Penny and Jenna have gotten off to. Maybe a walk with Penny's little girl in the stroller.

I sit down on the dock and take off my shoes, dipping my feet into the water.

I shiver and pull them back out. "Ooh, that's cold."

"It's hard to believe it's fall already," Leigh Anne says, leaning back on her hands. "Time seems to just be flying by."

"You'll be graduating after this year, right?"

She nods.

"Then what?"

Leigh Anne looks out over the water and shakes her head. "I have no idea," she says. "Knox is just starting to get his woodworking business off the ground, so I'm sure he wants to stick around Fairhope. I haven't given it much thought, though. I guess I better get on that."

I laugh. "Maybe so," I say. "You'll figure it out. Just follow your heart."

"Thanks," she says.

"Hey, Leigh Anne? Can you come in here for a second?" Knox calls from the house. "I want you to show Rob that video you took the other day. I can't find it."

"Be right there," she says.

Leigh Anne stands up and brushes her hands off on her jeans.

"That's really good advice, you know."

"What?" I ask.

"To follow your heart," she says. "Maybe you should really think about that restaurant thing."

I nod, my stomach filling with butterflies all over again.

She takes off toward the house, and I lay back against the wood of the old dock.

A restaurant?

I stare up at the changing leaves and try to imagine what it would be like to run and own a restaurant of my own. It's a lot of hard work, but I can't think of anything more fun. I could spend all day experimenting in the kitchen with new recipes and combinations. I could put together fun menus and better than anything, I could cook as much as I wanted to.

My heart races at the thought.

I love tending bar and taking care of my dad's place, but adding a restaurant would make it my own in a way I never even dreamed about until now.

Is this really something we could do?

"Good idea," Colton says, interrupting my daydream. He

sits down beside me and leans all the way back until he's lying down beside me with his arms propped under his head. "I could probably use a nap, too, after all the food. I'm stuffed."

"Feel free to take some of the leftovers home with you, if you want."

"Oh, I most definitely want," he says. "I want to get a piece of that chocolate cake I heard about, too."

I laugh. "I figured everyone was so full from lunch that it could wait a bit," I say. "We'll cut some up in a few minutes if you think you can handle it."

"Have you always loved to cook?" He rolls onto his side and props his elbow against the dock.

I turn my head toward him, painfully aware of just how close we are right now.

"Growing up it was just me and Dad, and he doesn't know the first thing about cooking," I say. "I guess I picked it up out of necessity after Mom left. Lucky for him, I was pretty good at it."

"I'm glad I got a chance to come over today," he says. "I would have been sad to miss it."

"If you missed it, you would have never known it was worth being sad about," I say.

He laughs. "Don't you know better than to talk in riddles when a man has a full belly?" he says. "I was trying to say I loved the food."

"I appreciate it," I say. I glance up, and the way he's staring down at me sends a jolt through my heart. I suddenly want very badly for him to kiss me.

My gaze dips to his mouth, and I feel like I can't breathe.

For months now I've been trying to deny that there was anything real between us. It was a simple flirtation, and that was as far as it would ever get. That was all it would ever mean to me, period.

I've denied it, because I don't want this. I like my life just the way it is. It's safe and simple and comfortable. Relationships make everything messy and confusing, and in the end, someone usually ends up getting hurt. I don't need that in my life.

But sitting out here on the dock with the cool autumn breeze blowing across my skin and the afternoon sun peeking out from behind a cloud, this feels like the simplest thing in the world.

I want Colton Tucker to kiss me.

Something I haven't wanted from any man in as long as I can remember.

My lips part so that I can draw a breath, but my heart is pumping so hard, it catches in my throat. Not once does Colton look away from my face, and as he moves toward me, half my body lights on fire in anticipation.

"Jojo, get up here," Daddy calls from the porch. "You've got to see this. It's hilarious."

Colton pulls back and stands so fast, I'm surprised when he doesn't fall backwards into the lake.

I sit up and run a nervous hand through my hair. "Coming," I yell back.

Daddy disappears into the house, and Colton holds his hand out to me, helping me get back to my feet.

"Maybe we could—"

"I should go—"

We both start talking at the same time, and then laugh like awkward teenagers. The perfect moment has passed, and as we make our way back up to the house, I wonder if it will ever come again.

CHAPTER 12
COLTON

"**H**ow many of y'all are ready for some good music tonight?"

The crowd at Rob's is epic this weekend. Rob told me there was a line of fifty people still waiting outside when they had to close it down. I told him we better work on getting a bigger place, and he just laughed. But from the way things are going, Rob's is quickly becoming the place to be on a Saturday night.

"I couldn't hear you guys, I said who's ready for some music?"

The screams get louder, and I search for those deep brown eyes behind the bar. Jo smiles and shakes her head, but I know she loves it.

"Okay, settle down. Y'all don't have to scream. I can hear you," I say, and everyone laughs. I turn to put my arm around the lead singer of this week's band. "Let me introduce y'all to one of the best up-and-coming bands in the South. Out of Athens, Georgia, let's give it up for Woodland Pride."

The music begins and everyone goes wild. I heard the band during their warm-up, and they're pretty darn good. Mostly covers with a few original songs thrown in, but I've got something really special in mind for a few weeks from now. If I can pull it off.

I can't wait to tell Jo about it. She's going to totally freak out.

I jump down off the stage and make my way through the crowd, my eyes on her.

It's been a week since the day out at the lake, and I haven't been able to stop thinking about her. There was a moment there where I felt so connected to her, it scared me. I was pulled toward her, as if I couldn't control myself or think of anything but wanting to kiss her.

If her father hadn't come outside at just the wrong moment, we would have kissed. And there hasn't been a minute since then that I haven't wanted to do it again.

We worked together a few times over the past week, but we never had any time alone. There's a part of me that wonders if it wasn't a blessing that her daddy interrupted our kiss. She's technically my boss, and this job is the best thing to come around for me in a long time. I can't afford to mess this up, and the one surefire way to do that is to get involved with her.

It's stupid, right? A fling with Jo would be amazing, and there isn't a part of me that doubts how good it would be to turn that girl's world upside down for a little while.

But what happens when it ends?

Because with me, it always ends.

Most of my ex-girlfriends—if you can even call them that since I don't think I've ever been in a truly committed relationship in my life—are still good friends of mine. Something tells me it wouldn't be that way with Jo. She's not exactly the type of woman who goes out every weekend and fools around with a lot of different guys.

If we start something up, it could get complicated. Am I ready for complicated?

But as I walk toward her, I really don't care. I just want to jump in head-first and enjoy the ride.

"You're a natural on stage," she says when I hop over the counter and join her behind the bar.

"Yes, I do believe I am," I say. "I think now would be the perfect time to ask for a raise."

"Don't press your luck," she says. She pulls a few beers from the cooler and passes them to a group of college guys.

"What if I told you I might have a band coming in next month that currently has a song on the Top 100 Country Music Charts?" I say.

"I'd say you need to lay off the booze while you're working."

My lips curl into a smile, and I wait, arms crossed casually.

She serves a few more people and then turns back to me. She shakes her head. "Wait a second. You're not serious, right?"

"Serious as a heart attack."

She eyes me. "Who? And how?"

I shrug. "I mean, if you don't have faith in me, maybe I ought to tell them not to come," I say, walking away.

She grabs my arm and spins me around. "Colton Tucker, you tell me right this second. Who?"

Oh, man, I love teasing her. Her cheeks get rosy and her

brown eyes sparkle as if there are fireworks going off somewhere inside.

"Long Road Ahead," I say. "But if you aren't interested—"

She screams and throws her arms around my neck. "Are you serious right now? I mean, Long Road Ahead here at our little hole in the wall bar?"

A group of people standing at the bar applaud, and I realize they're staring at us, not the band. I throw my hands up, pretending to be exasperated, and roll my eyes.

"Women, right?" I say.

The group laughs, and Jo pulls away and smacks my shoulder.

"Stop playing around." But she's laughing, and it's music to my ears. "Long Road Ahead?"

"Yes, ma'am," I say. "Nothing's set in stone yet, but I'll know for sure in a couple weeks. Now, can we talk about that raise?"

Her smile is so wide, it reaches into my soul and lights me up.

"I'll seriously think about it," she says. Someone down at the end calls her name, and we're starting to get a backlog of drink requests. "We need to get to work, but we'll talk about this after, okay? Not the raise part, but the band part."

"Or both, you know, if you're feeling frisky." I watch her turn and walk to the other side of the bar, a spring in her step that wasn't there before.

Her hair is up in braids again tonight, and I find myself obsessed with the idea of taking it down and sinking my hands into it.

"Can we get some drinks over here? Or are you too busy checking out your co-worker?" My friend Mike is standing near the counter shouting so loud, I'll be shocked if Jo didn't hear him.

"Is that any way to treat the guy you're hoping to get drinks from?" I say, laughing. "What can I get for you?"

"Tequila shots, all around," he says.

His girlfriend Jenny gives me a little wave, but she's singing along with the band.

"Just the two of you?"

"No, we're over there with Grant and Avery," he says, pointing to our other set of friends standing a little closer to the stage. "You should come out with us tonight when you knock off work. We're going down to the beach to build a bonfire."

"I'll think about it," I say, pouring out four shots of Tequila.

He throws a twenty on the bar and gathers up the glasses. "See you out there if you can make it," he says. "You know the spot."

I raise my chin. "Yep."

I glance down at Jo, and wonder if she'd come with me. There's probably no chance in hell, but that isn't going to stop me from asking her.

"Rum and coke."

I turn to the next guy in line, and stop short. "Hey, I know you," I say. I pour his drink, but I'm trying to put my finger on where I've seen him before.

He smiles. "Owen in the Mornings," he says, naming the local radio station's popular morning show. "I'm Owen."

He reaches across the bar and we shake hands.

"Owen, that's right," I say. "Drinks on the house for a local celebrity. Thanks for coming in tonight."

"I appreciate that," he says. "What you guys are getting started here is really something special. It's good for Fairhope."

"I couldn't agree more."

"And so are you," he says.

I glance up, trying to figure out if he's hitting on me or what. I have had my fair share of invitations at this bar, but this would be the first time it was coming from a guy.

"Um, thanks," I say.

He laughs. "I mean that you've really got a stage presence," he says. "I had a friend in the crowd last week who told me I should come check you out, and I'm glad I did. You've got the right kind of voice and personality."

"I'm confused, but flattered," I say.

He pulls a card from his wallet and pushes it across the bar. "My sidekick, Scottie, is leaving the show in six months, and I've got to find a good replacement," he says. "I'm inviting DJ's from all over to come in and audition, but I would love to have a hometown voice on the show."

I pick up the card and stare at it, not really sure I heard him right.

"You want me to audition for your radio show?"

"Yes, sir. I think you would be a natural for radio."

I slowly shake my head and put the card back down on the bar. "I'm more of a sleeping-in kind of guy," I say. "But I appreciate the thought."

"Think about it," he says. He picks up his drink and starts to move away. "I think you're exactly what I've been looking for."

I nod and pick up the card again. Me on the radio?

There's a nervous knot in my stomach just thinking

about it. A job like that could be fun, but it would be a lot of responsibility, having to get up crazy early in the morning and perform for people every day. I'm not sure I'm cut out for it.

"What's that?" Jo asks. She presses her arm against mine as she leans in to get a closer look.

"Nothing," I say, tossing the card into the trash.

But as I stare after the radio guy, I realize this is the first time in my life someone thought I was better than nothing. It's the first time I actually felt like something.

CHAPTER 13

JO

"**G**oodnight Slim," I say, standing on my tiptoes to hug him one last time. "Thanks again for tonight."

"Anytime, Miss Jo," he says. "It was fun."

"Might be an even bigger crowd next week, so I hope you're ready."

"I can handle it." He smiles and makes his way out to his car.

I close and lock the door behind him, collapsing against it with a sigh of relief.

"We did it," I shout. "Another successful Saturday night in the books."

"Have you looked at this tip jar?" Colton says, whistling.

"As good as last week?"

"Better than good," he says.

I'm exhausted, but giddy. A year and a half ago we were scared we were going to have to close the doors on this old place, so to be booming is a dream come true.

"We need a drink to celebrate," I say.

Colton raises an eyebrow. "Before we even count the money and clean up?" He glances around. "Who are you and what have you done with Jo?"

"Haha, very funny," I say, sitting down at one of the barstools across from him. "I know I can be tough sometimes, but I think we both deserve a break tonight, don't you? We'll get this place cleaned up before we go home. I'll come over tomorrow on my day off and finish up if I have to."

"Scotch?" he asks.

"Not tonight. Tonight I want a Corona with a lime," I say. "And a shot of tequila. The good stuff."

He pretends to stumble backward, clutching his chest. "Oh my God, a woman after my own heart," he says. "You are not playing around, are you?"

I laugh. "I'm happy and tired and I'm not going to let anything ruin it tonight," I say. "Not even me."

He opens the Corona and pulls a fresh lime from the cooler, taking his sweet time cutting it up before he squeezes one slice into the top of my beer. He sets up a couple glasses and pours two shots of Patron.

"To the best night yet," he says, meeting my eyes.

I can't help but wonder if there's a double meaning to his toast.

I pick up my glass and touch it against his. "To the best night yet."

AN HOUR LATER, WE ARE BOTH THREE SHOTS AND TWO beers deep into the night. We've managed to clean up most of the mess behind the bar and set all the chairs and tables back up, and now we are just sitting together alone, enjoying the silence.

"So, I want to know more about what Owen Kanton was over there talking to you about earlier," I say.

"Oh, him? He just wanted a recipe for my Fairhope Iced Tea," he says, avoiding my eyes. "It's famous around here."

"Tell me the truth," I say. "You guys were standing there talking for a while."

"Really, it's nothing important," he says.

"I want to know, and if you don't tell me right now, I'll cut your shifts for a week," I say, teasing of course.

He gives me his lopsided smile and his eyes light up. "You never let up, do you?"

"Not when I can tell *'nothing important'* is really something special," I say. "What did he want?"

He messes with the label on his beer bottle, pulling pieces off and rolling them into tiny balls that he sets on the bar top.

"Well, Mr. Owen seemed to agree with you. He thinks I'm a natural on stage and had some crazy idea about me coming in to audition for the morning show."

"What?" I scream and stand up. "Are you serious?"

"It's nothing, Jo, really."

"That is not nothing," I say. "That's huge. When is the audition?"

"I'm not going to audition for some morning show," he says. "Do you realize how early those guys have to get up?"

I roll my eyes. "Don't be ridiculous. Sleep all afternoon

if you want to sleep," I say. "You don't turn down an opportunity to be on the radio. That's one of the most popular morning shows in the state. There are rumors they're going national soon, but I heard there was some kind of hold up."

"Losing his partner would probably qualify."

"I would bet," I say. "So he's scouting out talent, and he came here tonight to see you? Colton, that's big news. You have to go."

"I wouldn't be able to work the bar at night and go into work again at the crack of dawn," he says. "And I like tending bar."

"Come in on the weekends," I say. "We could work it out. But if you got that gig, you probably wouldn't need a second job. I bet it pays pretty well."

He takes a long breath through his nose and shakes his head. "It's just not me. It feels too much like a career, you know? I like living with the illusion that I'm a free man," he says. "I can go anywhere and do anything I want at any time I choose. With a real job like that, I'd be stuck in this town every day of my life."

"First of all, this is a real job, thank you very much," I say. I'm afraid I'm slurring my words a little bit, but I take another sip of my beer anyway. "Third of all, you never really go anywhere now."

He smiles. "You skipped second of all."

I frown and finish my beer. "Second of all," I say, searching my mind for another point I was trying to make, "I like having you stuck in this town."

"Do you?" His eyebrow flicks up and my heart flutters.

My face flushes and the back of my neck feels like it's on

fire. "I mean, I'm glad you came to work for us, but that's a good opportunity. I think you should go to that audition."

He shakes his head and sits up straight. "I'll think about it."

"Good enough," I say. "How's the apartment working out for you?"

I've specifically been avoiding the garage, because I didn't want to be tempted to go hang out with him. That doesn't mean I haven't been thinking about it, though. In fact, it's been driving me wild.

"It's great," he says. "Thanks again for letting me stay."

I hand him my empty beer and he reaches into the cooler for another.

"No more," I say. "I'm starting to get a little giggly, and when that happens, it's time to call it quits."

His smile drops for a second, or did I imagine it?

"Let me get you some water, instead," he says. "Don't want you trying to walk the long journey home without sobering up."

I giggle and then quickly cover my mouth, embarrassed. He cuts a sideways glance at me.

"See?"

He pours an ice water and pushes it toward me. "You have a nice laugh."

I sip my water and the room gets quiet. We both seem to realize the night is winding down. It's after three in the morning, and everyone else is long gone. Pretty soon we're going to run out of excuses to be hanging out this late. It's either admit there's something more between us or part ways.

And I'm not sure whether I'm being stupid or what, but I

don't get up from my seat. I just wait and hope he doesn't make some excuse about being too tired and wanting to get home.

"Let's see. Last weekend you quizzed me about my family. So what's your story?" he asks, coming around the bar and settling down on the stool beside me. "You're an only child, right?"

I exhale. I so didn't want this night to end just yet.

"Growing up it was just me and my dad for as long as I can remember," I say.

"What happened to your mom? If you don't mind me asking."

The strange thing is, I didn't mind. I usually hate talking about my mom, but with Colton, everything is easy. He has a way about him that just puts everyone at ease, including me.

"She left us when I was a little girl," I say. "I had just turned five when she told us she was going to go visit her parents for a few days in Tennessee. She said she'd be gone a week, tops, but she never got there. And she never came home."

"Wow, where did she go?"

"I have no idea," I say. "After about two days, Dad was worried out of his mind. He'd called her parents about a thousand times asking about her, and they just kept saying they hadn't heard from her. She apparently had never even told them she was coming there to visit. Dad was convinced her car had broken down somewhere on the road and she'd been murdered or something horrible. It was one of the scariest weeks of my life. I swear neither one of us slept a wink. He'd called nearly every hospital from here to Nashville trying to find her, but no one had any information."

"I can't even imagine that," he says. "Did you ever find out where she was?"

"She called him about a week later out of the blue, acting like nothing was wrong," I say. "I still don't know everything they said to each other that night, and I was too little to really understand what was happening. I just remember Dad yelling for what seemed like forever, telling her she needed to come home and talk about this instead of running off like a coward. She never even said goodbye to me, really. She just called that one time to tell him she was gone and that he shouldn't come looking for her. We never heard from her again except when Dad got the divorce papers in the mail."

"Holy shit," Colton says. He runs a hand across his forehead. "I'm so sorry. I had no idea."

I shrug, and the simplicity of the gesture tells me how far I've come toward accepting what happened between my mother and me. It has taken me years to come to terms with her leaving, but now it just feels like something that was always meant to be.

"It's okay," I say. "I've come to believe that it was for the best, really. I hardly even remember her now. It's always just been me and Daddy, like two little peas in a pod."

"You two look out for each other, huh?"

"Always," I say. "I can't even imagine life without him."

"He's a good man," Colton says.

"I guess I should probably go home and check on him again," I say. "It's getting pretty late, anyway."

"Don't go," he says softly, touching my hand. It's the first time he's touched me so deliberately, and it flows through me like warm honey. "Stay for one more drink. I'm buying."

He raises an eyebrow and smiles, but I shake my head.

I've already stayed too long and said too much. I've already opened up my heart a little more than I intended, and I'm afraid if I don't walk away now, it's going to lead to something messy and complicated and painful. I don't have room in my life right now for all that, and it isn't right for me to lead him on and think there's more to this than there really ever can be.

So why do I want to stay?

"I really need to get going," I say. "But thank you for this. I had a nice time."

"I'll walk out with you," he says.

He clears the beer bottles off the top of the bar and sets the shot glasses next to the sink. I step into the office to shut down the computer and lock up the safe. When I come back out, he's waiting for me.

I lock the door behind us and walk with him across the back parking lot toward my house.

My heart is racing now that we're out here in the dark together. As much as I don't want it to, this feels like the end of a first date, and I can't help but feel nervous butterflies dancing around in my stomach.

"Well, I'll see you Monday, if not before," I say. "Enjoy the day off tomorrow."

"You too," he says. "What are you up to?"

"Inventory," I say.

"Doesn't sound much like a day off."

"No, I guess not."

Neither one of us moves, and I must look silly still standing here just waiting for him to say more. Why does it feel like there should be more?

I'm so mixed up, I'm not even sure what I want him to

say. Or if I just want him to say nothing and turn and leave before I do something stupid.

"Goodnight," I say, finally.

He takes a deep breath, and his eyes drop to my lips. I swallow back desire, knowing I need to get inside the house and forget what I'm feeling so that I can keep my life even and sane and safe.

But just as I force myself to turn away, he touches my arm and pulls me back.

There is only a breath of air between us as he moves his body closer to mine. I can feel his heart beating against the side of my arm as he clutches it to his chest.

He doesn't say anything, but this is not a moment that needs words. Right now, there is only a choice. Yes or no. Do we walk through this door, or do we let the possibility of what could have been pass us by?

I know what he wants, because he's telling me with his eyes and with the way he's holding so tightly to my arm. But he's waiting to know what I want. He's waiting for me to decide.

It's my heart that gives in, and I lean toward him, terrified, but excited at the same time.

All it takes is that one movement—that one moment of yes—and he wraps his arms around me. His warm lips descend on mine, and I melt into him.

Every inch of my body burns as he kisses me. I lift up, my hand touching his cheek and pulling him closer. I want more. I don't care how dangerous this is, I want to step into the fire and never look back.

When he pulls away, he takes my hands in his and holds them close to his body, warming them with his heat. "You have no idea how long I've been wanting to do that," he whispers.

I want to tell him to do it again, but the familiar fear is already creeping back in, telling me I'm in scary territory. That I should quit while I'm still ahead.

"You're trembling," he says.

I'm terrified. I don't say it, but I feel it down to my toes.

I haven't let anyone kiss me in years, which is ridiculous for someone my age to say, but it's the truth. I've avoided moments like this exact one with everything that I am, and now that it's here, I have no idea what to do next. My heart says stay, but my brain says run.

"Say something so I know I didn't just completely freak you out," he says with a nervous laugh.

"I don't know what to say." My voice sounds foreign and frightened, which I'm sure is not at all what he wants to hear from me, but I have nothing else to offer.

"It hasn't completely escaped my notice that you turn down any guy who gets within ten feet of you at the bar," he says, running his fingers across mine. "I know you're guarded and careful and focused, but all those things are part of why I absolutely cannot stop thinking about you."

I meet his eyes and shiver in the cool evening air. It's still early fall, and it's an unusually cool night for this time of year, but it's as if the kiss stole all my warmth and left me feeling vulnerable.

"I like you, Jo. More than I can possibly put into words," he says. "Tonight has been one of the best nights I've had in a long time, and I'd be lying if I said I didn't want more of that. But I don't want to rush you into anything you aren't sure about yet, either. If you're guarded, I know there's probably a reason behind that, too, and I'm not going to push you into telling me why. I just want you to know I understand and I see it and I'm willing to take this slow if that's what you need. I just want to be close to you."

His words take my breath away. I've never had a guy speak so plainly and honestly to me, just putting his heart out there on the line without holding anything back. I have no idea how to do the same thing for him.

I can't speak, so I rest my head against his chest, closing my eyes as his strong arms wrap around my body and hold me close. I listen to the rapid beating of his heart and lean into the rise and fall of his breaths. I concentrate on the way his fingers feel as they create lazy patterns across my back. I breathe in, loving the scent of him and the way his body warms me and makes me feel safe, despite my fear.

Colton is more patient than I expect him to be, and he holds me this way for a long few minutes as we stand together, just breathing and being. I try to imagine what it might feel like to have a man like him in my life. Someone I could depend on and have fun with and talk to. Someone I could fall in love with and trust with my darkest secrets.

For the longest time, I've refused to believe it was possible for someone like me. I thought that maybe I was just destined to be alone. But now, there's hope of something more.

Is Colton the kind of guy who's going to stick around, though? Or is he just looking for someone to have a good time with for a little while?

That's the question that keeps rolling around in my brain like a marble.

Life would be so much easier if I just had a crystal ball

and could glance into the future to see if this could work out between us. Will he love me? Or will he hurt me? The not knowing is what scares me most. I know what it's like to regret falling in love, and I'm not sure I could survive that a second time. It nearly destroyed me once, and I never thought I would want to give any other guy a chance to do it again.

Not until now.

I finally pull away and take a deep breath.

Colton smiles slightly and waits, not taking his hands from my waist.

"You're right. I'm scared," I say. "I'm not good at this kind of thing. I'm not good at anything that makes me feel out of control or uncertain, and getting into a relationship is just about the most out of control thing there is in my mind. All I know right now is that I liked the way it felt to kiss you."

His face breaks out into an even bigger smile. "Well, that's a good start, then," he says.

I can't help but smile back, which is what I'm always doing around him. He makes me happy, I realize, and how can I turn away from happiness?

"Tonight took me by surprise, and I might need some time to work out how I'm really feeling about all of this, but for now, I just want you to kiss me again before I change my mind," I say. If I thought my heart was racing before, now it was practically lifting off.

"You don't have to tell me twice," he mumbles before he tilts his head toward mine.

I giggle and throw my arms around his neck, holding on as he kisses me again.

I run a hand up the back of his neck and into his thick hair. He moans and his lips part.

I push aside my fears and let the kiss take over. I lean into him, open myself to him.

When he finally pulls away, I have no idea how long we've been kissing. I imagine my dad standing at the window like I was still a teenager, scowling at the boy who has me up late at night making out on the front lawn.

And I realize I feel young again. The thought brings hot tears to my eyes, and I dip my chin so Colton won't see.

So much of my youth was wasted on grownup concerns and sorrows. I haven't felt this light and free in years. It feels better than I care to admit.

I smile into him, hugging him and loving the way his scruffy cheek feels against mine.

"Okay, I really should get inside before this turns into something we don't want the neighbors to see," I say with a laugh.

"All the neighbors are asleep," he whispers, kissing my neck and not letting go.

"You obviously haven't met Mrs. Crosswell yet. She's practically a vampire, I swear. She never sleeps. She just sits at her window and watches everything that goes on in this town," I say. Still, I don't pull away from his kisses. "Half the town will hear about this by noon."

"Let them talk," he says. Then he pulls away and raises an eyebrow. "Unless you want to just come over to my place and keep this thing going?"

I smack his shoulder. "And to think I actually believed you when you said you were willing to take it slow."

He laughs and pretends to be hurt. "Hey, willing and wanting are two very different things."

The thought of going any further than this spins my head around. If his kisses have me this mixed up, I can't even think about what something more would do to me right now.

I'm definitely not ready for that just yet.

I lean in and kiss him softly. "I'm going inside," I say. "Thank you for a wonderful evening."

He takes my hand and kisses it softly. "Good night," he says.

I smile so hard it makes my cheeks hurt. It's nearly four in the morning, and as I pull away to walk toward the door, I realize I feel more awake and more alive than I have in years.

Colton watches as I put my key in the door and go inside. I offer up a simple wave and he smiles back, lowering his head as he lifts one hand in the air.

I close the door between us and lean against it, enjoying the way my heart's still racing. I touch my fingers to my lips, hardly able to believe this is anything more than a dream.

And thinking that if it is, I don't ever want to wake up.

CHAPTER 14
JO

I sleep until eleven and wake up pleasantly achy and sore from working so hard the night before. I still can't believe how well things are going with the live music nights, and the thought of expanding and turning our place into a bar and restaurant is actually looking like a possibility.

And then I remember.

My fingertips fly to my lips, and I smile and duck deeper under the covers.

I don't know whether to laugh or cry. Colton kissed me last night.

This is so not in my plan of how to control my life, but somehow it happened, and I close my eyes and let the memory replay in my head.

I want to see him again.

I have that funny feeling in my stomach that says I'm nervous to be around him, and excited to see what happens next. It's such a foreign feeling for me. Most guys don't even register. They flirt, and I tell them to hit the road. It's simple.

But things with Colton just got complicated.

How are we going to do this? Can we work together and date each other at the same time? Does he even want to date me? Or is this just a one-time that-was-fun type of thing?

My brain takes over, going through all the possibilities and every single consequence. Colton doesn't exactly seem to be a steady relationship kind of guy. I've seen him with several different girls since I've known him, and he's never with them for very long.

Do I really want to become just another girl in a long line of exes?

My heart sinks, and I close my eyes.

No, I really don't. And what would happen when it was over? I don't know that I could get involved with him and then go right back to working with him, watching him choose the next girl and take her out for a while.

If I don't put a stop to this now, I'm going to regret it.

But the thought of his lips on mine and his arms around me makes me feel alive, and I don't want to give that up.

I wish I could just see into the future so I would know how this ends. I'm terrified of getting hurt again, so if I could see a glimpse of my own devastation when he walks away, maybe I could convince my heart to stop wanting him so badly.

I throw the covers off my body and exit from my little cocoon. That isn't how life works. No one can see the future. The only way to protect yourself is just not to put yourself in a position where you might get hurt.

That logic has worked for me for years, so why does it suddenly make me sad?

"Good morning, honey bun," Daddy says, kissing my forehead. "Late night?"

"The latest," I say, not meeting his eyes. He knows me too well, and I don't want him prying into this until I've got it figured out.

He walks over to the window and takes a sip of his coffee. He's staring at something outside with a smile on his face.

"What are you smiling at?" I ask, rising onto my toes to see through the window. Colton is outside putting a bag into his truck, and just the sight of him makes my heart skip a beat and my face flush.

"I have a feeling it's going to be a very interesting day," he says with a smile.

"What's that supposed to mean?"

He walks over to the kitchen table and sits down to read the paper. "Oh, nothing," he says.

"Daddy, stop being all secret-y," I say.

"I'm just saying you might want to go get a shower before you run out of time to get ready."

I narrow my eyes at him. "What do you know?"

He simply shakes his head and takes another sip of his coffee. "You're wasting time," he says. "Just trust me."

I look from him to the window, where Colton is now loading up a couple of fishing poles from our garage.

Is he planning to take me out today? I can't think of any other reason my dad would be so cheery, and Colton wouldn't be taking our fishing poles if he hadn't come over and asked permission first.

Oh God, he's planning something. And Daddy's right. I am a mess.

I touch my hair and then make a run for the bathroom.

❧

COLTON RINGS THE DOORBELL JUST AS I'M BRAIDING MY wet hair. I brush some color onto my cheeks and look in the mirror. This is ridiculous. What in the world is he doing?

What am I doing?

I should tell him I'm busy, or that I'm too tired to go out all day.

But my pesky heart sends me out into the living room with a nervous little bump.

"Hey," I say as I open the door. "What are you doing here?"

He has a mischievous smile on his face. "Good morning to you, too," he says. "Rob."

My dad nods and gives him a wink. Partners in crime.

I give my dad an evil look and he just laughs and makes his way back to his bedroom.

"Have fun, kids," he says.

"What are you two conspiring about?" I ask. I step back so he can come inside, but he just hangs in the doorway, his arm propped against the threshold.

"I was thinking since it's our day off and all, and we've both been working so hard lately, it might be fun to get out and do something fun," he says.

I make a point to look around him toward the truck. "You want to take me fishing?"

"Knox said we are welcome to borrow his boat," he says.

"And your dad offered your old fishing poles. I thought we might go out on the lake and make a day of it. Your dad told me you guys used to go fishing a lot when you were younger."

"We haven't been in ages."

"Come on," he says. "I promise we'll have a good time."

I glance at his lips and think about last night's kiss. A good time is exactly what I'm worried about.

"I'm supposed to be doing inventory this afternoon," I say. "I have a million things to do, Colton."

"A million things that will still be there when you get home," he says. He holds his hand out to me, his eyebrows raised. "You can't work all the time, Jo. Everyone deserves to have a little fun."

I hesitate, my heart thumping against my ribs.

Do I take this risk?

I want to take his hand and jump in and forget the consequences, but there's too much of me that remembers what it felt like to be a fool. I'm too scared. And I'm too aware that sometimes a little fun comes with a price that's too high.

"I can't," I say. My heart protests, but I don't know what else to do. Going with him would be like stepping into a minefield.

His smile drops and he adjusts his weight from one foot to the other.

"Why not?" he asks.

I push an imaginary strand of hair behind my ears. "I told you. I'm busy," I say. I'm also too chicken to tell him the truth.

"Bullshit," he says. "You're terrified."

I look up. He's not supposed to call me on it. He's supposed to just say that's too bad and walk away.

"I am not," I say, lying like a dog. "If the inventory doesn't get done, we won't know what we need to order tomorrow morning. It's as simple as that."

"I'll have you know that Knox is already at the bar working on the inventory."

My shoulders tense. He's also not supposed to take away my excuses.

"Who told him he needed to do that, huh?" I put a hand on my hip.

Colton is completely unfazed by my anger. The right side of his mouth curls into a smile. "I was trying to do something nice for you, but if you honestly would rather sit in this house and let life pass you by without ever experiencing anything, I guess I'll leave you to it, then."

He turns and walks toward the truck, and I can't believe he's just going to leave.

I go after him, stomping every step of the way. I grab his arm and spin him around. "I experience things, thank you very much."

"Like what?" he asks. He motions toward the bar. "You go into work nearly every night and then you go home. You cook in your kitchen and you stay wrapped up so tight in your little comfort zone that you refuse to acknowledge what you're really doing."

"Oh? And what's that?"

"You're hiding," he says. "You're hiding from life, Jo, letting every day pass without ever taking any risks or stepping into the unknown. You have to have every little thing exactly as it was the day before, and I'll tell you what I think."

I clench my teeth, my breath coming faster. "What?"

He takes my arms in his hands and pulls me closer, the memory of last night's kiss rubbing up against my consciousness and spinning my world upside down.

He leans closer. "I think you're missing it," he says softly. "You're missing life, because you're too scared of what might happen if you actually lived it."

His words knock the breath right out of me.

"Haven't you wanted to know what it would feel like to just jump into the deep end for a while?" he asks. "Forget the past for a while and just enjoy this moment. This time in your life. This person standing right here in front of you."

I can't look away from his eyes. They have a hold on me that's too strong to release. And he's right. There's a part of me that wants those things so badly, I'm almost willing to risk my heart just to get them.

And there's no way he can know just how much that scares me.

I relax my shoulders, my mind made up.

"Well, if we're going to have some fun, don't just stand there staring at me like a lost puppy," I say, pulling away. "You're killing the mood."

His face breaks out in a huge smile, and as I run back to the house to grab my things, I feel more alive than I have in a very long time.

CHAPTER 15
COLTON

I feel like the champion of the world when Jo finally gets into my truck. I walk around to the other side and see that her father is standing in the kitchen watching us from the window. He lifts his mug and smiles, and I nod and wave.

I got up early this morning, because I couldn't get my mind off this woman. I wanted to do something fun that would give us a chance to step away from the bar for a while and really let loose outside of work. When I saw those old fishing poles leaning against the side of the garage, I got the idea of taking her out on the river for the day.

Coming up with a plan was the easy part. Getting her to agree to go instead of working all day? That was the only hang-up. But somehow, I managed to convince her to get in the truck and for the entire day, she's all mine.

I climb in and give her a smile.

"Alright, Boss, you ready for one of the best adventures of your life?" I ask.

She makes a face. "That's a pretty bold statement for a guy who's just taking me fishing," she says. "Are you sure you're up to the challenge?"

I start the truck and pull onto the road, heading for Knox's place on the lake. "Baby, I was born for this," I say.

I reach over and turn up the radio. WKTX Fairhope, and they're playing one of my favorite country songs. I start singing at the top of my lungs.

Jo laughs and relaxes into the seat. It's a cloudy day, but her laughter is like the sun coming out from behind the clouds and finally showing its face.

Kissing her last night has lit me up from the inside, and I feel like a brand new person. She's a challenge in the best way, and I cannot wait to see her relax for a little while. I got my first glimpse of a more relaxed Jo out at Knox's lake house last weekend, and even more of it last night when she got a little tipsy, but now I'm addicted. I want more.

I want to see her shed whatever fears she's got strapped to her shoulders. I want to see her truly be herself without always second guessing the consequences of every move.

When we finally pull down the bumpy dirt road toward Knox's house, she's singing along to the radio, her feet pulled under her on the bench seat of my truck. She looks happy, and it sends a zing of warmth through my body.

All I care about today is making her smile. As big and as often as possible. If there's anyone in the world who deserves a break, it's Jo.

I park behind Knox's house and we grab the gear from the back and make our way down to the dock. Knox is at the bar and Leigh Anne is hanging out with Jenna for the day, so we have the place all to ourselves.

It takes two trips to get everything settled into the boat, but when I reach for Jo's hand, she frowns.

"Uh oh, what is that about?" I ask.

She pulls back. "I don't know. I'm just worried about the inventory," she says. "Knox hasn't done it in a long—"

I place a finger over her lips and shake my head.

"No way," I say. "You are not going to ruin your own day by worrying about what's going on at the bar. It's your day off, Jo. Let the bar handle itself for a while."

"Colton, you don't understand."

"Oh, I understand completely," I say. "But you're the one who said you knew how to have a good time outside of the bar, am I right?"

She shifts her weight from one foot to the other and nods.

"Then prove it," I say, smiling. "First rule of the day. No talking or worrying about work."

"Well, if those are the rules, you better take me home right now," she says with a nervous laugh. "Besides, without work, I have nothing to talk about."

"And you don't see the problem with that?" I ask. "Josephine Warner, I'm going to make it my personal mission to see that you start living a little outside of that bar."

Her cheeks flush. "I like my life just the way it is."

I step back onto the dock and pull her into my arms. I allow a lazy smile to play across my lips. "Then darlin', you have no idea what you've been missing."

As I pull her into the boat with me and we shove off into the deeper part of the lake, I sincerely hope with all my heart that she lets me show her just how fun it can be to change things up every now and then.

CHAPTER 16
JO

I cannot believe he actually talked me into coming fishing. How exactly did he even do that? One second I was determined not to go, and the next I was in his truck headed for the lake.

I watch him as he steers the boat out into the middle of the lake. The wind whips his dark blond hair back, and there's a hint of a smile on his face. He's one of the most comfortable guys I've ever known. He's just easy and happy and free, like nothing's ever weighing him down.

I wish I could be like that. I wish I could just take these regrets off my shoulders and toss them out into the water, letting my hair hang wild and free. I wish I could shed the mistakes of my past and start over, but those mistakes are a part of me. I don't even know how to be me without them.

I honestly don't even understand how a guy like Colton could be interested in someone like me. I'm not at all the type of girl he usually dates, and if he knew the baggage I bring with me into any relationship, he might want to turn this boat around and take me home.

But we're here, and I'm determined to make the most of it.

What if he's right? What if all this time I've been pushing everyone away, I've been missing out on something important?

"Where are we going?" I have to shout over the sound of the motor and the wind.

"There's a little place about a mile from here where I've gotten lucky quite a few times, so I thought we'd start there," he says.

Gotten lucky? God, I really hope he's talking about fishing, and not about all the other girls he's brought out on his little river adventure. I don't even want to think about how many girls he's probably surprised with a fun date like this. Colton Tucker, always up for a good time.

I hate that twist in my gut when I think about what this all must mean for him. Why can't I just relax and have a good time?

But I already know the answer. I don't want to be just another notch in his bedpost. And I'm not sure he's looking for anything more.

I wish I could talk to him about all this, and tell him how worried I am. But you don't do that at the beginning of a... whatever this is. Do you? I always imagined it was supposed to be something natural that you just sort of fell into. But I'm not fond of the falling part. Or at least I'm not fond of the hitting the ground part of it. I just want to know where it's all going so that I can protect my heart from whatever's coming next.

"What in the world are you thinking about?" he says. "From the look on your face, I'd think your favorite kitten just died."

I take a deep breath. "I'm sorry," I say. "I was getting wrapped up in my head for a while there."

I don't dare tell him what I was thinking about.

He cuts off the motor and stands, the boat teetering back and forth. He laughs and holds his arms out for balance. He slowly makes his way over to where I'm sitting at the very front of the boat. He kneels down in front of me.

"Close your eyes," he says softly. With the motor turned off and the boat stopped, it's suddenly very calm and still out here.

I search his eyes, trying to figure out what he's going to do, but he reaches up and covers my eyes with his hand.

"Okay, okay," I say. "They're closed."

He doesn't move his hand. Instead, he moves onto the seat right next to me, his warm body pressed against my side.

"Just breathe," he whispers in my ear. "Listen. Don't think. Hear the water moving against the bottom of the boat. The wind rustling through the trees. The animals moving out there in the woods just off the bank. For just a minute, don't worry about work or responsibility. Just be, Jo. Just be a part of this."

I take a deep breath, filling my lungs with cold autumn air. I hear the slap of water against the side of the boat. Something moves, its feet crunching through the leaves in the woods to our left. I breathe again, my shoulders relaxing.

Colton's hand drops to mine, and my eyes flutter open. I turn my head to look at him, and his deep green eyes stare right into mine.

He's right. I never do this. I never let loose and just have a good time anymore. I never just enjoy anything.

What's happened to me?

"I don't know how to do this," I say. "Not just listen or breathe. I don't know how to date someone, or even if this is dating. I don't know what you want or how to—"

"Shhh," he says, placing a fingertip over my lips. "You don't have to know. Life isn't about knowing where every single step is going to take you before you make it."

"That's easy for you to say, you haven't..." I stop before I say anything more. I'm afraid I'm turning this whole thing into a huge bummer for him. I want to tell him that I'm simply not the right person for him, and that he needs to go find a girl who knows how to just have fun.

"I haven't what?" he asks.

I shake my head. "Nevermind," I say. "Do you want to go home?"

"Are you kidding me? I'm not going home until you've caught at least one fish," he says.

I laugh. "We could be here for weeks."

"Then we better get started," he says. He stands and moves to a seat closer to the center of the small boat.

"Here's your pole," he says. "Do you remember how to bait a hook?"

"You just put a worm or a cricket on it and go, right? How hard can it be?"

"My kinda girl," he says, handing me the fishing pole.

My stomach twists. I am so not his kind of girl. How can he not see that?

"Here." He also hands me a styrofoam cup full of dirt.

I set my pole across my lap and dig around in the dark,

moist dirt until a worm moves against my fingertips. I pull away and shiver. "Sorry, eww," I say.

"Want me to do it?" he asks.

"No, I can do it," I say. "I just need to work up to it."

I take a deep breath and dig into the dirt again, this time grabbing hold of a fat, juicy worm. I pull it out with pride and fiddle with my hook, finally spearing the poor worm. I wipe my hands on my jeans.

"Alright, now we're getting somewhere," he says. He's already got the bait on his own hook, and he casts out into the water.

It takes me several tries to get mine into a good spot, but once I've done it a few times, I start to remember what it was like fishing with my daddy all those years ago.

I keep my eye on the little red and white bobber floating on the surface of the lake. Colton passes something toward me, and I'm surprised to see he's got a steaming cup of coffee in his hands.

"Wow, you thought of everything, didn't you?"

"I aim to please," he says, and for some reason, that phrase sends a warm rush through my insides.

I have no doubt he knows how to please, and in more ways than one.

I bite down hard on my lip and take the coffee, not meeting his eyes. I'd die if he had any idea what I'm thinking. "Thank you," I say.

I'm trying to juggle the coffee in one hand and the fishing pole in the other when the bobber disappears.

"Oh!" I drop the coffee, spilling the hot liquid all over my leg, but I somehow manage to keep hold of the pole. I yank it toward me and feel the fish catch and begin to swim against me. "I think I got it."

"Reel it in. You got it," he says.

I spin the reel as fast as I can, pulling the fish toward the boat. Colton moves closer and grabs a small net from the bottom of the boat, waiting.

"I can't believe I actually got one," I say, smiling from ear to ear. I haven't caught a fish since I was a little girl. I forgot how exciting something so simple could be.

"Here it comes," he says. "I can see it."

He leans down and dips the net into the water, coming up with a large silvery fish who is not at all happy about his current predicament.

"Woohoo," I shout, my voice echoing off the trees that surround us.

Colton leans back. "Woooo."

I laugh so hard my side hurts. "Poor little guy," I say as he works to get the hook out of the fish's mouth. "We have to throw him back in."

"Are you kidding me? Some cook you are, wanting to throw a good fish like this back into the water?"

I stick my lower lip out and give him my best pleading eyes. "Please, let's not keep any of them today," I say. "I would feel bad."

He shakes his head and looks at the fish. "You are one lucky son of a gun," he says. He tosses the fish back into the water and it splashes and swims away.

"Sorry, but I just couldn't stand to watch it die," I say.

"But you have no problem cooking up a whole rack of ribs?" he asks. "You know those don't grow on trees, right?"

I roll my eyes. "I know. There's just something about

catching it yourself and having to watch the whole process," I say. "I'd rather just buy my food at the grocery store and try not to think about where it comes from."

"Okay, then we'll make a pact. Any fish we catch today we can throw back, but next weekend maybe we'll get some fish at the local market and you can cook something for me."

Next weekend? He wants to make plans with me again? Just like that?

I avoid his gaze and swipe at the coffee stain on my jeans. "I can't believe I spilled my coffee," I say.

"That's one way to warm up, I guess." He's smiling, and I wonder if there's anything he can't put a positive spin on.

"Do you always do that?" I ask.

"What?" He sits back down and checks his pole.

"Find the bright side?"

He shrugs as he reels his line in and casts again. "I guess growing up the way I did with six sisters all crammed into a small space, I realized I had two choices in life," he says. "I could complain about everything I had no power to change, or I could figure out the things that made me happy and focus on those. It didn't seem like a tough decision."

I put another worm on my hook and cast my line out into the water.

"Tell me about your sisters," I say. "What was it like growing up with six siblings?"

"It was like growing up with a pack of wolves," he says, laughing. "Seriously, most of us are only about a year or a year and a half apart, so we all grew up really close to each other."

"And where do you fit into the seven?"

"I'm the baby," he says with a smile.

"Of course," I say.

"Hey, what's that supposed to mean?"

"It explains your laidback attitude about everything," I say. "I imagine once you're the seventh kid to come along, you have to sort of learn to roll with the punches."

"Literally," he says, taking another sip of his coffee.

"What? Like your older sisters were into beating you up?"

"No, but they were into dressing me up," he says and pretends to shudder at the memory. "Which is really much worse, trust me."

I laugh. "I really hope there is photographic evidence of that."

"Don't even think about it," he says."

"And all your family lives on the land now?" I ask. I'm totally fascinated by his family. Growing up as an only child makes his life sound so exotic.

"Everyone except me, as of a few weeks ago," he says. "It's redneck central out there, believe me. Momma and Daddy live in a double-wide trailer. My sister Carley and her husband Jack live next door with their little girl, Mazie. Then my sister Claire and her husband live in a smaller single-wide with their two kids, Wyatt and Aubrey. My sister Caroline lives a little further back in the woods in a log cabin her husband Adam built himself. She stays home with their three little ones, Nathan, Maddie, and Caleb."

My eyes grow wide as he rattles off all the names. I can hardly keep them straight, but he keeps going.

"My oldest sister, Cora Mae, is married to Isaac and they live in a big trailer with their four children, Ainsley, Maddox, Peter, and Pressley. Chloe and her husband Matt live in the next trailer over with their one-year-old Lilly. And then of course there's my youngest sister Cammie and her husband West and their newborn baby, Emma. And that doesn't even touch on the aunts and cousins living out there."

I sit back, completely overwhelmed and amazed at everything he's just told me. I can't even remember well enough to count how many children are now living on his parents' property, much less all their names.

There's one thing that did occur to me as he was rattling them all off, though.

"Wait a second," I say, squinting and looking up, trying to remember all the names. "So you and your sisters are Caroline, Carley, Claire, Colton, Cammie, Chloe, and..."

I can't quite think of the other name, but he jumps in to help.

"Cora Mae," he says.

"Cora Mae," I shout. "All C's?"

He laughs. "My mom is Carol, and she claims she couldn't help herself. Named the whole lot of us with the first letter C in her pregnancy-minded haze."

I can't stop laughing. Not really at the fact that all their names start with C, but just more at the way Colton has no problem making fun of himself or his family. He's so carefree and easy, and I can't remember a time when I felt the same.

"I'm sorry to laugh. They sound lovely," I say. "How come they never come up to the bar so we can meet them?"

"Caroline's actually been up there a few times to say hello, but mostly everyone has their hands full with the kids these days," he says. "It's hard to get out for a night on the town when you've got three little ones to take care of."

"I'm sure," I say, slightly sobering at the thought. God, I could have a seven-year-old right now, if it hadn't been for...

But no, I refuse to let those kinds of thoughts ruin my night.

"Whoa, where did you go just now?" he asks, forcing me from my own dark past.

"Nowhere," I say. "I was just thinking what it must have been like for you, being the only boy with all those girls running around."

"I was my mother's pride and joy," he says. "She calls me her sunshine."

"I can see that," I say. He does have a certain sunshine quality that makes everything feel bright when he's around.

"Speaking of sunshine, we seem to have lost ours," he says.

I look up and see that the clouds have completely taken over the sky. As if on cue, thunder rumbles in the distance.

"Are we okay out here?" I ask.

A raindrop falls onto my face, followed by another. I laugh and lift my hands into the air.

We both reel in our lines and Colton starts the motor. I wrap my arms around my body and shiver as the boat begins to soar over the water.

"Where are we gonna go? It'll take us forever to get back to the dock," I say. "We're going to get drenched."

"I know a place," he says. "I'm hoping we can get there before the rain gets too bad."

Ten seconds later, the bottom falls out.

CHAPTER 17
COLTON

Going all the way back to Knox's will take more than half an hour in this rain, but I know another place we can go. I haven't been back there in a long time, and there are nervous knots in my stomach just thinking about it, but it will be a safe, dry place to hole up while the rain pours down.

I gun the motor and squint through the torrential downpour. In front of me, Jo has lifted her jacket over her head and is leaning over, trying not to get soaked, but it's impossible.

I probably should have checked the forecast before bringing her out on the lake, but it was sunny out, and I had no clue it was going to rain. Some romantic I turned out to be.

But hey, I promised the girl adventure, so if nothing else, she's at least going to get that.

I spot the rickety dock on the banks and memories of my past come flooding back to me. I can almost see my grandfather standing out there, a cup of coffee in one hand with the other raised in welcome.

Gosh, it's been a long time. Three years? Three years he's been gone, and I miss him just as much as the day he died.

I pull alongside the dock and cut the motor, and then throw a rope up onto the wooden surface. It takes me a second to tie both sides of the boat up to the dock, but once we're secure, I carefully step out and offer my hand to Jo.

She's laughing and completely soaked from head to toe. Her hand is ice-cold and she's shivering.

"What about our stuff?" she asks.

"I'll just grab the bag. We can leave the rest," I say. I kneel on the dock and grab my duffel back, which is also now soaked through. I hadn't even thought to bring a change of clothes or an umbrella.

"What is this place?" she shouts over the sound of thunder and rain.

I lead her up the small hill toward the ramshackle cabin where I spent so many days of my childhood.

The back porch that overlooks the lake is crumbling, the stairs warped and creaky, but they manage to hold our weight as we run under the tin roof overhang.

Once out of the rain, we both stop and shake off like two stray dogs, laughing and trembling in the cold. Jo stares out at the downpour while I search for the spare key hidden in a pile of wood at the other end of the porch.

"Aha, got it," I say, triumphantly holding up a key with a tattered red ribbon attached.

I unlock the door and push it open, holding my arm out for her to go inside. "Ladies first."

"Why, thank you," she says. She walks inside and looks around, finally flipping a light switch up and down.

"No electricity," I say. "Hasn't been for years."

"Where are we?"

I walk inside and set the duffel bag on the floor. The place looks almost just like he left it. A dusty plaid couch in the center of the room. A faded rug covering part of the scratched hardwood floor. I inhale, wanting to catch his scent, but he's long gone from this place.

"This was my grandfather's cabin," I say.

"Oh," she says. "He didn't live on the Tucker family land?"

"This was my mom's dad," I say. "Not a Tucker. He was a Wilson."

I pull open the drawer of a side table and smile. Bingo. There's a flashlight just where he left it, as if no time has passed at all. I grab it and pray the batteries still work after all this time.

A beam of light cuts through the dusty darkness, and my heart sinks.

The whole place is covered in dust and cobwebs, everything old and worn with time. I've let this place go to hell. Water drips somewhere inside the house, which means the roof is leaking. I guess it's no surprise, what with no one looking out for the place, but I had hoped to find it in better shape. I wanted it to be exactly the way it always was.

Jo walks in and strips off her wool hat and jacket, revealing nothing more than a black tank top underneath.

"I don't suppose your grandfather has any blankets?" she asks, running her hands up and down her arms.

SARRA CANNON

"Had," I say. "He passed away a few years back. But yes, I imagine I can find us something."

"Thank you," she says as I make my way to the small back bedroom. "And I'm sorry to hear about your grandfather."

I swallow a thick lump in my throat and disappear into the room. I ignore the pipe still sitting on the bedside table and open the closet, searching the top shelf for blankets. There's a whole stack of them, and I take them all and present them to Jo.

"Thanks," she says. "Now turn around, I'm going to peel these wet jeans off."

The cold shivering feeling is replaced by a hot need, like lightning flashing through me. Maybe not checking the weather will turn out to be the best thing I ever did.

I turn around and stare at the wall, but I listen as she unzips her jeans and pulls her legs free. I've seen her in a bathing suit before out at Knox's, but there's something so much more intimate about this moment. I want so badly to turn around and take her in my arms.

"Okay," she says.

I spin and find her wrapped in a soft blue blanket. She sits down on the couch and pulls it tightly around her body. I reach for a second blanket and lay it over her legs and feet.

"Aren't you cold?" she asks.

I raise an eyebrow, my heart pumping faster. "Trying to get me naked?"

She tries to hold back a smile, but fails. "I just don't want you coming down with pneumonia and dying on me," she says. "How would I find my way home?"

"Haha," I say. "I'm going to be just fine, so don't you

worry. I'm actually going to check that wood outside and see if it's dry enough to start a fire."

"Ooh, yes please," she says. "It doesn't look like this rain is going to let up any time soon, so we could be stuck here for a while."

"Worse things have happened," I say, just thinking about the possibilities. Jo and I stranded here in the cabin for hours, even all night?

I clear my throat and head to the front porch, trying to make sure I don't let my imagination and my libido get too far ahead of reality. There's no doubt how much I want her, but I haven't figured her out yet. I've never had to work so hard to bring a woman out of her shell. The kiss we shared last night was amazing, but I'm still wondering how she feels about me. She wasn't exactly jumping into my truck to spend the day with me. I had to almost trick her into it, so where does that leave us?

The wood on the porch is mostly dry, so I gather a few logs from the middle of the stack and bring them into the cabin. The red brick fireplace takes up nearly half the wall on that side of the living room. My grandfather never owned a TV, but he would spend hours just staring into the fire, as if it were telling a story of its own.

I dig through drawers until I find a set of matches. I take an old newspaper from a stack near the fireplace and crumple it up, strategically placing pages around the stack of wood I've arranged inside the fireplace. There's also a little box full of fat-lighter, so I break off a few small pieces and place it between the logs.

Here goes nothing.

I strike a match and light four pieces of newspaper,

watching as the fire spreads. The fat-lighter catches and, after a few seconds, so does the first log.

I smile and slap my hands together. "Now that's how it's done right there," I say.

Jo laughs and covers her mouth. "You are so full of yourself."

"I'm confident," I say, holding up a finger. "There's a difference."

"Well, either way, I'm glad you got a fire going," she says. She gets off the couch and moves to sit down in front of the fire. The blanket I'd placed over her legs falls to the floor, revealing the smooth white of her skin.

My mouth goes dry, and my heart races.

"I'm going to go see if I can find some dry clothes," I say.

I disappear into the bedroom again and lean against the wall. I hardly recognize this breathless, nervous me. I'm usually the one making all the right moves and sweeping girls off their feet, but Jo has me all mixed up. I don't know where to start or how to tell her what I'm feeling.

I just want her.

And for the first time in as long as I can remember, I'm afraid of being rejected. I'm scared to take that next step.

She's guarded and there's something in her eyes that's almost haunted, like she's been through something she can't let go of. I don't understand why I recognize that about her, but I see it as clear as day, and I know it means I have to be careful with her.

I take a deep breath and shake my head. Or maybe I'm overthinking this whole thing.

I search through my grandfather's closet and drawers, but most of his clothes were taken out of the house after he passed. I do manage to find a pair of gray sweatpants, but nothing else that's usable.

I peel off my wet clothes and slip into the sweatpants, feeling a little exposed going commando, but if I want to warm up, I have no choice.

I gather my clothes off the floor and bring them out into the living room where Jo is rubbing her hands together in front of the flames.

Her eyes flash as she looks at me, and for a moment, I think I recognize desire, and it drives me over the edge. I have to grab a blanket and wrap it around myself quickly so she doesn't see what she's doing to me with those looks of hers.

"If we lay our clothes out on the bricks, they should dry pretty quick," I say.

She nods and spreads her jeans, jacket, and hat out across the bricks. Then she crawls over to where I'm standing and grabs mine to do the same. The blanket she's wearing slips, revealing the side of her thigh, and my lips part. I can hardly breathe.

I don't care about rejection. All I care about is Jo and how much I want to know every part of her. I want to explore every inch of her body and make her mine.

I've never felt more wide awake in my life. This is something more. Greater than anything I've felt before, and as much as that terrifies me, I also know that I can't deny what my heart is telling me.

I kneel beside her and she looks over, startled. I take her bare shoulders in my hands and pull her up to her knees across from me. Her chest rises and falls with mine, both of us breathing shallow and fast.

"Colton—"

But I can't resist what I'm feeling any longer. I pull her to me, my mouth descending on hers. I wrap my arms around her and let my hand travel up the length of her back.

Her blanket drops to the floor, and I can feel her shiver against me. This time I don't think it's from the cold. The fire blazes next to us, filling the room with smoky heat. Our bodies come together, our hands exploring as we get our first real chance to let go of inhibitions and see where this might lead.

I reach for her braid, wanting to bury my fingers in her hair. The ends are still soaking wet, and I pull the elastic tie from them, carefully unbraiding her hair as I softly kiss her lips and cheeks and jaw. She's breathing fast, her heartbeat pounding against my chest.

"Colton, wait," she says, pulling away and putting her hand on mine.

She sits back and takes a deep breath. She turns her face toward the fire, and in profile, she's the most gorgeous woman I've ever seen in my life. She's vulnerable and trembling, and I struggle to find the words that will put her at ease.

"I know this is moving fast," I say. "I don't want to do anything that makes you feel uncomfortable, but I am sure that I have never wanted to know someone more than I want to know you."

My voice shakes a little, and I clear my throat. I'm so nervous I can hardly hear myself over the throbbing pulse that echoes in my eardrums.

"And it's more than that," I say, running a nervous hand through my hair. I want to touch her again so badly it hurts. "Please tell me I'm not crazy here. That you feel it, too."

She closes her eyes and pulls the blanket back over her legs. When she looks at me, her eyelids slowly lifting to reveal beautiful dark brown eyes shimmering with tears, my breath hitches.

"I do," she says. "And you have no idea how hard that is for me to admit."

I let out the breath I've been holding. I want to reach for her, but I am no longer smooth and confident Colton. I've become someone else in the intimacy of this moment. Someone I don't recognize.

"I'm not used to this," she says. "It's been a really long time since I've..."

Her voice trails off and she looks back toward the fire, avoiding my eyes.

"You can talk to me," I say, touching her arm.

"Can I?" she asks. Pain is written across her features, as if this whole scenario is agony for her.

"Of course," I say, moving closer. "What's going on?"

She shakes her head and swallows, looking down to her hands now cradled in her lap. "I know that you've been with a lot of women," she says, half-laughing, half-crying. "And it hasn't escaped my notice that you're not with them for a very long time."

I straighten. Is that what this is all about? She thinks I'm some kind of player who is just trying to score? And have I ever given her any reason to think differently?

My heart tightens. I don't know how to explain what I'm feeling and how different this is for me, but I also don't know how much I can promise her.

"And I'm sure you've noticed that I haven't exactly been seeing anyone," she says. "Not for a very long time."

"I'm guessing there's a reason for that," I say.

She nods and sniffs, wiping a finger under her eyes. "It's not something I like to talk about," she says. "Not to anyone. But I know even just talking about this is probably killing the mood."

"If you're not comfortable and you need me to understand what's going on, I'm here, Jo," I say. I don't know what she needs from me, exactly, but I'm willing to listen.

"Part of me wants you to understand," she says.

"And the other part?" I ask, holding my breath.

She looks up at me, then, her eyes wide and scared. "The other part wants you to just go away," she says.

It's not at all what I was expecting her to say, and the words punch me in the gut, leaving me hollow and lost. Is that what she really wants?

"I don't want to go away." The words have left my lips before I even thought about what I was going to say, but it's the truth. "I know you think I'm the kind of guy who just has fun with a woman for a while and then puts an end to it, but that's not exactly true."

I swallow and take a deep breath. This isn't something I've said out loud very many times, or hell, even admitted to myself very often, but I'm willing to fight for what we have. And as vulnerable as I feel right now, I know that opening up to her is the only way to fight.

"I like to have a good time," I say, half-smiling. "There's no doubt about that. But I want more, too. I've just never met the right girl."

I find myself repeating my sister's words, realizing just

how true they are. And realizing that the right girl might be sitting right in front of me.

"If you don't want to be with me, that's one thing," I say. "But if you're feeling the same way I am right now and you want to see where this might go, then you need to talk to me. I know it's scary and messy and there's no way to control the outcome, but there are some risks worth taking, Jo. If there's something you need to say, I'm listening."

My entire body is buzzing and aware, knowing that this is completely new for me. She's right. Sex for me is usually about having a good time and not thinking too much about the future. I'm used to just following my instincts and letting it go wherever it goes. But Jo is different. She's so guarded and works so hard to protect herself. I'm not sure if there's room for more with her, but I want to know if there's a chance of hope.

I give her time to respond, not saying anything. I just sit and wait, the fire warming my trembling body.

And finally, she speaks.

"Back in high school, I got really close to someone who hurt me," she says. "It changed me in ways I can't even explain to you. After that happened, I decided falling in love wasn't worth it. I haven't wanted to open myself up to that kind of pain again."

A tear falls down her cheek and she wipes it away quickly.

"Not until now," she says softly.

"I'm not going to hurt you," I say. I place my hand on her leg and she looks up.

"How do you know that?" she asks.

It's such a simple question, but as we sit here, I think we both realize that it's a question that has no answer. We can't possibly know what the future will bring. A relationship never begins with the knowledge of how it will end. Or if it will end.

"That's what I'm afraid of," she says. "If we take this step, it changes things between us forever. It changes me. And no matter how great things are at the beginning, I'm not sure I can handle the way it would feel to lose you."

"So you'd rather lose me now?" I ask, shaking my head.

"It's easier to lose someone before you truly love them," she says.

"But then you'd never know what it was like to love them. Isn't love worth taking the risk?"

As I stare at her, the fireglow caressing the side of her face, it hits me so hard I almost can't breathe.

I'm already falling in love with her.

Breathless, I move closer, placing my hand on her cheek and wiping a fresh tear away with my thumb.

"I don't know what happened to you in high school or who the jerk was who hurt you, but I can promise you one thing," I say. "If you are willing to let down your walls and give this a real shot, I will do everything I can to make sure you don't get hurt. If things don't work out between us, then we will at least know we both gave it everything we had. We can't see the future or know our fate, but I can't turn my back on the way I feel about you."

"I can't be another fling," she says, her tears falling freely now. "With me, things are going to be complicated, Colton. I can't promise you a carefree good time like those other girls."

"That's not what I want from you," I say. "All I want is for you to let go and give this a real chance. Take a risk that this could be real. This could be everything we've both been waiting for."

The room is charged with the tension of our words, as if a battle is being waged between our hearts. There is nothing but push and pull, fear and need. And one decision left hanging in the balance.

Is the risk of regret worth the chance at love?

My heart waits, every inch of me tense and trembling. I know my answer, my decision. I'm just waiting for her to make hers.

And when she finally meets my eyes, I know the answer is yes.

CHAPTER 18
JO

Colton takes me in his arms and his lips descend on mine.

I'm overcome by the passion of his kiss, his words, his body pressing against mine. I never expected things to go this far between us, but now that we're here, I want nothing more than to lose myself in him.

No, not myself. I want to lose my fear. I want to lose the pain of the past and step toward an uncertain future.

I wrap my arms around him, opening myself in a way I was afraid I would never be able to again. I shiver against him. Not from cold, but from release. I don't know if it will last, but in this moment, I release all the things that have held me back for so long. And with that release, a flood of passion breaks through the walls, washing over me with such force I cling to him for dear life.

My hands grip his back, digging into his bare skin, pulling him closer.

His lips break from mine and he kisses a trail along my

jaw and down my neck. I lean my head back, the motion opening my heart further. A moan escapes my throat, and I hardly recognize the sound.

It's the sound of desire and longing. It's the sound of need replacing fear.

It's the sound of truly letting go.

Colton's fingertips slide the straps of my tank top off my shoulders as he kisses his way down, caressing my skin. I pull back to give him access, letting my hands roam the muscles of his chest, feeling the hard ridge of his abs and playing with the space just above the band of his pants.

His eyes lift to mine, his lips parted and his breathing fast and heavy.

Without glancing away, he pushes my shirt all the way down my body, taking his sweet, torturous time.

No one has seen my body in this way in a very long time, and I'm nervous for him to see me. My instinct is to cover myself, my arms pulling back to hide my nakedness.

But he takes my hands in his and moves them to my side, letting his own hands travel up and down my bare arms, his fingertips like a brush, painting me with strokes of desire.

When his hands move to my breasts, they are warm and soft, each touch igniting something inside me. Trust. Confidence. Hunger.

He grabs a large pillow from the couch and sets it on the floor in front of the fire.

"Lie down," he says.

I suck in a breath, wanting this more than I can say, but knowing there is one thing that could ruin this moment. I'm almost embarrassed to ask, but I can't go any further without it.

"Do you have a condom?" I ask softly.

Please say yes.

He smiles that deliciously sexy half-smile that teases at the corners of one side of his mouth. "Just a second," he says.

He leans forward to grab his jeans and rummages in the pocket for his wallet. I release my breath when he pulls a condom from inside, one eyebrow raised as he looks at me.

He sets the packet beside the pillow and lowers me all the way to the floor, the soft blanket now warm beneath me.

My tank top is still wrapped around my midsection, and he slowly pulls it down my legs and off my body. His fingers tease the waistband on my underwear, and his eyes meet mine, asking for permission.

I nod, my heart fluttering like the wings of a humming-bird in my chest.

He bites his lower lip and slowly pulls the last of my clothes down and away, leaving me naked beneath him. I try to sit up, but he shakes his head, taking in the sight of me.

My face and neck flush with warmth, nervous of what he must be thinking. He has so much more experience at this than I do, and I'm terrified I somehow won't measure up.

But when he lowers himself to the floor at my side, the feel of his skin against mine sets me at ease.

"You're so beautiful," he says, his hands moving up and down my body slowly.

I hide my face behind my hands, embarrassed and happy. I'm so used to pushing men away that I don't know how to handle compliments.

I'm giggling and giddy, but when his hands explore below my waist, so close to the warmth between my legs, my laughter fades. I stare up at him as he touches me, my body naturally lifting to meet him. I'm on a rollercoaster ride, wanting it to go both fast and slow at the same time.

I move onto my side, facing him, and he kisses me again.

The room spins, heat pulsing off of us as the rain continues to pound against the tin roof of the cabin. I move my hands to his chest, unable to drag this out any longer. I want him.

My fingers find the drawstring on his sweatpants and fumble with the knot as we kiss. He moans against me, his hands growing impatient as he grips my back. I finally manage to free the knot and with one motion, slip my thumbs into the waistband of his pants and push them down.

The last barrier between us falls away and a promise is made as he pushes me back against the floor and positions himself above me. It's an unspoken promise, but it's real just the same. I can see it in his eyes and feel it in the way my heart beats against his.

It's a promise that no matter what happens between us, we will always have this moment where our hearts were truly open.

As his body joins with mine, a cry sounds from deep inside me and tears flow from my eyes. But they are not tears of regret or fear or sadness.

They are tears of surrender.

CHAPTER 19
COLTON

Jo is asleep next to me on the floor, her body snuggled against mine under the blanket.

Our fire is down to a few smoldering embers, but I don't want to wake her. Her hair is dry and rolls in waves around her face and over her shoulders. I run a finger along her cheek and she nestles closer, her hand resting on my chest.

There is an invisible force pulling my heart toward her now. It's unlike anything I've felt before, and I'm not sure whether to be ecstatic or terrified.

What exactly am I getting myself into?

I meant every word of what I said to her, but what if I am not enough for her? What if I screw this up like I've done so many other times?

Hurting her would destroy me.

But we've gone too far to turn back now. We're connected in a way we can't erase, so there's no choice but to move forward and see what lies ahead for both of us. I have no idea how it will affect things at work. Her father seems to like me, so that's a huge plus, but now my job depends on this relationship. My home depends on it, too, considering I'm living in her garage.

If I mess this up and lose her, I'll lose everything.

That's a lot riding on this step we've taken together.

Lying here, though, watching her sleep, I know it's worth it. I just hope I can be the man she needs for me to be. I hope I can be worthy of her.

A chill goes through me, and I realize the fire has completely gone out. It's still pouring rain outside and the sun is going down, which means it's going to get much colder very quickly. With no power out here in the cabin, we're going to need a fire to make it through the night.

I sit up, carefully moving my arm from behind her head. She stirs and smiles, her eyes closing again as I cover her shoulders with the blankets.

My clothes are dry, so I slip back into my boxers and jeans and pull my t-shirt over my head before I go out to get more wood from the pile. I stand outside for a few minutes, watching the sun set over the lake.

I used to love coming out here. Why did I stop? It's so peaceful and quiet except for the sound of the rain falling. I glance over at the pair of rickety wooden rocking chairs and smile. I can still picture my grandfather sitting out here for hours. Sometimes we'd play checkers or cards, and sometimes we'd just sit talking about life and family. He had a lot of stories to tell, and it didn't matter that I'd heard them all a hundred times.

Standing here, my heart open, I miss him so much it hurts.

The door to the cabin creaks open and Jo walks out, yawning. She's wearing nothing but my plaid button-up, and it sets my heart racing all over again.

"Wow," I say, whistling. "You're killing me here."

She blushes and laughs. "It was dry and warm," she says. "I forgot to put my tank top by the fire, so it's still a little damp."

She walks over to where I'm standing and wraps her arms around my waist. Man, I could get used to this.

"Speaking of our fire, I'm going to have to start over," I say. "We might be here for a while, and it's supposed to get pretty chilly tonight."

"Oh my gosh, I need to call my dad," she says, pulling away and running toward the house. "I bet he's worried sick."

I follow her inside and get her phone from my duffel bag where I stashed it earlier to save it from the downpour.

"Crap, it's almost dead," she says, dialing. She bites at her thumbnail as she waits for him to answer. Finally, she shakes her head. "He's not answering."

"He's probably at the bar still doing inventory," I say. "Or watching TV."

"He's always forgetting to take his phone with him," she says. "I'll try the bar."

She lifts the phone to her ear, and I duck back outside to grab the wood. When I come back in, she's talking to Knox.

"Hey, Knox. It's Jo. Is Daddy there with you?" she asks. She frowns. "Is he okay?"

I stack the wood in the fireplace, but keep an eye on her reactions.

"Okay, well can you let him know that Colton and I got stuck in the rain?" She shifts her weight from one foot to the other. "No, we're fine. We couldn't make it back to your house, so we're hiding out at his grandpa's old cabin for a while. We'll head back once the rain stops."

She pauses and laughs. I release the breath I've been holding. For a second there, I thought maybe something had happened to her dad. In my mind I was already brainstorming ways to get her home in this rain.

"No, you don't have to do that," she says. "Listen, there's no power out here and my phone is almost dead, so if you don't hear from me in the morning, maybe come get us, okay? I'll put Colton on the phone and he can tell you where we are."

She holds the phone out to me.

"It's Knox," she whispers.

"Hey," I say. "Do you know where Old Porter Road is?"

"Not a clue," Knox says with a laugh.

The phone beeps telling me I'm almost out of time to explain it.

"About a mile down from where we turn off to get to your house, there's a little dirt road on the left with no sign," I say. "It's across from the Martin's farm. If you go down that way for a bit, the road will come to a T. Turn left and follow it all the way down. That's where you'll find us. Hopefully the rain will cool off at some point and we'll be able to make a break for it."

"I didn't realize you had a cabin out there," Knox says.

The phone beeps again.

"This phone is about out of juice, so I'll have to explain it to you later," I say. "But we'll text you if we make it home."

"If I wake up in the morning and the boat's back, I'll

know you made it," he says. "If not, I'll head out there and check on you guys. And Colton?"

"Yes?"

"Take care of my cousin, okay? She may act tough, but she's more fragile than she seems."

I nod even though I know he can't see me. "I will," I say.

And as I watch her loading more wood onto the stack, her hair wild and free and a smile on her face, I realize I've never wanted to take care of anything more than I do her.

"What did he say?" she asks. She looks so good wearing my shirt, I can barely answer.

She has me breathless.

"He said if we aren't home by morning, he'll come rescue us," I say. Although I swear I could spend the rest of my life right here in this cabin with her. No rescue necessary.

"So, are you going to get this fire going, or what?" she asks with a smile.

"Yes, ma'am," I say. "I am at your service, Boss."

She narrows her eyes. "We're not going back to that again, are we?"

"If the shoe fits," I say with a shrug.

She smacks my arm, but the smile on her face tells me everything I need to know. She's happy, and right now that's the only thing in the world that matters to me.

I turn my attention back to the fire, but with her sitting close, it's awfully distracting. Her knee is touching mine, and all I want to do is run my hand along her thigh. Talk about playing with fire.

Just when I think I won't be able to focus enough to get this thing going, Jo stands up and grabs an old oil lantern off the mantel.

"Does this thing still work?" she asks.

"Let's light 'er up and see." I pull the glass off and turn the key to lift the wick. It lights right up, throwing fresh light around the darkening room.

"Cool," she says when I hand it to her. "I want to explore."

"There isn't much to see, but have at it," I say.

"You said this was your mother's father's place?" she asks. "Did she grow up here?"

"No, they had a house in town over in Westbrook. She and her three sisters grew up there. My grandpa built this place with his own two hands when she was in elementary school," I say. "They used to come out here on the weekends to fish and swim in the lake. After the girls were grown up and my grandma passed, he sold the house and came to live out here permanently. He loved this place."

After I get the fire going again, I follow her to the kitchen, signs of my grandfather everywhere I look. His old work gloves sitting on the counter. Loose change in the mason jar on top of the fridge. A picture of him with a big catch out on the dock, his dusty overalls bringing back so many memories it nearly knocks me over.

I pick up the photo and shake my head. Now I remember why I haven't been back here much. It's too hard to think about him being gone.

"When did he pass away?" she asks softly, looking over my shoulder at the photograph.

"Three years ago," I say. "He was going in for what they said was a routine surgery to put a stent into an artery. He called me the night before he went in. He was so scared."

SARRA CANNON

Tears threaten to spill, and I take a deep breath. I can't let myself go back to those dark thoughts.

"I'm sorry," she says.

I put the picture back on the kitchen counter. "He's everywhere in this place," I say. "I miss him so much."

"Who does it belong to now?" she asks. "Your mom?"

We walk back through the living room to the two small bedrooms in the back.

"No, he left this place to me," I say.

One of the bedrooms still has two sets of bunkbeds, ancient remnants of those summers my mom and her sisters spent here. I slept in those bunkbeds so many times I lost count.

There's a leak in the corner of the room and water is dripping onto the old wood floor.

"Crap," I say. I run back into the kitchen and grab a large pot to collect the water. I position it under the leak, and it starts a high-pitched tinkling sound every time a drop hits the metal. "Looks like it's been leaking for a long time. Must be a problem with the roof."

The wood underneath the pot is warped and obviously water damaged. The small rug thrown across the floor smells mildewed, too, and probably will have to be thrown out.

"I bet Knox would be glad to take a look at it," Jo says. "It's probably an easy fix."

"I can probably do it myself," I say. For some reason, the thought of Knox having to come out here and take care of the problems with this place makes me angry. It's an irrational feeling, but this is my place. My responsibility.

I glance up at the ceiling and listen to the water dripping. Just one more thing I've screwed up.

142

"How come you don't come out here very often?" she asks. "It's a really beautiful cabin. Very warm."

I smile. "It's freezing in here."

"That's not what I meant," she says, bumping my arm as she moves into my grandfather's bedroom. "It has a well-loved feel to it, like there are a lot of happy memories here."

"There are," I say, feeling the tears sting my eyes again. I can't believe I've let things get so bad around here.

A thin layer of dust covers every surface. There's a second leak in the hall bathroom. I wouldn't be surprised if there were plumbing and electrical issues after it sitting here unused for so long.

"If you fixed this place up, you could easily move out here instead of living above our garage," she says.

"You ready to get rid of me so soon?" I ask, leaning against the doorframe.

"Hardly," she says, pressing her lips together to hide a smile. Her cheeks flush, and with the light from the lantern, she looks so vulnerable and beautiful.

An image pops into my mind of us coming out here on Sundays and in the evenings after work, spending our mornings out on the lake or the dock. Maybe sitting on the back porch playing cards or checkers and watching the leaves change.

"I think you could make a life for yourself here, that's all," she says. "This place could really be something special with a little bit of love."

I look around and know that she's right. This place has always been special, and I've been avoiding it for far too long. Maybe it was fate that brought us back here in this rainstorm. A place for new beginnings and a fresh start.

"Hey, look at this," she says. She sets the lantern on the bedside table and grabs something from the closet.

"What?" I ask.

She's so excited, I half expect to see a stash of gold nuggets or something, but when she turns around, my heart stops. She's holding my grandfather's old guitar case.

She places it carefully on the bed and snaps it open.

I hold my breath, memories rushing back. The honey-colored guitar sits inside the case, as perfect and well-worn as the day he died.

"Did he play?" she asks. She runs her hand across the smooth surface of the Gibson guitar.

I move next to her to sit down on the bed. My heart is so tight in my chest, I can hardly breathe.

"He did," I say. My voice cracks, and I have to look away.

"Hey, what's wrong?" she asks, placing her hand on mine. "Did I upset you somehow?"

I shake my head and close my eyes, images of my grandfather sitting on the front porch playing through my memory.

"I'm okay," I say, squeezing her hand. "It's just hard coming face to face with all these memories."

"I'm sorry, I didn't mean to make you sad," she says. "Want me to put it away?"

I look over at the old guitar, half its strings missing now. God, I miss him so much it's physically painful. My grandpa was my anchor in a chaotic life where there was never enough to go around. He always had time for me. Lord knows what might have become of me if he hadn't been there for me every time I needed him.

And the one time he needed me most...

Tears finally push through my resolve and I have to stand up so that Jo won't see. Crying in front of a woman isn't exactly the sexiest thing a guy can do. I don't want her think I'm weak.

"Colton?" she asks. She moves behind me and places her arms around my waist.

The warmth of her against me means the world in this moment.

"I'm sorry," I say. It's too late to hide these emotions from her. The tears are flowing freely, and there's nothing I can do to stop them. "I don't want you to see me like this."

She holds me tighter, placing her head against my back. "It's okay," she says. "I understand how difficult it can be to lose someone you loved so much. Do you want to talk about it?"

This is usually the type of thing I avoid talking to any girlfriend about. I want to be the one who makes them laugh. Someone they can have a good time with without worrying about things getting messy or emotional.

But things have been different with Jo from the very beginning. I want to open up to her, but we've just gotten started. I don't want to bring her down when things were just getting good and happy between us.

"No. It's nothing, really," I say. I force a smile and turn around, taking her in my arms. "Let's go back by the fire. You've got to be getting cold."

"A little," she says. She lifts up and kisses me on the cheek. "Just know that I'm here for you if you need to talk about it."

I walk over and shut the guitar case, letting my hand

linger for a moment on the clasp. The last thing I want to do is burden her with my sadness. Especially tonight.

"I can think of a few things I'd love to do more than talking," I say, spinning toward her. I pick her up and she screams, laughing.

"Wait, grab the lantern," she says.

I turn her all the way around and go back for the lantern. She's laughing and the dark mood is gone just like a shadow in the light. I dare a glance at my grandfather's cherished guitar, sending up another apology to his spirit as I carry her out of the room, where we make love until the rain finally stops.

CHAPTER 20
JO

The rain lets up just as the sun is peeking above the horizon. We gather our things and make a run for the boat. I almost slip on the muddy banks of the lake, but Colton holds tightly to my hand.

I laugh, realizing my cheeks actually hurt from smiling so much in the past few hours.

I'm sad to see the cabin disappear through the trees as we make our way back down the lake, but I hope we'll come back soon. Right now, it's the most magical place in the whole entire world.

We tie the boat off at Knox's dock and quietly make our way back to Colton's truck. Knox is home, but we don't want to wake him up. He'll see the boat and know we made it back safely.

When we get back to my house, Colton walks me to the door and pulls me into his arms.

"Thank you for one of the best nights of my life," he says. "I'm never going to forget this as long as I live."

"Me, too," I say, looking up at him. He's got a little stubble growing on his face and his hair is wild from laying by the fire snuggled against me all night. He's never looked so good.

"You going to be okay working tonight?" he asks, kissing my forehead.

"I'll be fine," I say. "It'll probably be slow, anyway. You know, if you want to come by and hang out for a while."

"Definitely," he says. He pulls me into a kiss, and my heart feels so light I think it might simply fly away.

"Try to get some sleep," I say. "I'll see you tonight."

He kisses me again, and then holds onto my hand as long as he can before I disappear inside.

I practically float to the kitchen and grab a bottle of water from the fridge. The sun is fully awake now, and even though I barely slept a wink last night, I feel more alive and awake than I can remember ever feeling before.

I haven't opened my heart, or my body, up to a man in so long, but it's not at all what I expected. I thought I would be a nervous wreck. But instead, I feel like I'm a brand new person.

I'm happy, and all I want to do is crawl under the warm covers and dream happy things.

I down the water and carry what's left of the bottle toward my room, but something stops me before I go inside.

The light in the bathroom at the end of the hall is on, which is odd. Dad never leaves that light on. Is he already up?

I walk down the hallway to let him know I'm home, but as soon as I turn the corner, the water bottle falls from my hand and I scream.

I rush to my father's side, panic tearing at my heart.

He's lying on the floor, a large gash on his forehead bleeding a pool of bright red across the tile.

"Daddy?" I say, lifting his head into my lap. "Daddy, can you hear me?"

I lean down and put my cheek against his face, thankful when I feel a rush of warm breath against my skin. I pull the towel from the rack and place it against his wound. It isn't bleeding too badly, but it's impossible to tell how long he's been lying here.

Oh God, the whole time I've been with Colton, my father's just been bleeding on the bathroom floor?

"Daddy," I say louder, stroking his cheek. His eyes flutter open, but close again. I look around, trying to figure out what happened. He must have fallen and hit his head on the edge of the bathroom counter.

I feel his forehead, checking for fever, but he doesn't seem to be hot.

My hands are shaking, and I don't know what to do. He wouldn't want me to call an ambulance, but I have no idea how long he's been out or if he has a concussion.

My cell phone is still dead but there's a cordless in the kitchen, and as much as I hate to leave him, I don't have any choice.

"I'll be right back, Daddy," I say. I rest his head gently on the towel and run to the kitchen for the phone.

Someone is beating on the door, and I dial as I run to open it.

Colton is standing on the front steps, his eyes wild with worry. "I heard you scream," he says. "What's wrong?"

I leave the door open as I run back toward the hallway.

"It's my dad," I say. "I came home and he was passed out in the bathroom. I think he hit his head. I'm calling 9-1-1."

"I'll talk to them," he says, reaching for the phone. "You just sit with your dad."

I nod, tears now streaming down my face. Dad still hasn't woken up, and he looks so pale lying there on the floor. I never should have left him here alone when he's been acting so strange lately.

Guilt weighs heavy on me as I hear Colton telling the 9-1-1 operator our address.

The one night I decide to let loose and have fun and this is what happens? It's like fate is punishing me for thinking I could ever have any sort of normal life.

I belong here with my father, and he means more to me than anything else in this world. If anything were to ever happen to him, I would never forgive myself.

"They're sending an ambulance right away," Colton says. He brings a blanket from the couch in the living room and rests it over my father's legs. "What in the world happened? Did he slip and fall?"

"I don't know," I say, barely able to contain my hysteria. "I have no idea how long he's been like this. I can't believe we were out all night while he was just here by himself."

Colton touches my arm. "It's not your fault," he says. "Accidents like this happen. You couldn't have known he was hurt."

I pull away faster than I mean to. "I should have checked on him earlier," I say. "I know he hasn't been feeling right lately, and I should never have left him alone."

The sound of sirens in the distance brings fresh tears to my eyes. How could this be happening?

"I'm sure it's nothing too serious," he says calmly. "Just a bump on the head. They'll get him in and check everything out, make sure he doesn't have a concussion. It's going to be okay. I can't see how this would be related to what's going on with his hands. Arthritis wouldn't make him fall. Everything's going to be fine, Jo."

"How can you know that?" I snap.

I close my eyes and sit down hard against the cold tiles.

"I'm sorry, I didn't mean to snap at you," I say. "I'm just scared. I've never seen him like this before."

I don't want to say it out loud, but there's a part of me that knows there's more to this fall than just an accident on the way to the bathroom. He's been acting strange a lot lately, having a hard time picking things up with his hands or running credit cards at the bar. I've seen him trip up and nearly fall a few times in the past couple weeks, and I just dismissed it at the time, but the worry has been there in the back of my mind, brewing.

What if this is really something serious?

I'm shaking so hard, my teeth are chattering. I simply couldn't handle it if anything happened to my father. He's everything to me.

Colton sits on the floor in the hallway and places his hand on mine. I keep one hand on the towel pressed against my father's forehead to stop the bleeding. The gash doesn't look too bad, but any kind of blow to the head is bad news.

The ambulance can't get here fast enough, and even though I can hear the sirens wailing, it feels like it's taking them forever to actually arrive.

When they finally pull up and the flashing lights pulse

across the dark hallway, Colton stands and lets them in the front door.

I recognize the paramedic who comes down the hallway. We used to go to school together, and his father is good friends with my dad.

"Josh, thank you so much for coming," I say. "I don't know what happened."

Josh drops his bag in the hall beside the bathroom door. "How long has he been out?" he asks.

"I don't know. I was caught up in the storm all evening and just got home and found him like this," I say.

"I'm sorry, but I'm going to need you to step out here so I can get into the bathroom and check his vitals," Josh says.

I nod and wipe the tears from my face with the back of my hand. I carefully step around my father's body and move to stand beside Colton. He puts his arm around my shoulder, and I lean against him. My knees feel weak and I'm completely unsteady.

Josh checks Dad's temperature and blood pressure, takes a look at his wound and quickly bandages it up. His partner —a woman I don't recognize who looks several years older than us—wheels a gurney down the hallway.

"Vital signs are strong, but he's unresponsive, so I think we need to take him in," Josh says. "Do you want to come with us in the ambulance or meet us there? You'll need to fill out some paperwork at the hospital."

"I'll come with you," I say. I run into my bedroom and grab my purse. I stuff my wallet, keys, and phone into it and grab my hoodie off the back of my desk chair. There's no time to change clothes.

"I'll meet you there," Colton says as they put my father into the ambulance.

"You don't have to do that," I say. "I'll be fine. I'll just call you this afternoon."

"I want to be there for you," he says softly. "You shouldn't be alone."

I swipe at my tears and nod. "Thank you," I say.

I wonder if I should call Knox, but I hate to wake him up this early in the morning. Maybe Colton's right and this will turn out to be nothing serious. Just a slip and fall, nothing to worry about. He'll be home by lunch.

I think it like a prayer, trying to convince myself that everything is going to be okay. But in the deepest part of my heart, there's a nagging terror that says nothing is going to be okay ever again.

CHAPTER 21
JO

I ride to the hospital with my father's hand in mine. He opens his eyes a few times, but closes them again. Even when Josh tries to get him to keep his eyes open, it's as if the weight of them is just too great.

"Does he have a concussion?" I ask.

"Yes, it appears that he does, but we're going to do every-thing we can to keep him awake and get him talking," he says. "It's good you found him when you did. I'm pretty sure this happened recently."

I hear the words he's saying, but all I can think is that it's bad I didn't find him sooner. That I wasn't with him last night. Knox had told me on the phone that Dad left the bar early because he wasn't feeling well. I should have made Colton bring me home, even in the rain.

When we get to the hospital, they take my father away to a room to see the doctor, but hold me back so that I can fill out all the insurance forms and information in the waiting room. I hate for him to be out of my sight even for a few minutes, but they assure me they'll come for me as soon as they can.

Colton arrives shortly after I do, and as much as I said I didn't need him to come, I'm so thankful when he walks through that door. He sits down beside me, takes one look at my trembling hands, and pulls the clipboard and insurance card onto his lap.

I rest my head on his shoulder and clasp my hands together nervously as he asks questions and finishes filling out the form for me.

I hate acting weak in front of someone else like this, but it feels so good to have him to lean on right now that I don't much care. "Thank you for coming," I say.

"Did they tell you anything?"

"He has a concussion," I say. "They're trying to wake him up and get him talking. They said they'll come out and get me as soon as they can."

He finishes the form and hands it back to the lady at reception.

"Do you want something out of the soda machine?" he asks.

"If they have water, that would be great."

He comes back in a minute with two cold waters and hands one to me. He puts his arm around my shoulders and pulls me close.

"It's going to be okay, Jo," he says.

"I hope you're right."

I don't know how long we sit there together. It feels like years before the receptionist calls my name and tells me I can go back to see my dad.

"Next of kin only," she says.

"I'll be here," Colton says.

I follow her back to my dad's room and nearly cry out when I see him sitting up, his eyes open and an IV in his arm.

"There's my Jojo," he says. "I kept telling them to go get you, but they took their sweet time about it."

I throw my arms around him, wet tears leaking onto his hospital gown. "I'm so glad to see you awake," I say. "How are you feeling?"

"Better," he says. "Just took a little tumble, that's all."

"What happened? When did you fall, do you know?"

He shakes his head. "Sometime early this morning," he says. "I'm not sure what time. Maybe around four or five? I got up to use the bathroom and my legs just gave out from under me. I don't know what happened, but next thing I knew I was waking up here with half a dozen people standing over me. Just about gave me the fright of my life."

"I rode here in the ambulance with you, but they made me wait outside," I say. "I tried to get in, but you know hospitals."

"Yes, I do, and I'll be happy to get out of this one as fast as possible," he says with a laugh.

And I think that laugh is just about the best sound I've ever heard in my life. I squeeze his hand and sit down on the edge of the bed.

"Did they say you'd be going home today? Or are they going to keep you here for a while?"

"They want to keep me overnight just to make sure I stay awake and alert, but the doctor said I can go home tomorrow morning," he says. "He doesn't think there will be any lasting or permanent damage, so that's good news."

I smile from ear to ear, so relieved I almost start to cry again. "Did he say anything about why your legs gave out on you?"

Dad's smile fades and he clears his throat. "Well, that's the real mystery, I guess," he says. "He wants me to follow up later this week with Dr. Taylor. Maybe run some tests."

"What kind of tests?"

He shrugs. "I have no idea. Just to make sure nothing seems out of the ordinary."

I think about the trouble he's been having lately with his hands. Whatever it is, it's something we'll be able to deal with. I'm just so glad he's okay now, and that it's nothing too serious.

"I'll call first thing this morning after they open and get you in for an appointment," I say. "But seeing how we're going to be stuck here for a while, what do you want to do? Want me to turn on the TV? I could see if Colton could bring us a deck of cards or something, if you want. We could play a round of Gin Rummy, just like old times?"

"Colton?" he asks, raising an eyebrow and studying me, the corner of his mouth tweaked upwards. "I take it you two were out all night?"

I blush and look away. Damn. He totally knows what happened between us. "He's in the waiting room," I say.

"And where exactly were you two all night?" I know he already knows the answer, but he just wants to hear me say it.

And what choice do I have but to humor him? He is sitting here in a hospital gown all hooked up to machines and IV's.

"Not that it's any of your business, but we got caught in the storm and had to hold out in a cabin that used to belong to his grandfather. Didn't Knox tell you I called?" I say. "We sat there for a while until the storm passed and then headed home as soon as the sun started coming up."

"Mmm-hmm, I see," he says, a glimmer in his eyes.

I pull my hand from his and roll my eyes. "Don't go getting any of your crazy ideas," I say. "We were just hanging out."

Which is such a lie, but like I said, it's none of his business.

"Hanging out with a boy while your poor old dad was passed out on the floor of the bathroom."

"Dad!" I would have swiped his arm if there wasn't an IV sticking out of it. Tears spring to my eyes. "You have no idea how guilty I feel right now. Don't even start to tease me about something like that."

He laughs hard, but then winces and raises a hand to his forehead. "I'm sorry, Jojo. You know I'm just giving you a hard time," he says. "I've been dying for you to finally give in to that boy and spend some real time with him. The way he looks at you?"

He shakes his head and whistles.

"What?" The warmth of a blush is creeping back into my cheeks.

"If you can't see it, there's no use trying to explain it to you," he says. "But I see it. And all I have to say is it's about damn time. I just hate that I ruined your fun night with all this nonsense."

I lean over and kiss the part of his head that isn't bandaged. "You didn't ruin anything, Daddy," I say. "I'm just glad you're okay."

"Well, if he's here anyway, why don't you bring Colton

back here with us?" he says. "No sense in him sitting in the waiting room all by his lonesome."

"They told me we could only have next of kin back here in the room with you," I say.

"Bullshit. Just go tell Kelly you're bringing your friend back," he says. "She'll get him through, no problem."

"Kelly's working today?" I haven't seen her in ages, it seems like. She and my dad dated for a while when I was in high school. She's really the only woman I've ever seen him head-over-heels for, and I still don't quite understand why it didn't work out between them. I always liked her.

"She's here," he says. "You can imagine how excited I was to have her see me in here looking the way I do."

He pats his hair, and I laugh. "Handsome as ever," I say. "I'll be right back."

I find Kelly by the nurse's station and she stands to give me a hug.

"Your daddy gave you quite the scare tonight, huh?"

"You have no idea," I say.

"I couldn't believe it when I saw them wheel him back here. Nearly had a heart attack," she says, touching her hand to her chest. "Thank goodness he's going to be okay."

"I've never been so relieved in my life."

"Does he need something?"

"I hate to ask, because I know they told me next of kin only, but I've got a friend in the waiting room and Dad said to ask if he could come back with us?"

She smiles. "It wouldn't happen to be that tall drink of water with the dark blond hair and the eyes to die for, would it?"

I blush again, thinking that this is probably the most I've

ever blushed in my life. It's beginning to be a nuisance. I'm sure everyone can see right through me.

"His name is Colton, and before you go getting any ideas, he works for us at the bar."

"Whatever you say." She smiles and bumps my shoulder. "You can bring him back with you. Anything that'll help keep Rob alert and awake for the next few hours will be a big help."

"I don't suppose you guys have a pack of playing cards back here anywhere, do you?" I ask.

"Believe it or not, we actually do," she says. "Some of the doctors like to play poker on the slower nights, which is sadly not often enough. I'll go see if Sandy can find them for me."

"Thank you."

I duck my head out of the double doors leading to the emergency wing and Colton looks up. I crook my finger at him and he smiles and stands.

"How's he feeling?"

"Back to his old self, mostly," I say. "Thank the good Lord. He sent me out here to ask if you want to play a few rounds of cards since they're wanting to keep him awake the rest of the morning. I understand if you want to go home, though. It's been a long night."

"What? And miss the opportunity to play some Blackjack with you and your daddy in the emergency room? I wouldn't dare."

He smiles and my stomach flips in the most pleasant way.

The receptionist sitting at the desk gives me the evil eye, so I grab the front of his shirt and pull him through the doors with me. I lead him to the room where they're keeping my dad, glancing around like a thief in the night, trying not to get caught breaking the rules.

Kelly is already there, double-checking the IV and chatting with my father.

"There they are," she says. "I'll leave you guys to it. Take it easy, now. No betting or anything. Rob doesn't need the disappointment of losing too badly after taking a fall like that."

"Haha, very funny," Dad says. "I happen to be very good at cards, thank you very much."

"I remember," Kelly says with a smile, and maybe a hint of something like regret in her voice. "Y'all have fun. I'll be back to check on you in about an hour. Just call if you need anything."

Dad watches her leave, and I can't help but wonder again what happened between the two of them. I don't understand how sometimes perfectly good relationships fall apart when you least expect it.

"Colton, I'm sorry you have to see me like this, but I guess this officially makes you a part of our family at the bar," Dad says.

"I always used to say it isn't a real party until someone ends up in the emergency room."

Dad laughs and Colton pulls a chair closer to the bed. He takes the deck of cards from the table and shuffles.

"I'm not sure I like the sound of that saying," I tell him as I sit down on the end of the bed. "What kind of parties have you been having, anyway?"

"The kind you've been missing out on your whole life, apparently," he says.

I know he's just joking, and to hear the sound of my

father's laughter is all I need to hear to be grateful for Colton's light-hearted humor. How does he always seem to know just what to say?

"Well, let's keep this party going, then," I say. "What should we play?"

Dad touches my arm and winks. "I'm thinking hearts."

CHAPTER 22

COLTON

Thank God for comfy beds and blackout curtains.

Exhausted from spending most of the morning in the ER, I fall into bed, looking forward to at least four hours of uninterrupted bliss before I have to show up at work. I told Jo I'd take her shift tonight so that she could look out for her dad. About fifteen minutes later, though, someone is banging on my door. I grumble and roll over, tempted to just pull my pillow over my head and wait for them to go away.

But what if something else has happened to Rob? He was in good spirits after they moved him to his hospital room this afternoon, but I'm still worried there might be something more serious going on with him.

I get up, pull on my jeans, and rush to the door.

Only, it isn't Jo. It's my dad.

I run a hand over my face, my stomach in knots. What have I done now?

Reluctantly, I open the door. "Hey, Dad. What's up?"

I assume my most casual stance. It's a good defense against my father, who always seems to be wound up tighter than a jack in the box. I'm nowhere near calm on the inside, but I don't want him to know that.

He pushes the door open and blows past me. "Colton, what the hell is wrong with you, son?"

I swallow back the words that come into my brain. I don't even dare open my mouth for fear that I'll say something that will only make this worse.

"Imagine my surprise when I get a call from Neal this afternoon saying that you didn't show up for the very important interview this morning?" Dad says.

I close my eyes and breathe in, exhaustion weighing me down.

"I'm sorry, Dad, I completely forgot."

Which is just about the worst thing I can say. I realize it after the words have passed my lips. Dad's entire face tenses, and if he was the hitting type, this would have been the moment he balled his hands into fists and let it rip.

"You forgot?" He adjusts his jeans on his hips and points a finger at me. "Do you have any idea just what I had to do to get you this interview? I went out of my way to get you in when they were already full up, Colton. They had to pass on some other guy who actually cares about this job, and you forgot?"

He shakes his head, disgust written so clearly on his face, it brings a bad taste to my mouth.

"Well, now I never asked you to do that, did I?" I say. Not that my father really cares what I want. He never has. All he thinks about is what he wants for me. What he thinks is best for me.

And in his eyes, I'm already the type of loser who misses interviews and takes everything for granted. So why even bother telling him about Jo's dad? To him it would just be another excuse, and I'm too tired to drag this out.

"You really plan to spend the rest of your worthless life serving beer at some dive bar?" he asks. "You are so much better than that, Colton, and you know it. But if you want to party your whole life away, never taking any responsibility, then by all means, go ahead. Just don't bother coming back home when it all falls apart."

His famous line. My whole life he's been telling me I'm worthless. Telling me that I am free to make my own choices as long as I don't expect him to be there to help pick me up when I fall.

"Don't worry, Dad," I say, not backing down this time. "I never expect you to be there for me. Especially not when I need you most."

He draws his eyebrows together and steps back. "Now what the hell is that supposed to mean?" he asks.

As if he didn't just tell me the same thing in so many words.

"I've had a very long couple days," I say. "And before you lash out at me again, I wasn't up all night partying. I was at the hospital with a friend who needed me. Not that you care or probably will even believe me. Either way, I haven't had much rest, and since I have to work my very irresponsible and worthless job tonight, I'd appreciate it if you would leave so that I can get some sleep."

Dad doesn't move at first. He stares at me, shaking his

head. He's not used to me talking back to him or standing up for myself, and it's possible he's in shock.

I walk to the door and open it wider, leaning against the wood and waiting for him to get the message. Finally, he turns and walks toward me.

"Colton, I didn't—"

"Dad, just stop," I say. "Please. I'm sorry I missed the interview and made you upset. Please apologize to your old boss for me."

He nods. "I'll see if we can set something up for the end of the month."

I don't even bother arguing. "I'll see you later, Dad."

"Take care of yourself, son," he says. "This is a nice place you've got here, by the way. Very grown up."

I want to laugh. "Thanks," I say.

Dad claps a hand on my arm, starts to say something else, but then turns and stomps his way down the stairs and out into the cold.

I slam the door so hard the whole apartment rocks. I'm not worthless, but no one is as good at making me think I am than my own father. Maybe he really does just want the best for me, but what makes him think he knows what I need better than I do?

I lock the door and undress again, collapsing into the bed where I toss and turn all afternoon.

CHAPTER 23

JO

I spend the next few days focused one hundred percent on my father. He had to spend the night in the hospital, but I called to make an appointment with his regular doctor for this morning.

"You almost ready?" I call back to his bedroom.

"Stop hovering over me," he calls back. "I'll be ready when I'm ready."

There's frustration in his voice, and I understand it, but he needs to come on. I don't want to be late.

"Finally," I say when he emerges from his bedroom.

"Can you get these last few buttons for me?" he asks. He shakes his hands. "I swear, I'm falling apart these days."

He says it with a laugh, but I know this man better than I know myself, and the worry in his tone makes my stomach hurt. I reach up to button the last few buttons of his shirt.

"Everything is going to be fine," I say. "Which is why we don't want to be late to this appointment. We need to figure out what's going on so we can just get it fixed and move on with our lives."

My hands are sweaty, but I hope I'm managing to keep my fear out of my voice. My father has always been the strong one. He's always been there for me when I needed him, even when I've made the worst mistakes of my life. I want to be here for him now, too.

"Let's get going, then," he says. He kisses my forehead and runs a hand down my hair, just like he used to do when I was a little girl.

I smile and wrap an arm around him as we walk out to the car.

Colton is standing by his truck talking to Knox, and they both turn as we come out of the house.

"Hey, beautiful," he says. His smile slays me.

I hate that we haven't been able to spend any time together for the past few days, but he's really been helping out. He's taken all of my shifts this week, and between him and Knox, we haven't had to worry about a thing.

"Hey," I say, the familiar flush of warmth creeping up the back of my neck.

Dad whistles, and I'm tempted to punch him in the arm. He's obviously getting a kick out of watching me squirm.

"I'll be in the car, just in case the two lovebirds need some privacy," he says, winking at Colton.

"Daddy, if you know what's good for you—"

He lifts his hands in surrender and gets into the passenger side of his old Buick.

"Sorry," I say, kicking at the dirt as Colton approaches me.

"Don't apologize," he says with a laugh. "It's a father's job to tease his little girl when she's got a boyfriend."

I look up at him. Boyfriend? My stomach fills with butterflies.

We haven't had a chance to talk about anything official between us, but I definitely like the sound of that.

"Thanks for taking my shift again tonight," I say. "The doctor said they're going to run a bunch of tests today to try to rule a few things out. It might take a while, and I'm sure we'll both be exhausted by the time we make it home."

"No problem," he says. "Whatever you need, you know that."

He's either too good to be true, or I've died and gone to heaven.

"Thank you," I say. "I'd love to spend some time with you soon, though."

"Why don't I swing by tomorrow night?" he says. "Knox said he'll take over for the night, and we'll both work the weekend."

"I don't know," I say, glancing at the car. "I don't really want to go out and leave him home alone. Not until we figure this out, anyway."

"Who said anything about going out?" he says, taking my hand. "I was thinking I'd bring over a few movies and maybe a couple games. We can order pizza and make a night of it."

I smile and shake my head. "You're wonderful, you know that?"

"I've heard it a time or two," he says, a wide smile lighting up his entire face.

"I need to get going," I say. "I was just giving Daddy a hard time about running late."

"Okay, call me if you need anything," he says.

He leans down and places a soft kiss on my lips.

He and Knox disappear into the bar to get things ready for tonight, and Daddy and I make our way to the hospital. My stomach is in knots as we wait for the doctor. When he finally comes out, I've worked my mind into all sorts of terrible possibilities. I'm ready to just find out once and for all so we can start treatment.

My father is my life, and I just want him to be okay.

He squeezes my hand as we sit down beside each other in the doctor's office.

"Alright, doc, what's the plan?" Daddy says. "How do we figure out what's going on?"

Dr. Taylor leans forward, picking up a manila folder. "Let's go through your symptoms one more time," he says. "I know you were concerned about the strength and coordination in your hands?"

"Yeah, lately I've just had a hard time getting a grip on things. I thought it might be arthritis," he says.

"I think we can rule that out since your fall the other night," the doctor says. "What else has been going on?"

"Just those things, really," Daddy says. "You think maybe it's something muscular?"

"Could be," he says. "Today we're going to get you in for an MRI, take a blood and urine sample, and do a few simple tests here in the office once you're done."

"How long will it be before we find out what's going on?" I ask.

The doctor smiles, but there's no joy behind it. "Jo, I know you guys are both anxious to know what's going on, but you need to be aware that this could take some time to properly diagnose. Hopefully it will be something simple, but it could take a few weeks to get all the tests back on this first round."

"And if we don't have answers at that point?" I shift in my seat.

He shakes his head. "If the tests we run today don't give us a clear answer about what's going on, we'll keep looking. I've already put a call into a neurologist friend of mine. Depending on what we see in the MRI, I might refer your father over to him."

"A neurologist?" My hands feel numb. This all sounds so complicated, and I'm afraid that if this takes weeks or months to figure out, I'll lose my damn mind.

"It's going to be fine, Jojo," Daddy says. "Let's just get this over with and see where we are."

The nurse leads my father to one of the patient rooms and asks me to sit in the waiting room. I brought a good book with me to read, but I find myself fidgeting and getting up several times to just walk around. I can't stand the waiting, and I was really hoping we'd have some answers today.

Why can't this be easy?

When will things go back to normal? Daddy keeps telling me it's nothing serious and not to worry, but he's crazy if he thinks I'm going to take this lightly. What in the world would be making him lose control of his hands and his legs?

I sit back down and cross my legs. Uncross them. Take a sip of water. Check my phone. Cross my legs again. I can't sit still.

Daddy's been gone for about two hours now, and I can't focus on anything else.

I look down at my phone, pulling up Colton's number on

instinct. It's just after eleven in the morning, so he's probably just sitting at home watching TV. I don't want to become the needy girl who's always bugging him, but I could really use a friend right now.

I dial his number before I can second guess myself.

He picks up on the second ring. "Hey, what's going on? Everything okay?" He sounds about as worried as I feel, and for some reason, it makes me feel better.

"Hey. Yeah, it's fine, I guess," I say. I glance around again to make sure I'm alone in the waiting room. People have come in and out all day, but overall it seems to be a pretty slow day in the office. "I've been in the waiting room alone for two hours, and I'm kind of losing my mind."

"Where's your dad?"

"They took him back to do some tests and to get an MRI," I say. "They said I couldn't go back with him."

"Why didn't you call me earlier?" he asks. "I'm on my way. Which doctor?"

"No, you don't have to do that," I say. "I know you've been working a lot lately. You're probably tired."

"I am literally sitting here doing nothing," he says. "I'd much rather be there with you. Just give me a few minutes to get over there. Do you want me to bring you something to eat?"

Tears spring to my eyes. I didn't realize how much I needed him right now.

"There's a cafeteria here at the hospital," I say. "The nurse said I could grab a sandwich there."

"And you really want to eat hospital food?" he asks, and I can hear the smile in his voice. "Just tell me where to go, and I'll be there as soon as I can. I'll bring some good food."

"Bring something for Daddy, too," I say. "Just in case."

"Will do."

"And Colton?"

"Yes, Boss?"

I smile. "Thank you."

"Sure thing, gorgeous," he says. "See you soon."

I hang up and feel more calm and centered than I have in two hours. I close my eyes and lean back against the couch in the waiting room.

I sit still for a full twenty minutes, my monkey mind finally calm, until Colton walks through the door, two bags of Abby's BBQ in his hands and that familiar smile on his face that seems to set everything right, if just for a little while.

CHAPTER 24
JO

The next few weeks pass slowly. We're in limbo with Daddy's health. None of the tests have come up with an easy diagnosis, so we've been back and forth between the hospital and the new neurologist's office half a dozen times.

Things at the bar have been as busy as ever with two more successful live music Saturdays coming and going, but this weekend is the one that matters.

"Are you serious that Long Road Ahead is coming in this weekend?" Penny asks. She and her husband Mason are sitting at the bar on a Thursday night. "Tell me again how exactly you guys pulled that off?"

"Ask him," I say, jerking my thumb toward Colton.

"I'll never tell," Colton says, raising an eyebrow as he pops open another beer and slides it toward Mason.

"I seriously can't get him to tell me his tricks," I say. "I have no clue how he managed it."

"Hey, didn't one of the guitar players in Long Road Ahead go to high school over in Westbrook?" Mason asks.

"Did he?" I ask. I look at Colton. "Did you go to high school with one of them? I had no idea they were from around here."

"Like I said, I'm not giving up any of my secrets," he says, smiling.

"You're not supposed to keep secrets from your girl-friend," I say, wrapping my arms around him.

He plants a kiss on my cheek.

Working at the bar with him has been amazing. At first, I was afraid things might be awkward or complicated, but it's actually been as easy as breathing. Obviously we don't want to constantly be kissing and touching behind the bar, but every once in a while sure is nice. Besides, it's still early in the night and other than Penny and Mason, we only have a handful of regulars in the whole place.

"You guys are too cute," Penny says.

"Young love," Mason says. He puts his arm around his wife. "Not like us old married folk."

"Shut up and kiss me," Penny says.

I laugh. I love it when they come by the bar. I never in a million years thought I would have a friend in Penny Wright. She's always been the richest girl in school. Hell, the richest girl in Georgia. She always had this air of betterness around her, like she just didn't see things the way they really were.

But ever since she disappeared about a year ago to run away with Mason, she's been a different person. She never mentions how expensive her clothes are or how she just bought the newest Prada purse, anymore. She and Mason live in a modest house not too far from the bar, and she's been really working her ass off to get her own business started. Not to mention all the work she does for charity in Fairhope to help kids in need.

"Where is your little one tonight?" I ask.

"Believe it or not, Preston and Jenna took her for the night," she says. "I love her more than life, but it's so nice to have a break every once in a while. You cannot imagine how tough it is to have a baby and be working full time. Especially now that she's walking."

I shift uncomfortably and get to work washing a few dirty glasses in the sink. I can imagine it more than she knows.

"Well, we really are grateful for how much you've done to help us get the bar back on its feet," I say. "Saturdays have been packed for two months, but this weekend is going to be the biggest we've seen yet. I've been putting flyers up all over town."

"It's too bad you don't have a bigger space for the crowd," Penny says. "I heard you guys have been turning people away."

"More and more every weekend," I say.

"See, Penny sees the potential," Colton says. "You guys really ought to think about expanding."

"I'm not saying it's outside the realm of possibility, but it seems complicated," I say. "Permits and contractors and inspections. It would take forever to put that together, and I can't imagine how we'd get the money for the new construction."

"I told you I could help you with the paperwork," Penny says. "It wouldn't be too hard. You could take out a small business loan to get things going. You've got plenty of equity built up in the bar now, so you could put the property up as collateral."

I sigh. It sounds wonderful, but it's still so scary. With everything up in the air now with my dad and this new relationship with Colton, I feel like I've got enough life-altering things to deal with than I can handle as it is.

"Maybe it's something we can revisit in a few years, but for now, I don't think we should mess with a good thing, you know?"

"If you ask me, it's the best time to expand," Penny says. "Business is good and adding a new restaurant with your recipes would bring people from all over the state, I'd be willing to bet."

"Which is exactly what I keep telling her," Colton chimes in.

"If you decide you want to seriously consider it, let me know," she says. "I'll come by one afternoon and we can talk about all the details. I'd love to help you out."

"Thanks," I say, and I mean it. I'm just not ready for something like that. I like the bar the way it is.

"Well, I'm excited to hear Long Road Ahead this weekend," Mason says. "I love that one song they had out last year. Picking up the Pieces."

Colton clears his throat and looks down at the floor. I could swear I see a blush forming on his cheeks, which has me interested. What in the world is going on with him and this band?

"What's gotten into you?" I ask when he steps away to ring up someone's tab.

"What do you mean?"

"The secret connection you have with this huge country

band, convincing them to come all the way down to our little bar and play for peanuts," I say. "And that strange look on your face when Mason mentioned that song. What am I missing here?"

"I have no idea what you're talking about," he says.

But there's a look in his eyes that says there's more to this story than he's telling. I hope I get a chance to question the band about it this weekend. There's some kind of history here, and I'm going to figure it out if it kills me.

Before I can question him further, the door to the bar swings open, and my stomach turns.

Bryan and two men I don't recognize walk in. My entire body tenses.

Why couldn't this be a night when Slim is working the door? I so don't want to deal with this jerk tonight. How many times do I have to tell this slime that he isn't welcome at this bar?

I've been lucky not to run into him anywhere around town, but I heard from a friend that he's been looking for work and having a hard time of it. He's on probation for something he pulled with a couple buddies of his a few months back, which is why he's stuck here in Fairhope for a while.

"What?" Colton asks, looking at me.

I nod to the guys who just walked in. "Unwelcome customers," I mumble.

He turns and his fist curls around the stack of cash in his hand. "That's the guy we had to throw out of here awhile back?" he asks. "What was his name, again?"

"Bryan," I say, the hatred bitter on my tongue.

"I'll handle this," he says, taking a step in their direction as they settle on a few stools at the end of the bar.

I shake my head and grab his arm. "Don't," I say. "I'll deal with them."

"You sure?" he asks. "Because I'm more than happy to put him in his place."

"You'll only make it worse, and I really don't want things to get out of hand," I say.

He shrugs, but keeps his eyes cut toward the group of three obviously drunk guys. "You're the boss," he says.

"Yoohoo, what's a guy gotta do to get a damn drink around here?" Bryan says. His eyes land on mine, and there's a challenge there. He knows exactly how to get under my skin, and he's here to play his little games.

Well, I've had enough of his shit.

"Bryan, you'd have to wait until hell freezes over to get a drink here ever again," I say, walking over to him, glad there's a bar between us. "Whatever trouble you're looking for tonight, you're not going to find it here."

"I'm hurt, Josephine," he says, clutching a hand to his chest. "Is that any way to treat an old friend?"

His two buddies laugh, but I don't take my eyes off Bryan's. I refuse to back down or give in.

"You're no friend of mine," I say, teeth clenched. "I'd appreciate it if you'd leave. You're not welcome here."

The smile fades from Bryan's face, and I recognize the anger that replaces it.

"Listen, you little bitch, don't forget that I know how to put you in your place," he says. "Now, I came in here with my friends to have a good time, and you're going to be polite."

"You're in my bar, in case you forgot," I say, my hands

trembling. "And no one talks to me that way in my own place. You can either choose to get the hell out of here, or I'll call the police and make sure they help you find your way back to whatever hole you crawled out of."

"Ooh, well, lookie who finally grew up and got herself a spine," he says, slapping the top of the bar. "Guys, I do believe we have a live one here."

"Come on, man, we can find another place to get a drink." His dark-haired friend stands and pats him on the shoulder.

"Nah, man, shit. I'm not leaving," he says. "Sit down."

"Bryan, it's not worth it," the guy says. He shoots me a look of apology, which makes me wonder why a halfway decent person is hanging out with such scum.

"From what I remember, it was well worth it," Bryan says, licking his lips when he looks at me.

Rage erupts inside me like a bomb that's been waiting years to explode. There's a corkscrew lying on a towel next to me, and I want to jab it in his eye and watch him bleed. This man has caused me far too much pain for me to stand here and let him even look at me the way he is right now.

I resist the urge to grab the corkscrew and step closer to the bar, leaning forward so I know he can hear me loud and clear.

"If you value your life, you will turn around and walk out that door," I say. "If I ever see you in this bar again, I'll get a restraining order on you, and with your record, I imagine that would be a very bad thing for you right now."

He glares at me and leans forward, so close I can smell the alcohol on his breath.

I never wanted to be this close to him again in my life,

but there's no way I'm backing down. I want him to know I'm not the same weak girl he messed around with all those years ago.

"Fine, I'll go, but you better watch your back," he says. "All you would have had to do was treat me with a little respect after all this time, but since you refuse to let bygones be bygones, you just made my shit-list."

"You've got five seconds," I say, glancing pointedly at my watch.

"Come on, Bryan, let's bolt," his friend says, pulling on his arm. "We don't need to be dealing with the cops tonight, man."

Bryan makes a point to glare at me one more time before he finally stands and wobbles toward the door.

"And I better not see you guys driving out of my parking lot," I say. "Get a cab or walk it off, or I will be calling the cops."

Bryan curses and pushes the door open with such force it hits the brick wall outside and rebounds right in his face. His head knocks all the way back and blood pours from his nose.

"Dammit," he says, walking out.

Serves him right. I don't even offer him so much as a napkin.

"Want me to make sure they don't drive off?" Colton asks.

I jump and hold a hand to my heart. "I didn't realize you were standing there," I say.

"I really wish you would have let me put those guys in their place," he says.

He slides over the top of the bar and takes a quick look

outside. When he comes back, he nods. "They were walking down the street," he says.

I relax a little, but my hands are sweating and my heart's still racing.

"When are you going to explain to me who that guy is to you?" he asks.

"He used to work here," I say. "A long time ago."

Colton takes my hand. "Is he the one who hurt you?" he asks.

I nod. "And I don't like to talk about it," I say. "Hopefully that's the last time we'll ever see him in here."

"I hope so, too," he says. "But maybe we need to make sure you aren't working here any nights by yourself for a while."

"I can take care of myself," I say, busying myself with straightening things behind the bar. I'm rattled, but I don't need a babysitter. I don't want Bryan to think he can shake me up the way he used to.

"I don't doubt that, but that guy's got at least a hundred pounds on you," Colton says. "I don't like those odds, and he doesn't seem like the kind of guy who takes no for an answer."

You have no idea.

I clear my throat, avoiding his eyes. I feel exposed and weak, and I want to just put it behind me. I've got enough on my plate right now without worrying about Bryan-freaking-Thompson.

"If he shows up again, I'll just call the cops," I say. "I can handle it."

"You know the cops in this town," Colton says, refusing to drop it. He puts his hand on my wrist. "It could take them half an hour to get over here. Maybe you should go ahead and put in a call to make sure they're aware."

"Drop it," I say, snapping at him and pulling my arm away.

"Jo, I heard him threaten you," he says. "You really expect me to drop it?"

"He's not going to mess with me," I say. "Not anymore."

I try to sound confident, but it's getting into my head all over again.

"I don't trust that guy as far as I could throw him," Colton says. "I know you're determined to prove how tough you are, but I care about you, Jo. I'm not going to drop this. I think we should call the cops and let them know what he said to you."

I lean against the counter and take a deep breath.

"If it will make you feel better, I'll put a call in to my dad's friend Alan tomorrow morning," I say. "I'll let him know Bryan was up here causing trouble."

"You think he'll take you seriously?" he asks. "Maybe you should file an official report. Or get a restraining order like you said."

"Alan knows some things about what happened with Bryan a long time ago," I say softly. "He'll take it seriously."

Colton studies me, and I can feel his gaze burning a hole in my heart. "Jo—"

"Colton, I know what you're going to say." I stand up straight. "Please, I'm asking you to let it go, okay? It's important to me."

He lets out a frustrated sigh and runs a hand through his hair. "Okay, if that's what you want," he says. "But I wish you'd talk to me about it. If I'm going to be a part of your life, that means you have to actually let me into your life, Jo. If you can't even trust me with this, what exactly are we doing here?"

I don't answer, because I don't have an answer for him. It's not about trust. Is it?

"I'm going to take a break," he says. He walks away, disappearing into the back room for a few minutes.

I stare down at my hands and realize I've been holding them in tight fists ever since Bryan walked in. My fingernails have dug crescent-shaped craters into my skin.

I open them and my fingers tremble as I take another deep breath.

I glance toward the door to the back room.

This is exactly why I've avoided getting involved with anyone for as long as I have. My past is messy, and as much as I like to pretend I'm over what happened when I was younger, Bryan coming in here proves that it can all come back in an instant.

But telling Colton the truth and admitting just how messed up I was in high school, and how many terribly stupid decisions I've made in my life, is more than I'm willing to confess to someone right now. If he knew the whole truth, he'd probably run so far from me I'd never see him again.

And that's just not something I'm willing to risk.

CHAPTER 25
COLTON

"**G**ood evening, ladies and gentlemen. Welcome to Rob's." I clutch the microphone and stare into the crowd of more than a hundred people. I knew the bar would be completely packed tonight, but from what Jo says, there's a line of at least a hundred more still outside. It's insane and the energy in the room is electric.

"I heard a rumor that some of y'all were expecting to hear Long Road Ahead tonight," I say, the crowd hanging on my every word. "Now, I'm not sure where exactly that rumor got started, but I hate to tell you guys..."

I wait for a second, watching the mixed expressions and anticipation on everyone's face. A couple girls in the front row are holding onto each other so tight, their knuckles have turned white.

I smile. "The rumor is absolutely true."

The crowd erupts into screams and cheers so loud it vibrates the stage under my feet.

"Now, I know y'all can do better than that," I say.

The screaming gets even louder. When they settle down, I lean into the mic.

"Some of you guys might not know this, but my good friend Greg is the lead guitarist of Long Road Ahead. Some of y'all may have heard of him?"

Another cheer erupts throughout the room. Greg is a legend in country music these days. Good looking, charming, and a favorite of ladies everywhere. I smile, thinking of what my best friend from high school has accomplished in such a short time.

"Well, Greg grew up just a few miles away over in West-brook," I say. "So when I asked him if he wanted to come play for the folks living in his old stomping grounds, he dropped everything to come play for you guys. So let's give Greg and Long Road Ahead the best damn welcome home they've ever heard."

Throughout the bar people raise their cups and bottles into the air, screaming at the top of their lungs. I turn and wink at Willow, the lead singer. She shakes her head and smiles as I hand her the mic.

"Good to see you again, Colton Tucker," she shouts into my ear. "Find me after?"

"Of course," I say.

She kisses my cheek and steps around me, the lights dimming in the rest of the bar as the stage lights come up.

She settles the mic in its stand and plays the first notes of their first big hit. The crowd goes insane. I nod at Greg and he smiles. It's damn good to see him again.

I jump down to the dusty floor and weave my way through the crowd toward the bar. I hop across the bartop and find my place behind the counter, nodding my head at the familiar song. The energy in here tonight is addictive, and it kind of makes me miss my days travelling with the band.

"They sound amazing," Jo shouts, throwing her arms around me. "I don't know how you pulled this off, but I'm sure as hell grateful you did. Thank you."

I smile and hug her back. "You're welcome, Boss," I say. "Now, get to work. We've got customers for miles."

I grab a white towel from a stack of clean ones and stuff it in my back pocket.

She rolls her eyes, but the smile that teases her lips sends an electric jolt straight through my heart. Does she have any idea just how gorgeous she is tonight with her hair down and her tight black tank top and jeans? How anyone is able to concentrate on the band instead of her is a mystery.

I stare a little too long before I realize there are at least ten people shouting for drinks. I tear my gaze away and concentrate on the customers, letting the next few hours pass in a blur of good music and nonstop, old fashioned hard work.

I love everything about this job, and it's hard to remember why I almost didn't take the offer. Working over at Brantley's was fun, but it was much slower paced most nights. Sometimes I loved the quieter atmosphere, but here at Rob's, I am in my element. Especially on nights like this where the crowd is hot and the drinks are flowing.

But more than anything, I love working with Jo. She may have been a hardass in the beginning, never letting me slack off and never letting up, but I think that's what made me start falling for her. She throws her whole heart into this place, and she does it with a smile on her face, never complaining about sore feet or being exhausted every night when it's time to close up.

Her passion shows through in everything she does, and sometimes I think I must be the luckiest man alive to be the one she's chosen to trust with her heart.

We've fallen into a rhythm together, communicating behind the bar in looks and gestures, barely having to say a word. We understand each other, and I've never been more comfortable around someone.

A few weeks ago we even started playing around with throwing drinks back and forth behind the bar, and the crowd around the bar appreciates the show. I catch her eye and lift a shaker full of margaritas. She nods and turns around, holding one hand behind her back.

I toss the silver shaker toward her and she catches it one-handed, flawlessly spinning around and catching it in her other hand in front of her.

A few people near the bar break out in applause and Jo lights up from the inside. Her smile and energy is contagious, and I realize with a sudden certainty that I've fallen hopelessly, head-over-heels in love with her.

The thought knocks the breath from my lungs.

It's happened so quickly, I didn't realize just how much my feelings for her have grown over the past few months.

She shoots me a concerned look, but I just wave her away and turn back to the customers. I was not expecting this, and I don't completely know how to handle it. I've never fallen in love before.

I want to tell her how I feel, but I also don't want her to think she has to say she loves me, too. What if she isn't in love with me at all?

She has so much going on with her dad right now, I don't want our relationship to be just another thing she has to deal with.

I glance over, watching her work. I'll tell her when the time is right. I have to trust that somehow, I'll know when that is.

"I think it's starting to slow down now," she says to me several hours later. "The band should be wrapping things up pretty soon, and I'm sure it'll be a madhouse until last call, but just a few more hours and we'll be home free."

As if on cue, the band ends their song and Willow steps forward to hold onto the mic.

"Well folks, this has been an amazing night, and I can't tell y'all how much we have loved being here in Fairhope," Willow says. The roar of the crowd subsides as nearly everyone in the bar turns to listen. "It's almost time for us to say goodbye, but before we go, we wanted to play an oldie but goodie. Some of y'all will recognize this tune. It's called Picking Up The Pieces, and was written by a good friend of mine named Colton Tucker, which some of you will know as the guy who's been serving you drinks most of the night."

Half the room turns to look at me, and I raise my hand in acknowledgement, half wanting to slink behind the counter and disappear. Willow's eyes meet mine across the distance and I nod to her as she winks.

"Colton, this one's for you," she says.

The music begins and the crowd cheers, everyone in the room recognizing the song that put Long Road Ahead on the map a few years ago. It was the song that launched them, really, and whenever I hear it playing, it brings me back to those days when I wasn't me unless I had a guitar in one hand and a beer in the other.

Willow's voice echoes through the room, and couples come together on the dancefloor.

Jo appears at my side, and I don't dare look at her. My cheeks are bright red, I'm sure. I wasn't expecting Willow to call me out like that, and as much as I sometimes like being the life of the party, I don't always like being pushed into the spotlight.

"Colton Tucker, you sly dog," she says, pushing her hip into mine and making me splash vodka all over the counter. "You never told me you write music. Much less that you wrote a hit song that's actually been on the radio."

I scoop ice into four cups and start pouring my signature drink for a group of ladies at the end of the bar. "I'm a complicated man, Josephine Warner."

"I'll say," she mumbles. "Don't think I'm letting this go so easily."

"I wouldn't dream of it."

She moves away to take care of a fresh rush of customers, and I shake my head. The secret is out, and I have no doubt she'll grill me about it for weeks.

I sing along to the lyrics I wrote back when I was really just a kid, and for a moment, wonder what happened to the part of me that used to love making music. Tonight, it somehow feels like coming home again to something I didn't realize I was missing.

CHAPTER 26
COLTON

When the band finishes their last set, they all come to sit down on my end of the bar, and I treat them to drinks on the house.

"You guys were amazing up there," I say. The crowd is starting to thin out a little now that the music has stopped.

"Brings back old times," Willow says.

"Yes it does," Greg says, taking the barstool next to hers. His hair has grown out down past his shoulders now. "I missed home more than I realized."

"You're not getting tired of living out of a suitcase just yet, are you?" I tease. "Because we could probably use another good bartender around here if you're looking for a job."

He laughs. "No offense, man, but I'll keep this gig a little longer," he says. "I can't imagine going back to slinging drinks after all this."

"No offense taken," I say. "I'd probably kick your ass if you quit now, after all you guys have accomplished."

"It's been a ride, I'll tell you that," Willow says. "Three years ago if someone had told me we'd have two hit records and be touring the country, I probably would have laughed in their face."

"Well, I'm proud of all you guys," I say. "How long are you planning to stick around?"

"Believe it or not, we've got a full week off, and we're thinking about sticking around here for a while," Charlie, the bass player, says. "I like the vibe of this town, and it'll be nice to hang around and relax for a change. We'll be going back into the studio in a couple months, and we're hoping some down time will help inspire a few new songs."

"If you're up for it, we'd love to have you come over and play with us," Willow says. "Maybe dust off your guitar?"

I shake my head and clear my throat. "I haven't been playing much lately, to tell you the truth," I say. "No time these days."

"There's always time for music," Charlie says. "Come on, now. You've got to at least come out to Greg's place on the beach sometime this week and jam with us. Just like old times."

It's definitely a tempting thought. Greg and I used to sit around playing for hours when we were in high school. When I used to tour with the band in the early days, before their music really took off, we had a lot of good times. But I feel like a different person than the guy I was back then.

"Let me know what you guys have planned, and I'll see what I can do," I say. "I'm usually here at the bar every night, but I could maybe spare a few afternoons."

"Shit, you better do more than that," Greg says. "I'm sure

this place could manage without you for a few nights this week."

I glance over at Jo still working to get drinks out to the late crowd. With everything going on lately, I know she needs me to be here. And hanging out with these guys means a lot more than just playing music.

The last time we partied together, I blacked out and lost an entire week to a massive hangover.

"Hey, remember that night we played at that little hole in the wall bar just outside of Birmingham?" Willow says. "It was maybe two and half years ago now, I think, and the owner actually had a chicken coop right there beside the bar."

"Wait, is that the place where the guy had a pasture full of cows right by the parking lot?" Charlie asks.

"Yes, remember we got so drunk after the show we decided to go cow tipping? Man, was he mad." Willow laughs and takes a shot of whiskey. "Those were good times, though. We were so wild back then."

"I miss it," Greg says. "These days our manager is up our ass about keeping to our schedule and getting to sleep at a reasonable hour. He never lets us be free like we used to."

"Come to think of it, though, it was always our boy Colton here who was instigating such shenanigans," Charlie says. "I'm sure the cow tipping was his idea."

"No doubt about it," Willow says. She looks into my eyes and smiles. "You should really think about coming back out on the road with us again. It would be a lot of fun to have you riding with us."

The idea kind of throws me off for a second. "Nah. You

guys are big time now. What could I possibly bring to the table now?" I ask. "I'd just get in the way."

"Of course not, you'd be our lucky charm for one thing," she says. "Most importantly, though, we could start writing music together again like we used to. I've been in some kind of slump these days. I think it's all the pressure of the third record and trying to make it just as good as the first two. I feel like I don't have any good ideas left."

"Sure you do, you just need to relax and jar them loose," Greg says. He pats her shoulder and kisses the top of her head. "It's going to be fine. Besides, we've already got at least five or six really great songs for the next album."

"Five or six isn't enough," she says. She rubs her forehead, and I notice for the first time that she's got dark circles under her eyes that didn't use to be there.

"Stop stressing it so much," Charlie says. "Where's Aidan? He knows how to cheer you up."

"He's outside smoking and chatting up the hotties," Willow says. "I'll be fine. I just need a few good weeks of relaxation, and I'll be right as rain."

"You guys want another round?" I ask. "We're getting close to last call."

"Already?" Willow asks. "Damn, this night has just flown by. We can't let the party end here, gentlemen. What are we going to do after this? Should we head out to another bar? Or head to the beach house?"

"Every other bar in town is going to be closing," I say. "City ordinance."

"The beach house it is, then."

"Sounds good to me," Greg says. "I sent our assistant

over there this afternoon to make sure it was stocked with whiskey and snacks. We should be good to go for the night."

"You're going to join us, right Colton?" Willow asks.

"I wish I could, but I've got to help close this place down tonight," I say. I wonder what Jo has planned for after we close up. I haven't had nearly enough time with her lately. "Maybe another time?"

"You're not getting out of this that easily," Willow says. "Why don't you come over after you close up? We'll be partying all night, I'm sure. Just like old times."

The way she keeps looking at me and catching my eye, I have a feeling she wants me to come over for more than just the music and the partying. Is she really inviting me back into her bed after all this time?

A few months ago, I would have jumped at the chance to have a good time with my old friends. Spending a little extra time with a beautiful woman like Willow wouldn't have made me think twice. But now?

Not a chance.

I glance back at Jo and she looks over and smiles. She's the only one I want to be with tonight.

"It's tempting, but I'm afraid I'll have to pass on tonight," I say. "We'll get together later this week, though, I promise."

Willow sticks out her bottom lip in a pout. "Your loss," she says. "We're having a bunch of people out there tonight, and I can promise you it's going to be a night to remember."

"Yes, I'm sure it will," I say with a secret smile.

This is the night I realized I was in love for the very first time, and that's just not the kind of thing a guy ever forgets.

CHAPTER 27
JO

"Are they gone, already?" I ask. I was trying to get over to officially meet the band, but there were too many people still wanting drinks. Plus, I had to run home real quick and make sure Daddy was doing okay. Thankfully, he was sound asleep in bed already.

"Yeah. Greg has a beach house not far from here," Colton says. "Apparently they had it stocked with drinks and food and are heading out there to party."

"Darn," I say, pouting. "I've been so busy all night I didn't even get a chance to meet them."

He puts his arms around my waist and kisses the top of my head. "We have an invitation to go out there if you want," he says. "Just say the word."

I shake my head. "I'd love to, but I don't want to leave Daddy alone right now," I say. "But you can go if you want."

"I was hoping we could spend some time together," he says.

"Are you really willing to turn down a once-in-a-lifetime

party with a famous band just to hang out at my house and do nothing?" I ask. "I would never ask you to do that. I really don't mind if you want to go."

"Trust me, it's not once-in-a-lifetime," he says. "I used to tour with them back in the day. I've had enough party nights with them to last forever, but what I haven't had is enough time with my beautiful girlfriend lately."

I blush and tuck my head against his chest. He really is too good to be true.

"Let's get this place cleaned up, then, so we can do something terribly exciting, like watch yet another movie," I say, laughing. "I'll even let you choose tonight."

"I knew there was something special about tonight," he jokes. "My very own choice of DVD. I'm in heaven."

I smack his arm and turn to start working on getting the bar closed down. He grabs the belt loop on the back of my jeans and pulls me back toward him.

"Now, wait just a second," he says. "I need one more minute of snuggling before we get back to work."

I laugh as he wraps his strong arms around me and kisses my neck.

"Maybe you don't deserve any snuggling," I say. "You've been keeping secrets from me."

"Mmm-hmm," he says as he keeps kissing his way up and down my neck.

"I'm serious," I say, spinning around. "You really used to tour with them?"

He shrugs. "It's not a big deal."

"It is, too," I say. "When was this?"

"About two and a half years ago," he says. "Greg and I used to play guitar together a lot in high school, but we didn't see each other for a while when he moved off to go to college at UGA. He invited me to come up and spend a weekend with him to meet some new friends he'd made. That's where he met the other guys from the band and they'd been playing around a lot in their spare time. I was the one who suggested they start an actual band, and I guess the rest is history."

"You're kidding me?" I say. "You're the one who convinced them to start a band? I had no idea. And you're the one who wrote Picking Up The Pieces? Wasn't that their first hit single?"

It makes me wonder just how much I don't know about him. I can't believe he's acting like it's nothing to get excited about.

"Willow and I wrote it together, really," he says. "I wrote the lyrics, but she's the one who figured up most of the actual music."

I shake my head. I'm dating a songwriter and never even knew it.

I start gathering dirty glasses and empty bottles from around the bar. "So does that mean you get royalties from the song? How does that work?"

He frowns. "No, to be honest, my name isn't officially listed as a co-writer," he says with a shrug. "It's not a big deal, though."

My eyes go wide. "Not a big deal. Colton—"

"Let it go, okay?" he asks, and I can tell from his tone that he means it.

"How long did you tour with them?" I ask, even though I really want to give him hell about the royalty thing. He's been cheated out of a hell of a lot of money. Doesn't he realize that?

"About three months," he says. "I ended up moving up to Athens for a few months first. We rented a house together so the band could practice whenever they wanted, and I acted as a part-time manager, talking to local bars and getting gigs for them before they started travelling."

"Unbelievable," I say. "How come you never told me this before?"

He shrugs and turns on the water to start washing glasses. "I guess it didn't seem important."

"Bullshit," I say. "There has to be more to it than that."

He laughs. "You never let up, do you?" he says, shaking his head. "How do you always know when there's more to tell?"

"I've been working at a bar half my life," I say. "I've dealt with more bullshit than most people deal with in a lifetime, trust me. Now, spill it."

I grab two glasses from the stack of clean ones and pour a couple of shots.

Colton takes his glass and throws it back. "Thanks," he says. "I needed that."

"I had a feeling," I say, downing my own shot and pouring another round. "Tell me what happened."

"I was out touring with them for a while. Mostly dive bars and small-town fairs, stuff like that," he says. He closes his eyes for a second and takes a deep breath. "I hadn't been home for a while, but I knew my grandpa wasn't feeling so well. He'd been in and out of the hospital for chest pains and some problems with circulation."

I lean against the bar, listening. I'm pretty sure I know

where this story is heading, and it makes my heart hurt for him.

"He told me the doctors wanted him to go in for this procedure," he says. "All standard stuff. The kind of thing they've done a thousand times, you know? He was real nervous, though. He said he had a feeling things weren't right. I told him he was being silly and that he'd be around for a long time yet."

I reach over and place my hand on his.

"The thing is, I knew exactly when the procedure was scheduled, and I had a chance to come home," he says. "The band was playing in a town not that far from here, and I could have come back to be with him. He wanted me to be here, but I was young and stupid and having a good time. Hell, even though I was still underage, I was drunk nearly every night, going wild."

He pauses and wipes away a tear.

"He called me the night before he went in for the surgery," he says. "He told me he loved me and that he was scared he wasn't going to pull through."

He shakes his head and turns away, his shoulders shaking. I wrap my arms around him and place my head against his back.

"Colton, I'm so sorry," I say.

"I told him he'd be fine and that there was nothing to worry about," he says, his voice choking on sobs. "I said I'd come see him when he got home and that we'd be playing guitar on his back porch before he knew it. But he was right. The doctors said his heart just wasn't strong enough to handle the surgery, and he died on the table. I never got to tell him I was sorry. I never told him how much he meant to me. I could have been there, but instead I decided to hang out with my friends, playing guitar and drinking. I passed out until late the next day. I woke up to six missed calls from my mom telling me he'd passed away. I'll never be able to forgive myself for that."

He turns and wraps his arms around my shoulders, and I hold him as tight as I can as he cries. My tears soak into his shirt, and my heart aches for him and this regret he's been carrying inside for years.

"It's not your fault," I say. "From everything you've told me about your relationship with your grandpa, I have no doubt that he knew exactly how much you loved him."

He wipes a hand across his face. "I'm sorry, I didn't mean to get so upset," he says. He turns away from me, but I pull him back to me.

"I'm glad you told me," I say. "You shouldn't carry that burden alone, Colton. It's hard to live with regrets that pull our hearts apart. I understand that more than you know."

"I came home for the funeral and never went back to the band," he says. "I turned twenty-one a few months later and got that job at Brantley's. I haven't left home since."

"That's why it was so hard for you to see that guitar the other day at the cabin, isn't it?" I ask.

He nods. "I haven't picked up a guitar since the day he died," he says. "I can't bear to think of what he was going through while I was out there playing around and spending time with people that didn't matter nearly as much to me as he did."

"You're punishing yourself," I say. Which is another thing I understand with all my heart. "He wouldn't want you to give up music, though, Colton. Not if he's the one who taught you to play."

He holds his hand against his forehead. "I'm not sure I have music inside of me, anymore," he says. "It was something we shared that was so special to me, and I feel like I didn't honor him. I wasn't there for him when he needed me, and I don't know how to live with that."

"You can't blame yourself forever, either," I say. "How does that honor him? For you to give up something you both loved so much?"

He smiles, but it quickly turns to more tears. "The crazy thing is that I know you're right," he says. "I guess I've just spent a long time trying to avoid it. That's why I haven't gone back to his cabin in so long. Sometimes it's easier not to face it. But maybe you're right. Maybe it's time to start playing again."

I hold him close and hope that he can feel just how much I care for him. I never knew my own grandparents, but I remember how hard it was when my mother left. I blamed myself for her departure for a long time, thinking that if I had been a better girl and hadn't caused her so much trouble when I was young that she might have stayed.

Loss is one of the hardest things we have to deal with as human beings, and some losses are the kind you never recover from. But hopefully time can start to heal what hurts us most.

"Thank you for sharing this with me," I say. "I know it's not an easy thing to talk about, but it means a lot to me that you trusted me with it."

The moment the words leave my lips, I realize how much this echoes what happened between us the other night when

Bryan was here. He's shared something extremely personal with me when I couldn't do the same for him.

"It actually helps to say it out loud," he says. "I haven't told anyone about that last conversation with him, not even my mom or my sisters. I've been holding it in for so long, I didn't realize how much it would help to finally face it. To just tell someone."

I smile up at him and he leans down to kiss me.

His touch is so tender and loving that I feel it all the way through my body.

"I love you, Jo," he says when he pulls away, and the words rock me backwards. "I wasn't going to tell you, because I was afraid that you'd feel like you had to say it back to me, but I can't hold it in. I love you, and I've never loved any woman before in my life. Not like this."

"I love you, too," I say, tears spilling onto my cheeks.

I do love him. I've loved him for a while now, and I'm amazed at how much he's opened my heart and changed my life in the past few months.

I've avoided having a relationship or opening myself up to love for so long that I had forgotten how amazing it could feel to give yourself to someone. And how terrifying it could be when you weren't sure how they truly felt about you.

But Colton Tucker is in love with me, and I know I am the luckiest woman in the world.

He places his hands on my face and kisses me again, this time hungrier and more passionately.

I have never felt so connected and so free.

"Let's leave this for tomorrow," I say. "Take me to your place."

"You don't have to tell me twice," he says.

He picks me up and carries me to the back door of the bar. He turns off the lights and locks the door behind us as he carries me across the yard and up the steps to his small apartment.

I laugh as he fumbles with his keys and finally pushes the door open.

He takes me to the bed and I watch as he pulls his shirt off. I raise onto my knees and start working on the buckle of his jeans. I've never wanted someone so much in my life.

We undress each other in the dark and finally, when there's nothing between us but the love in our hearts, we confirm with our bodies what our mouths have already declared.

CHAPTER 28
COLTON

I'm still awake when the sun comes up. Jo is asleep at my side, and I love watching her when she's so peaceful and unguarded. We spent all day together on Sunday, cooking and watching TV with her dad, and she came over last night to be with me again.

I never dreamed that love could be this powerful, but now that I've told her exactly how I feel, there's a strange knot of worry growing inside.

I've never had a good thing in my life that I didn't screw up or destroy in some way. Even my most precious relationship with my grandpa was something I messed up when it really mattered. Jo is the best thing that's ever happened to me, but what if I make a mistake? What if I let her down?

She's known the best of me, but she's never been on the receiving end of one of my massive screw-ups.

It will break me if I hurt her in any way.

She rolls over and sleepily opens her eyes. "Good morning," she says, kissing my arm.

"Good morning."

"Did you sleep?" she asks.

"I'll sleep when I'm dead," I say, and she laughs.

"What time is it, do you know?"

I glance over at the clock by the bed. "Six-thirty."

She groans. "I need to go home and check on Daddy," she says. "He's got an appointment with the neurologist this morning."

"Another appointment?" I ask. "Man, when are they going to have some answers for you guys?"

She shakes her head and rubs the sleep from her eyes. "Your guess is as good as mine," she says. "I'm trying to be patient, but it's getting pretty frustrating. I think he's getting worse, too, but he's trying to hide it from me."

"What's going on?"

"He's slurring his words, lately," she says. "You haven't noticed it?"

I shake my head. "Have you mentioned it to the doctor?"

"I don't know if Dad's mentioned it or not," she says. "But I'll probably mention it today if he doesn't bring it up. He's having more trouble with lifting things, too, like he's getting weaker. I was really hoping this was going to be something simple, but now that the neurologist is involved and nothing showed up on the MRI or the other tests, I'm clueless as to what's going on."

I kiss her forehead and run my hand across her back. "Do you want me to come with you?"

She shakes her head. "No, we shouldn't be there too long," she says. "They're doing some kind of nerve conduction study today, but they said it will take less than an hour. We should be home by lunchtime."

"Okay, but call me if you need anything," I say. "Since we've got the day off, I was thinking about going over to Willow's beach house tonight if you want to come. Hopefully it will be more low key than whatever they had going on last night."

"I'll see how he's feeling and whether he has anything planned for tonight," she says "But if I can't go, you should definitely go hang out with your friends. I'm sure they miss you."

She stands and pulls on her clothes from last night. I lay back on the pillows and watch, enjoying the view. I could definitely get used to having her spend the night more often. Once things are more settled with her dad's health and he's feeling back to his old self again, maybe we could even talk about getting a place together.

Or fixing up my grandfather's cabin and moving out there for a while.

I smile, realizing that the thought of moving in with a girlfriend would have probably scared the crap out of me a year ago, but now it feels like the most natural thing in the world. I want this to work between us.

"What are you grinning about?" she asks, leaning over to kiss my cheek.

"Just watching you," I say. "You really are the most beautiful woman I've ever known."

She hides her face, but I can tell she's smiling.

"Call me when you guys get back this afternoon," I say. "If y'all are up for it, I'll take you both out to lunch at Brantley's."

"Sounds perfect," she says. She kisses me and heads for

the door. She pauses before she leaves the room, and looks at me with a smile on her face. "I love you."

"I love you, too," I say.

She giggles and practically waltzes out of the room. A few seconds later, I hear her footsteps on the stairs.

I roll over, happy, and let sleep wash over me. All morning I dream of music and slow dances with a beautiful girl, her long dark hair falling down her back like waves of pure silk.

CHAPTER 29
JO

Daddy's appointment with the neurologist is just more of the same. No new answers. No treatments. Just more questions.

"What else can we do?" I ask the new doctor.

This new guy doesn't exactly have the greatest bedside manner, and so far, he's been less than forthcoming about what he thinks we might be dealing with.

"More tests," he says. "The nerve conduction study has ruled out a few muscular diseases, but there are a few more tests I'd like to run before I can make a diagnosis."

I sigh, but Daddy takes my hand and I hold my tongue.

"When can I come back in?"

"Let's set up an appointment next week on Monday," he says. "Does that work for your schedule?"

"I'll be here," Daddy says. "Thanks, Dr. Walsh."

He stands and shakes the doctor's hand.

"Why don't you go get that appointment set?" I say. "I'll be out in just a second."

Daddy narrows his eyes at me, but heads out to see the receptionist.

"Dr. Walsh, I'm not sure if you noticed it today or if my father has said anything to you, but I've noticed another symptom that has me concerned," I say, my hands trembling slightly.

"What have you noticed?" he asks.

"His speech is slightly slurred sometimes," I say. "It might not be terribly noticeable to people who don't know him as well, but it's like he's got a lazy tongue sometimes. He hasn't mentioned it to me, but I've noticed it off and on lately. Is that related, you think?"

A look of concern crosses the doctor's features, and it makes my stomach tighten. I get the feeling he knows more than he's told us, and for some reason, that scares me to death.

"I think it's related, yes," he says. "Again, I have a few more tests I'd like to run before I make an official diagnosis."

"But you think you know what's going on, don't you?" I ask, holding my breath.

"I understand how difficult this must be, Ms. Warner, but I'm hoping I'll have more answers for you soon," he says, ushering me toward the door.

I want to scream. If he knows what's wrong with my father, why the hell isn't he telling me? Why isn't he getting started on some kind of treatment that will make him better? The longer we wait to diagnose this, the worse it's going to get before he gets better.

I don't like having to put my trust in strangers, and I definitely don't like it when things are so far out of my control.

"Dr. Walsh, if you suspect something, I'd rather know

about it sooner than later," I say. "We need to be starting some kind of treatment for whatever this is."

The doctor nods as if this is an argument he's heard a thousand times. As if my worry bores him.

"I'll see you and your father next week," he says.

I take a deep breath and let it out slowly. "Thanks," I mumble.

Daddy is waiting for me by the receptionist's desk, his coat thrown over his arm. "Now, are you planning to tell me what that was all about? Or have you become the parent in this relationship?"

I smile and lean into him as we walk out the door and into the windy morning air. I was so distracted this morning, I forgot to bring my jacket.

I shiver and Daddy places his coat across my shoulders.

I take his arm and walk with him to the car. "You'll always be my daddy, but I think it's okay if I take care of you every now and then, too," I say. "That's the way it's always been, right?"

"You got it, Jojo," he says. "It's always been you and me."

And for a little while, as we drive back to our house, I'm glad there's no diagnosis yet. There's a part of me that knows when the news finally comes, it may be worse than either of us have suspected.

I could see it in the eyes of that doctor today.

It may be windy outside, but there is a dangerous storm brewing in my life right now, and I feel as if everything is about to start spinning out of my control.

Daddy turns up the radio, and I realize it's Colton's song playing. I told him about it earlier while we were waiting in the office, and he smiles at me now, singing at the top of his lungs.

I join in, letting fear take a backseat so that I can be fully present in this moment, right here, right now. Because despite how much my childish heart wants to believe that daddy's are immortal and will be around forever, I know that no matter how intensely you love someone, there are some things love simply cannot do.

CHAPTER 30
JO

"Y ou sure you're feeling okay?" I ask.

"Will you please stop hovering over me like I'm your patient?" Dad asks with a smile. "Go, have fun with your boyfriend. I promise I'll be fine."

"First of all, who told you he was my boyfriend?" I say. "Second of all, I'm not hovering. I'm just worried about you."

"You're worry-hovering," he says. "And come on, Jo, I'm not blind. Anyone can see plain as day how the two of you feel about each other. You should go out and have a good time together. Besides, I may have a date of my own this evening."

My jaw drops open. I'm not sure I heard him right. "With who?"

He shrugs and carries his plate to the kitchen.

I follow close behind. "No way, you're not going to drop a bomb like that on me and just walk away," I say, playfully slapping him on the shoulder. "Speak up. Who are you going out with?"

Dad turns and leans his back against the sink. "If you promise to get out of my hair for a little while this evening, I might just tell you."

I cross my arms. Two can play at this game. "If you don't tell me, I might have to stick around all night just to see who shows up."

He laughs. "You are such a little stinker."

"I learned from the best," I say. "Tell me."

"Kelly said she wanted to stop by to check on me is all. So I suggested we could rent a movie and pop some popcorn while she was checking on me," he says. "She agreed."

My hand goes to my mouth, because I know it's hanging open again. "Are you serious? That's great news," I say. I throw my arms around him. "I thought I saw a little spark between the two of you last time we ran into her. I have to say, I never did understand what happened between the two of you all those years ago. I thought you were perfect for each other."

My father's face falls just a little and he turns back around to rinse off our plates and stick them in the dishwasher.

I watch him carefully, trying not to hover or offer to help. He's dropped a few dishes lately, so we switched to using plastic ones for now, but I know he wants to do it himself.

"Don't go getting ahead of yourself, Josephine," he says. "I asked her to come watch a movie. Nothing serious. Just two friends catching up after a long time."

"Right. Because you have no feelings for her whatsoever."

"I didn't say that, either."

"I knew it." I come up behind him and hug him tight. "I'm so happy for you, Daddy."

When he finishes with the dishes, I can see he's smiling from ear to ear. "I'd be lying if I said I wasn't a little bit excited."

"You little devil. You probably faked that fall last month just to go in and see her," I say with a wink. "Pretty dramatic just to get a girl to go out with you, if you ask me."

He laughs. "Yep, you got me. It was all an act, so see? Nothing to worry about," he says, kissing my cheek. "So you might as well go out with that boy you swear is not your boyfriend and have a good time hanging out just as friends."

I bite my lower lip and study him. He does seem to be feeling good tonight. I've been nervous to leave him alone too long after he fell, but he hasn't had another accident like that since.

"Stop staring at me like I'm some kind of invalid," he says. "I'm fine. Good as new."

"If you say so," I mumble.

"You can't stay home with me for the rest of your life," he says. "You finally have an opportunity to go out and spend some time with a guy you like without having to take people's drink orders while you're doing it. Go out. Meet some new people. When else are you going to have the chance to hang out with a famous country band?"

"Are you sure?" I ask. There's no doubt I want to spend a night out with Colton and get to know his friends, but going to a party where there are going to be lots of people? It's not exactly my comfort zone. I may work in a busy bar every night, but I've got a counter between me and everyone else. A safety net. My hands are sweaty just thinking about a house full of people I don't know.

"I'm more than sure. I'm insisting on it," he says. He

squeezes my hand. "You've been cooped up in this house your whole life. It's time to put yourself out there and make new friends. A girl your age—"

"Shouldn't sit at home alone with her old man. I know." He's only been telling me this every weekend for the past five years or so.

"If you know, then prove it. Humor me for once," he says. "Call Colton and tell him you'll go. I promise you'll have a great time."

"Don't make promises you can't keep," I say as I walk back to my bedroom.

I know he only pushes me because he cares about me and wants me to be happy, but he of all people should understand how hard it is for me to put myself out there. Change is difficult for me, and I've already stepped so far out of my comfort zone with Colton that I'm not sure how much more out there I am willing to go.

Of course, I should have thought of that before I let myself fall in love.

I fall across my bed with my arms out and sigh. I am hopeless. I really did try to protect my heart, but with Colton, I think I was a goner the second he walked into my bar. The heart simply wants what it wants, and fear never had a chance.

My cell phone rings, and I glance at the screen. My heart skips a beat at the sight of Colton's name. Crap, what am I going to say to him? Should I go with him?

"Hey," I say, my voice catching on the knot of nerves in my throat.

"Hey, yourself," Colton says. "So what's the verdict? You want to go?"

I take a deep breath. "Here's the thing. I absolutely want to spend time with you. I want to meet your friends and be the model girlfriend, but I'm not super comfortable at parties," I say. "I'm used to spending my nights at the bar or here at home with Dad. I feel like I'm going to be totally out of place there with a bunch of people I don't know."

"You know me," he says, and I can hear the smile in his voice. "You're not going to be out of place, Jo. I promise. And if you're having a terrible time, we'll leave. Deal?"

I'm nodding, but scared to say the words out loud. When did I become such a chicken-shit?

"Okay, deal," I say finally. My heart is racing.

"Awesome. How much time do you need to get ready? Did you already eat dinner, or do you want to grab something before we head out?"

"I already ate," I say. "We have some leftovers if you want to swing by here and eat first."

"You know I can't resist your cooking," he says. "Be there in ten?"

"Sure. See you in a few."

When I hang up, I'm out of breath like I've been running. Why does the thought of one simple party terrify me so much?

But I already know the answer to that. A simple party is what started that whole mess for me when I was just fifteen years old.

Logically I know this isn't at all the same type of situation, and I'm twenty-two now for goodness sake. Colton is not just some one-night-stand who is going to toss me to the side once he's done with me. He loves me.

Still, I'm nervous about going to a party where I hardly

know anyone. What if they hate me? What if Colton thinks I'm boring and changes his mind about me?

None of these fears make sense, but that's the thing about fear. It's not exactly logical.

All I know is that I barely made it out alive last time I fell in love, and I've been so good at avoiding the possibility of that ever happening again. Now that I've opened myself up to someone again, I want to keep things as safe and comfortable as possible. I'm like a new kitten who's been hiding under the bed, scared to come out for the longest time.

I may have finally stepped out into the open, but my claws are still stuck firmly to the carpet.

I sigh and sit up, staring at my closet. I guess there's no time like the present to let go and trust that everything is somehow going to work out fine. Besides, Colton's already on his way and my dad has a date coming over in an hour.

I change into my favorite pair of tight jeans and a simple red top. I pull my black leather jacket over it and slide into my black converse high-tops. It's not all that different from my typical work outfit, but at least I'm wearing a little color instead of all black. That has to count for something, right?

I go to braid my hair, but decide to leave it down. I know that's the way Colton likes it best. I brush a little bit of color onto my cheeks and apply simple eyeliner and mascara. I've never been to a party with a famous country band, but if I'm going to step outside my comfort zone, I'm going to just be myself and hope that it's enough.

The doorbell rings, and I hear my dad say Colton's name.

I take a deep breath and chance one last look in the mirror.

What are you so afraid of?

I stick my tongue out at my own reflection and join the men I love most in this world, refusing to let my own fear hold me back any longer.

CHAPTER 31

COLTON

Jo's hair is down and flowing around her shoulders and down her back when she appears. No matter how much time I spend with her, her beauty always takes my breath away.

"I see you found the food," she says with a laugh.

I have to search for my voice. "You look stunning," I say, standing to put my plate away.

She ignores me, turning away to say goodnight to her dad. "Promise me you'll call if you need anything or if you find you aren't feeling well," she says. She lifts onto her toes to kiss his cheek. "And I want you to text me when Kelly gets here, okay? Promise."

Rob rolls his eyes and hooks his thumb toward her. "Do you see what she's been putting me through?" he asks.

"She's relentless," I say.

"You got that right," Rob says, like they are partners in crime. "I'll text when Kelly arrives, I promise. Have fun you two."

"Thanks, Daddy," Jo says.

"Goodnight, Mr. Warner."

"Oh, so it's Rob when you're working, but tonight it's Mr. Warner?" he says, nodding. "This must be more serious than I thought."

Jo groans and pulls the door closed, leaving the two of us alone on the front porch.

"Ignore him," she says.

I laugh. "Well, I am taking his daughter out," I say. "It's his fatherly right to heckle."

"He was heckling me more than you, trust me," she says. "He's just happy to see me going out for a change."

I lead her toward the truck and open the passenger door so she can climb inside. I go around and get in, grateful when the old thing starts right up. I've had this truck for five years, and it already had a hundred thousand miles on it when I bought it. It still runs most of the time, but I've had a few problems with it lately.

Luckily, it looks like it's going to cooperate tonight.

"So should we call this our first official date?" I ask. "I mean, technically this is the first time I've taken you out."

"I think the fishing trip counts as a date," she says. "I might rather do that again, instead."

"Definitely a day to remember," I say.

She laughs and scoots a little closer on the seat. I grab her hand, and it's ice cold.

"If you don't want to go, we can turn around," I say. "I just want to be with you."

She shakes her head. "I want to go," she says. "It'll be fun to meet your friends."

But she doesn't sound so sure. She's always so confident

at the bar that it seems strange she would be nervous about going to a simple party. I make a mental note to stick by her side so that she's comfortable and having a good time. Greg assured me it was going to be a small, low-key kind of crowd tonight, so hopefully it will be fun.

When we get to the beach house, though, there are so many cars parked along the street that it's obvious this is a little more than low-key. I open the door for Jo and take her hand to help her down.

"Who all is going to be here tonight?" she asks. "That's a lot of cars."

"I'm not entirely sure," I say. "Greg told me it would be the band and a handful of old friends from high school. I wasn't expecting so many people. He made it sound like a small gathering."

"Maybe this is small for them these days," she says.

"True," I say. Either that or word got out that they were hosting friends and the whole damn town showed up.

The music booming through the trees makes me think this won't exactly be the kind of gathering where people are quietly sitting around talking about old times.

Seeing the beach house again brings back some strong memories. It used to belong to Greg's dad, but when he passed away a few years ago, he left it to him. I imagine it mostly goes unused throughout the year with the band touring so much lately, but it's definitely getting some use tonight.

"Man, I haven't been back here in years," I say. "I used to spend nearly every weekend of my life camped out on that back porch."

"I didn't realize you guys were so close," she says. "It must have been tough when he left."

"He was my best friend," I say. "Plus, it was nice to get away from the estrogen in my house. It wasn't exactly a picnic to be the only boy in a house full of girls."

"I imagine this was a pretty cool place to hang out," she says. "It's gorgeous out here. Was it hard for you when he left to go to college?"

"In some ways," I say. "But in other ways it was good for me."

"How so?"

"Greg's parents were divorced, and his mom was pretty strict with him, but his dad was another story altogether," I say. "He was out of town on business a lot, so when we used to come out here, we had free reign of the place. Things got out of hand a lot."

"Drinking?" she asks.

"Drinking. Smoking weed. It's a miracle I ever graduated from high school the way we used to party," I say, wincing at the memory of how out of control I used to be. "Imagine being almost black-out drunk on a nightly basis. It was fun for a while, but believe me, it gets old."

"I can't even imagine it," she says.

"Not your style?"

"Not even a little."

"Come on, you didn't party and drink even when you were in high school?"

She shakes her head. "I guess I got a little bit into the party scene when I was fifteen or so, but Dad put a stop to that pretty quickly," she says.

"Ah, the overprotective father."

"Sort of," she says. She clears her throat. "I guess you could say I got mixed up with some of the wrong people back then. It kind of killed the whole party scene for me."

There's an edge to her voice, and I wonder if this has anything to do with that Bryan guy. I want to ask her more about it, but we're almost to the house when someone on the back porch spots us and starts calling out for us to hurry up.

"Colton Tucker, is that you? You better get your ass up here."

It's dark, but I recognize the voice instantly.

"Wesley, is that you?" I shout back.

"You know it, bro," he says.

We make our way up the steps of the porch and Wesley slaps his hand into mine.

"What you been up to, man? I haven't seen you in ages."

"It's been a while," I say. "I've been working at Rob's. What are you up to?"

"That hole in the wall in Fairhope? Man, I thought you left town or something. You never come by our old haunts anymore."

I cringe and put an arm around Jo. "This is Rob's daughter, Jo."

"Ouch," Wesley says, reaching out to offer his hand to Jo. "No offense meant by that. I've only been in there a couple times, but I heard it was going under."

"None taken," Jo says, smiling and taking his hand. "We were in a rough spot a while back, but things have really picked up."

Nice, so I convince her to finally go out with me to meet my friends and she gets insulted about two seconds in. Not exactly the start I was hoping for, but she doesn't seem to be too bothered by it.

"You should have come out last night. The band played," I say.

"What band?"

I roll my eyes. "Long Road Ahead, dummy. Why else do you think they're back in town? Just to hang out with you?"

"What? Seriously?" He takes a long pull on his beer. "I had no idea. I thought they were just on a break or something. I totally would have come out if I'd known they were playing. Since when do you guys have live music out at Rob's?"

"Since a couple months ago, I guess," I say. "Jo's been doing an amazing job getting the place back on its feet."

"So you're Rob's daughter, eh? What's that like, growing up with a dad who runs a bar? I bet you were sneaking a lot of booze when you were younger, am I right?"

"My dad would have killed me," she says.

"Yeah, and trust me, you do not want to mess with Jo's dad. He's a big guy."

"Guess you better treat this girl right, then," Greg says, coming out onto the porch. He smiles and offers his hand to Jo. "I met your dad briefly last night when we got in, but I don't think I had the pleasure of meeting you. I'm Greg."

Greg and Jo shake hands and Wesley throws his arm around my shoulders.

"It's so freaking awesome to have the old gang back together," he says. From the way he's slurring his words, he's obviously already had several of those beers by now. "What's it like out there on the road all the time? Is it awesome?"

"It's exhausting," Greg says. "But it'll be nice to take some time to slow down and be home for a while."

"I bet you get all the women, though, man. What's it really like out there?" Wesley asks.

"Busy all the time," Greg says. "You can't imagine how much pressure there is to constantly be on. I'm looking forward to relaxing for a little while."

"How long is a little while?" I ask. "Willow said something about spending a week here?"

"Yeah, we're hoping for at least a week off," he says. "We've really got to focus on getting some new music nailed down."

He looks around and shakes his head. "She needs to seriously cool it with these parties, though," he says. "It was insane out here last night and the night before. I'm surprised no one called the cops."

"Yeah, I thought you told me it was just going to be a small get-together tonight," I say.

"Well, apparently the word got out that we were having some people over, and everyone just showed up. What can you do?"

"I had a feeling that might be what happened," I say. "It's your house, though, man. You can ask people to leave, if you want."

"Nah, it'll be fun to see some old friends," he says. "We'll settle down after tonight and get to work. Speaking of work, where's your guitar? I was hoping you'd play something for us tonight. You been writing much lately? I know you said you've been busy, but the Colton I know wouldn't be without a guitar in his hand for very long."

I catch Jo's eye, knowing she's the only one who really understands what I've been going through.

"I really haven't been playing much at all," I say. "I'm not even sure I remember all the chords."

"Shit, man, you never forget how to play," he says. "Once the music is in your soul and in your fingers, you never forget it. Maybe when things settle down later, we'll pull out our guitars and get you to play something for us."

I nod, but I know I won't be playing anything tonight. Not like this.

"Hey, you guys want something to drink?" he asks. "Come on in, and I'll serve you guys for a change."

I take Jo's hand and we walk inside together.

The living room and entryway are packed with bodies, so I hold tight to her hand and lead her through the crowd toward the kitchen.

"I'm sorry," I say in her ear. "I had no idea it was going to be this many people. Are you okay?"

She nods, but sticks tight by my side.

Greg hands us a couple of beers and we make our way around the kitchen, saying hi to old friends I haven't talked to in years except in passing. Jo seems to be hanging in there, even if she hasn't said much.

About an hour later, I excuse myself to go to the bathroom and leave her talking to a few girls in the living room. I've had three beers already, and I'm dying for the bathroom, but there's a line downstairs about a mile long.

I make my way up to one of the bedrooms on the second floor, thankful no one else seems to realize there are three more bathrooms up here. I wash my hands and start back toward the stairs, but Willow appears out of nowhere and throws her arms around my shoulders.

"Colton, there you are," she says.

"Hey, girl, I was wondering where you were," I say. I glance toward the stairs. I hate to leave Jo for too long. I know she's fine on her own, but I don't want her to be uncomfortable even for a second.

"I've been up here listening to some of our most recent recordings," she says. "Colton, we are totally screwed with this next album."

"It can't be that bad," I say. "Come downstairs and hang out for a while. You're probably just letting all the pressure get to your head. Take a break."

I start toward the bathroom again, but Willow grabs my hand pulls me back to her side.

"You don't understand," she says, her eyes searching mine. "I've got serious writer's block, and nothing I do seems to break through to anything good."

She's got a death-grip on my hand and she moves up real close to me. I back up, but she comes with me, pressing me up against the wall.

"Stay with me for a while," she says. She presses her body hard against mine. "I need you, Colton. You were like magic for me once. Maybe you could be again."

I smell the alcohol on her breath and realize too late she's extremely drunk.

She lifts her hands to my face and tries to kiss me, but I turn away and grab her hands in mine.

"Willow, you've had a lot to drink," I say. "You're not thinking straight. Come on, let's go downstairs and get you some water."

She pouts. "I have missed you so much, Colton," she says. "There's never been another man in my life like you."

I try to maneuver around her, but before I can convince her to follow me down to the kitchen, I hear footsteps on the steps. I look up to see Jo standing a few stairs from the top.

"Oh," she says, her lips parting and her hand gripping the handrail. "Greg said I might be able to find you up here."

She shakes her head and turns around, running down the stairs and out the back door.

"Dammit," I say. I pull away from Willow and run after Jo, but Willow calls after me, and I hear her footsteps right behind me.

I push through the crowded entry and search the back deck for any sign of Jo, but by the time I catch sight of her, she's already down the back steps and in the parking lot.

Willow grabs my arm and won't let go.

I turn around and shake my head. "I have to go," I say.

"What's your problem?" she shouts, drawing the attention of everyone within hearing distance.

"That girl on the stairs? She's my girlfriend and she thinks something was happening between us just now," I say. "I have to go explain to her that there's nothing going on, Willow. Please, just go get yourself some water and sober up."

"Hey, what's going on?" Greg asks, making his way through the crowd. "You guys okay?"

I pull my arm away from Willow's grip and nod to him. "Can you take care of her, please?" I say. "I'm sorry, but I have to go."

"Colton," he says, but I'm already running.

I catch up with Jo on the road, and when she turns her face toward the light, I can see she's crying.

"I'm sorry," I say. "She's drunk and I was trying to get her to come downstairs so she could get some water or coffee or something. I swear to you nothing was going on."

"But you used to date her, right?" she asks.

I swallow and run a hand across my jaw. "A very long time ago," I say.

"And you didn't think maybe that was something you should have told me before you asked her to come to the bar?" she asks. "No wonder they were willing to come back to this area to play at a hole in the wall place in Fairhope. She wanted to see you."

"It's not like that," I say. "Things were never serious between us. They came back because Greg's been one of my best friends since I was a kid."

"Well, the fact that you had a thing with the lead singer of the band was probably something you should have told me before you brought me here tonight," she says. "Instead, I had to hear it from someone I just met. They told me you wrote that song for her."

I groan, my shoulders tense. This cannot be the thing that screws it up for the two of us. Not my past relationship with Willow. It was never anything compared to what I feel for Jo.

"I didn't think it was important," I say. "It's been over for years."

"Did you?" she asks. "Write that song for her? Those lyrics were about the two of you?"

I shake my head. "It's a dramatization of what was going on between us back when I was living in Athens with the band," I say. "I wasn't in love with her, if that's what you're asking. I've never been in love with anyone but you, Jo."

"Well, apparently Willow still has a thing for you," she says. "She was all over you. Not exactly what I wanted to see when I came looking for you."

"I know. I'm sorry," I say. "But I swear to you I wanted nothing to do with it. She just had a little too much to drink."

Jo closes her eyes, and wipes the tears from her face.

"Look, I don't want to be this girl," she says. "I don't want to be irrationally jealous and a pain in the ass. I want to believe you that there was nothing going on between you guys, but I really don't want to go back to that party right now."

"Do you want to go somewhere else?" I ask. "We could go walk on the beach for a while. Anything. I don't want the night to end like this."

"I just want to go home," she says. "It's been a rough few weeks with all these doctor's appointments and the busy nights at the bar. Maybe I just need some rest."

"Okay," I say. "I wasn't expecting to have to drive so soon, though, and I've already had a few beers."

"I'll drive," she says, holding her hands out for the keys. "Oh, dangit. Dad's got Kelly over for a movie. I don't want to ruin their night, too."

Her words are like a punch in the gut. Our first official date is ruined. Of course. Leave it to Colton to screw things up. It's always just a matter of time with me.

"Let's go to my place," I say. "We can put on a movie, too, and relax on the couch. I don't want to say goodnight with you still angry with me."

She stops beside my truck and leans against the door. "I'm not angry," she says. "I mean, I'm annoyed that you didn't tell me you guys used to date, but I'm not mad. I was just surprised and hurt. And when I saw the two of you together like that, it was too much. I was so scared that maybe you..."

Her voice trails off and she looks down at her shoes.

"You're the only one I want," I say, lifting her chin. "I would never do anything to hurt you like that, Jo. I may be a screw-up sometimes, but I'm not a cheater."

"I know," she says. "I'm sorry I ruined the party. Everyone probably thinks I'm a nutcase."

"Who cares what anyone else thinks?" I say. "And you didn't ruin anything. If I had known it was going to be a huge party like that, I never would have suggested we go in the first place."

"I think my nerves are on edge too much lately," she says. "This whole thing with Daddy has me all mixed up. I'm sorry I stormed out like that."

I pull her close and rest my chin on the top of her head, loving the way she fits perfectly in my arms.

"I'm sorry I didn't tell you about Willow sooner," I say. "From now on, I promise to be an open book."

She pulls back and smiles. "Just promise me one thing," she says.

"Anything."

"Someday, when you start playing music again, you'll write a song for me, too."

I smile and lean down to kiss her.

"You got it," I say. "It'll be the biggest hit song ever written."

"I don't care if it ever hits anyone's top one hundred list," she says. "All I want is for it to come from the heart."

"That's the only place a song for you could ever come from," I say. I pull her close again and hold her for a long time, letting the ocean breeze carry our worries away. "Dance with me."

She looks up, tears still lingering on her lashes. "What?"

I smile and grab the keys from her. I reach into the truck and turn on the radio, dialing the volume up so we can hear it over the wind.

I offer my hand to her and she laughs, shaking her head.

"This is ridiculous," she says.

"Then be ridiculous with me," I say.

There's a perfect slow song playing on the local station, and slowly, she places her hand in mine.

CHAPTER 32
JO

"Any news?" Knox asks when we get back from Daddy's appointment later that week.

"Still nothing," I say, taking off my coat and setting it on the chair in the office. "More tests. I swear this is taking forever."

"You guys know I'll be happy to help out and pay for a specialist," he says. "There's a guy in Atlanta who works exclusively with neurological disorders. I made a few calls and he said they could get your dad in as soon as next month."

I touch his hand. "Thank you," I say. "I hate to ask for your help with this, but the bills are really starting to pile up and our insurance is crap. If you could go ahead and make that appointment, I would really appreciate it. Even if this Dr. Walsh comes back with a diagnosis, it might be a good idea to get a second opinion."

"When do you guys go back in?" he asks.

"Next Tuesday," I say. "He said he hopes to have some

answers by then. I'm just ready to get him into treatments, physical therapy, whatever might help."

"Hang in there," he says. "How are you holding up with all of this?"

"I'm doing okay," I say. "It's just been a lot to take in. A lot of waiting and worrying, but hopefully it will get better soon. Thanks for picking up so many of the shifts lately. If it wasn't for you and Colton, we probably would have had to shut down a few nights lately."

"You know I'm here for you guys, whatever you need," he says, pulling me into a hug. "You guys are all the family I have left in this world, and you mean everything to me."

"You coming home to Fairhope was one of the best things," I say. "I don't know what we would have done without you."

"It worked out pretty good for me, too," he says with a laugh. "I'm thinking of picking out a ring for Leigh Anne, and I could really use a female perspective."

My hand goes to my lips, and my eyes fill with tears. "Oh my God, I'm so happy for you."

I hug him again.

"Just say the word, and I'm there," I say. "I don't know how good I'll be at ring shopping, but I'll help however I can. Does she have any idea?"

"I don't think so," Knox says. "Of course we've talked about the possibility of marriage a few times. We both want to have a family together someday and now that the house is all fixed up and my restoration business is getting off the ground, it seems like the right time to take the next step."

"Well, I'm very happy for you guys," I say.

"What about you and Colton?" he asks as we head back into the bar to get the tables set up for the night.

"Whoa, don't get ahead of yourself, there," I say with a laugh. "This is still really new for me. I can't even think about marriage right now. That feels a million years away, if I'm being honest."

"Are you guys having trouble?" he asks.

I shake my head. "No, nothing like that," I say. "Just that I don't have a lot of experience when it comes to matters of the heart. I have no idea what I'm doing most of the time."

"No one does," he says. "That's the truth no one tells you about relationships. We're all just going in blind and hoping for the best. Sometimes we get lucky and meet the right person."

I think about my parents and how they must have been in love with each other at some point. Once upon a time they thought they were going to last forever, and they committed their lives to each other. So where did it all go wrong? Why does love disappear? And how can you trust in something that you can't ever be sure is going to last?

I pull chairs off the top of the tables and arrange them, thinking about last night.

Things have been going so well with Colton, I knew it was only a matter of time until we ran into some rocky times. We managed to survive our first real argument, but when I saw him standing there with that girl, their hands entwined like that, it reminded me just how fragile a thing love really is.

The deeper I fall, the harder it's going to be if something goes wrong between us.

I can't bear to think of it.

I finish setting the bar up, worry gnawing at my insides. Part of me misses the safety of my life before Colton turned it all upside down. But part of me knows I wouldn't trade my time with him for anything in the world.

"Are you good?" Knox asks. He glances at his watch. "I promised Leigh Anne I'd be back by five so we can try to catch a movie tonight."

"Yep, thanks for helping out this afternoon," I say. "I've got it from here."

He smiles. "I'm going to head out then," he says. "Tell your dad hi for me. I'll be back Saturday night to help out."

"I will. Say hi to Leigh Anne for me," I say.

Knox leaves just as Colton arrives for his shift. They say a quick hello and then Colton joins me behind the bar.

"Sorry I'm a little late," he says. "I was on the phone with my mom and she would not stop talking."

"She's probably missing you," I say. "It has to be hard for her when she was used to seeing you every day. When was the last time you went out to see your family?"

"That's part of what I wanted to talk to you about," he says. "My birthday is coming up this weekend, and Mom wants us to come for dinner. What do you think?"

"She wants me to come, too?" I ask.

"Of course," he says.

Our first customers come through the door, and Colton gets them started with a couple drinks.

I can't stop smiling, thinking that his mom even knows about me. I hadn't realized he'd told his parents about our relationship.

"So will you come?" he asks when he comes back.

"Of course," I say. "I didn't know your parents even knew about me."

"Shoot, are you kidding me?" he says with a laugh. "You're all I can talk about."

I blush and look away, trying not to smile too wide. It's silly, but it means a lot that he's talked to his mother about me. It somehow makes this whole thing feel more real.

"When? And should I bring something?" I ask.

"Sunday night," he says. "And only if you want to. I'd love for my family to taste some of your amazing cooking. I've already bragged to my sisters about your barbecue, but you don't have to go to any trouble."

"You bragged about my barbecue?" I ask.

"You're my girl," he says. "That's what you do."

I laugh and grab a few beers for the two regulars who always come in about this time. They say thank you and go back to their conversation.

The door opens again and the night is a steady stream of customers. I barely have a chance to get back to our conversation all night, but I can't stop thinking about it.

I'm finally going to meet Colton's family this weekend, and I can't stop smiling.

Just when I start to let my fears take over, fate steps in to give me a little push in the right direction. It's a journey, but I'm slowly learning to trust again.

CHAPTER 33
COLTON

I head downstairs with a spring in my step. I cannot wait to introduce Jo to my family. Hopefully they will be on their best behavior. It's been a long time since I brought a girl out to meet them. Not since I asked my first girlfriend to prom.

I know they are going to love her.

I'm surprised to find Jo outside standing beside the truck. She catches sight of me, and quickly throws a blanket over something in the back of the truck.

"Okay, sneaky, what are you up to out here?" I ask.

She laughs. "You'll find out later," she says. "You look handsome."

I spin and kick my cowboy boots out for her to see. "I bought myself some new boots for my birthday," I say. "I figure I deserve it after all the hard work at the bar."

She whistles. "Very nice," she says. "Of course you do realize that other people are supposed to buy you presents for your birthday, right? You're not supposed to have to buy them for yourself."

"Well, I've always been a rebel," I say.

"I've heard that about you," she says, and she smiles so wide it lights up her eyes.

I step around the truck and do a double-take. She's wearing a dress, and it's the first time I've seen her in anything but jeans in all the months I've known her, with the very memorable exception of the night she wore my plaid button-down.

"Wow," I say. "Let me get a look at you."

She blushes and steps away from the truck, taking my hand as I spin her around.

The dress is bright yellow, and it looks amazing in contrast to her dark features. She's wearing a blue-jean jacket over the top, and I'm dying to know if there are spaghetti straps on that dress. I really hope I get to find out at the end of the night, because I can't wait to push them down her shoulders.

"You're stunning," I say.

"Thank you," she says. "I wanted to look nice to meet your family. I'm nervous."

"They are going to adore you," I say. "You ready to get going?"

"I'm just going to run in and say goodbye to Daddy," she says. "Kelly's coming over again tonight."

I raise an eyebrow. The two of them have been spending a lot of time together lately, and I can see how happy it makes Jo to see them together. She's told me that her dad and Kelly used to date years ago, and it seems like there's possibility of them rekindling that romance.

I'm happy for Rob. He deserves it with everything he's been going through lately. Jo's taking his mysterious illness pretty hard, but Rob is always in good spirits whenever I see him. He's really an incredible guy, and I hope they get the answers they're looking for soon.

Jo disappears into the house for a few minutes, and I'm so tempted to look under the blanket she's put in the back of my truck. Just what does she have up her sleeve for tonight?

I resist temptation, though, and wait patiently until she comes back out, carrying a large covered plate.

She sits close as we make the drive out to my family's land. It takes a good twenty minutes to get all the way out there, and I have a knot of nerves in my stomach as we pull onto the wooded road that leads down to the trailers.

Part of the reason I haven't brought many women out here is that it's not exactly a typical family home. There's no white picket fence and big brick house. I've been called "trailer trash" more times than I care to remember. A lot of people around here don't understand why we all live out here in a bunch of rundown trailers and hand-built cabins.

Growing up, we never had much money, but what we lacked in material possessions, we more than made up for in family loyalty and love.

My dad has always been hard on me, but I know he loves me. And I wouldn't trade my close-knit family for all the gold in the world. I hope Jo loves them.

We pull up to my parents' trailer, and my mom comes running out, her arms wide open.

I step out of the truck and she throws her arms around me.

"There's my sunshine," she says. "Oh, Colton, I'm so glad

you're here. It's been weeks since you came to visit. I miss you so much."

She takes my face in her hands and squeezes.

"Happy birthday, baby," she says, hugging me again.

Jo comes around the other side of the truck, and my mom squeals.

"Honey, get yourself over here so I can hug your neck," she says.

I laugh as I watch Jo tense and finally give into my mother's relentless hug.

"Nice to meet you, Mrs. Tucker," she says.

"Girl, you better call me Carol," Mom says. "We don't entertain a lot of formalities out here, as you'll soon see."

"Oh, I almost forgot," Jo says. She rushes back to the truck and grabs the plate of appetizers she made for tonight. "I hope you don't mind that I brought something for dinner."

"I've been dying to try some of your cooking," Mom says. "Colton has told me all about your passion for food. We've all been crazy to try some of this food. What did you bring us?"

Mom pulls the foil off the top of the plate, and Jo raises an eyebrow at me. I shrug and laugh. If she's going to spend some time out here, she's going to learn real fast that my mom wasn't joking. Other than saying grace before every meal, we don't have a lot of rules or boundaries in our family. People say what they're thinking and everyone does exactly as they please most of the time.

It's part of what I love most about my family.

"Colton, I'm already in love with this girl," Mom says. "Did you tell her how much I love deviled eggs?"

"I may have mentioned it a time or two, but I had no idea she remembered," I say.

"When it comes to food, I remember everything," Jo says with a laugh. "This is my own special recipe, so I hope you like it."

"I know I'm gonna love it," Mom says. "Come on, everyone's dying to meet you."

As we head toward the house, my brother-in-law Isaac comes out, beer in hand. "There's the birthday boy," he says. clapping a hand on my shoulder. "This must be the illustrious Jo we've all heard so much about. I'm Cora Mae's husband, Isaac."

Jo blushes and holds a hand out to him, but he grabs her into a hug, nearly knocking the plate out of her hand.

She laughs as I take the plate from her. "Nice to meet you," she says.

"You, too," Isaac says "The girl who finally tamed Colton has earned a special place in my heart."

"Well, I don't know that you can tame a guy like Colton," she says. "But I'm happy to be along for the ride."

Isaac raises his beer to me. "I like her already," he says.

"See, I told you they would love you," I say in her ear, placing a hand on her elbow and leading her up toward the trailer.

It takes a while to go through all the introductions, and I'm sure she's feeling overwhelmed, but she seems to be taking it all in stride. She's much more relaxed than she was the other night at the party, as if she naturally fits here.

My brother-in-law Matt and I go out to get the fire started, and everyone gradually joins us. Luckily it's a beautiful fall evening, and not too cold out even though the sun's going down.

The family is so big, it's hard to find room for everyone inside, so when we all get together, we tend to gather around the fire and eat at the big picnic tables my dad built in the yard.

My sisters work to get all the food and plates and silverware set up on the tables while the guys get the fire and the grill started. Dad sets a couple coolers near the tables. They're filled with ice and beer, cans of soda, and bottled water. There are kids running all over the place, and before long, we're all settled into our routine of laughter, music, and standing around the fire.

My dad hasn't said a word to me since we got here almost an hour ago, and I know he's still angry at me for never setting up another interview with his old trucking company. I'm hoping to get a few minutes to talk to him tonight so we can clear the air, but for now, I'm just enjoying the company of my sisters and my extended family.

I keep Jo close to my side, wanting to make sure she's having a good time, but my sister Cammie steals her away to help with some kitchen emergency.

"I'll be right back," she says.

I pull her into a kiss, which elicits a couple cheers from the peanut gallery.

Jo covers her face as Cammie takes her hand and drags her toward the house.

She turns to give me one last look before she disappears into the house, and I smile. Life has never been so good, and I wonder how in the world I got so lucky.

CHAPTER 34
JO

C ammie takes my arm and pulls me toward the trailer. I laugh and follow along. I'm not used to having a lot of girlfriends to hang out with, so when I find myself surrounded by Colton's sisters, I'm completely overwhelmed.

They are all inside, gathered in the kitchen, giggling and cooking and shouting back and forth. Music plays from a small radio on the counter. The house is filled with smells of bacon and beans and homemade bread, and between the smells and the noise and trying to remember everyone's names, my brain is about to explode.

How on earth did Colton survive growing up with so many people around all the time?

It's so different from my small house with my dad. Sure, we always had the loud bar and lots of customers, but inside our home, there was always peace.

I get the feeling this house rarely knows the meaning of the word.

"Taste this," Cora Mae says, practically pressing a wooden spoon to my lips.

One of the other sisters has her hand on my shoulder and is telling me about a great deal she was able to get on Colton's birthday present.

I open my mouth to taste the sauce, but just as I do, someone pushes me from behind and the spoon smacks against my chin, sending marinara all over my yellow dress. I stumble forward, hot sauce burning my chest. I suck in a breath and Cora Mae catches me.

"Oh my word. Chloe, look what you did, you dork," she says. "Jo, I'm so sorry, darlin', are you okay?"

I try to say that I'm fine, but everyone is making such a fuss, I can hardly think straight.

Chloe grabs my arm and spins me around. "Here, let me get that," she says, pressing a cold washcloth on my stomach and rubbing the sauce spots. The water is freezing in contrast, and I bite my lip, involuntarily trying to scoot away.

"Girls, give her some space. You're crowding her." Colton's mom waves her hands in the air and the girls scatter backward. She clucks her tongue. "Oh my, look at that dress. I'm so sorry. Here, come with me a sec."

She grabs my arm and leads me back to one of the bedrooms. My mind is spinning, and I feel like I can hardly catch my breath.

"Take that jacket off and let me help you unzip that dress," she says.

"Excuse me?" I ask. "No, really, I'm fine. Don't worry about it."

"If you don't get that stain out, that dress is going to be ruined," she says. She's digging in her closet and finally comes out with a much larger pink dress. She shoves it toward me. "Put this on. I'll get the other one in the wash for you."

Reluctantly, I take the dress. I really don't want to strip down in front of Colton's mom less than an hour after meeting her, but she's just standing there with her hand out. I'm frozen, unsure what to do, exactly.

His mom stares at me as if she has no idea what's wrong, but then finally shakes her head. "What am I thinking? Let me give you some privacy," she says. "Just give me a holler when you're done."

She walks from the room and shuts the door behind her. I can hear her in the kitchen scolding Chloe for bumping into me, but everyone is laughing and having a good time, teasing each other.

I don't know whether to laugh or cry.

I'm so far out of my comfort zone, I don't even recognize the zip code. I slowly shrug my jean jacket off my shoulders and unzip my dress. There is no way this pink one is going to fit me, but I guess I can try to make it work.

I slide it over my head and look for a mirror, finding one in the small bathroom.

I stare at my reflection and shake my head. This is awful. I don't want to be rude, but the dress is about three sizes too big and makes me look like I'm a preteen trying on her mama's clothes. I can't go out there looking like this.

Someone knocks on the door and before I can even answer, Carol walks in.

She brings a hand to her mouth, trying to hide her smile. "Well, that's not going to work, is it?" she asks. "Cammie? Come in here for a minute."

Cammie, holding her newborn baby, walks into the room and begins laughing. My cheeks flush and tears spring to my eyes.

"Oh, don't cry, sweetheart," she says. "Are we scaring the crap out of you?"

I shake my head, afraid that if I try to speak, I'm going to collapse into sobs.

"Mama, why on earth did you put her in this old thing?"

"I don't know, it was the first thing I grabbed," Carol says. "I'm sorry, Jo, you're such a tiny little thing, I doubt any of my clothes are going to fit you. Cammie, you're probably my smallest girl. Do you think you may have something that will work?"

"I'm sure I do," she says. "Here, why don't you hold Emma while I go look."

Before I can protest, Cammie passes the baby into my arms and turns away. Someone in the kitchen calls for their mom and Carol excuses herself, leaving me alone with Emma.

I am breathless.

My heart is tight in my chest. My body shivers.

I sit down on the edge of the bed, unable to hold myself up or trust my knees not to collapse.

I don't hold babies. I haven't in years. In fact, I avoid them at all costs. It's just easier not to think about it.

A tear slides down my cheek and I force air into my lungs.

Baby Emma squirms a little, her tiny pink foot escaping from the blanket. I swallow and stare down at those perfect little toes, kicking back and forth. She coos and pushes her tongue against her lips.

I hardly know what to do with her.

I'm terrified I'm going to drop her or hurt her somehow.

Carefully, I hold her against my chest as I use my other hand to wrap the blanket around her feet again. The baby begins to cry, and on instinct I bounce her up and down slowly in my arms.

"Shh, shh, shh," I say softly. "It's okay, Emma."

She calms, her dark blue eyes staring up at me.

It's the strangest moment. Our eyes meet and a hidden part of me opens wide, letting her in. This tiny little person. Regret and fear pours over me like a rainstorm, but there is something else, too. Something like forgiveness. Hope.

"Here you go," Cammie says, rushing back into the room. She hands me a black dress that looks much more my size.

"Thank you," I say.

She reaches for the baby, and for a moment, I don't want to give her up. I feel like in the span of two minutes, she's changed me somehow.

Or maybe it's time that has changed me. Maybe it's Colton.

Either way, the pain of my past doesn't hurt quite as much as it used to.

She leaves me alone in the room to change. I wipe my tear-stained face and pull my jacket on over the dress, all the while feeling like a piece of my past has just rushed back. A memory of what might have been. A sign of what might someday be possible.

CHAPTER 35
COLTON

When Jo finally comes back out of the house she's wearing a completely different dress. I thought I saw Cammie running back and forth from her trailer with a black dress, but I had no idea it was for Jo. What did my sisters do to her?

She looks shaken up, so I cross over to her, offering her a beer.

"What happened to the yellow dress?" I ask, eyebrow raised. "Did my sisters do something?"

"I spilled spaghetti sauce on it," she says, but I know there's more to that story she isn't telling me.

I take her hand. "You okay?" I whisper.

"I'm fine," she says, but there's an edge to her voice that wasn't there earlier.

"You can tell me if you're not," I say. "I know my sisters can be a little hard to take in a group like this. If you want to go, we can scoot anytime. Just say the word."

She smiles and shakes her head. "I would never ask you to

leave your family's party," she says. "You're the guest of honor. Besides, it's honestly no big deal."

"Well, you look beautiful in black, too," I say, kissing her cheek.

The rest of the night goes off without a hitch. The family gathers around the picnic tables, the fire roaring and the stars above us decorating the sky. Everyone is drinking and laughing and having a good time, and I'm glad to see Jo begin to relax into the evening.

Whatever must have happened earlier with my sisters seems to have left her mind now, and she's laughing and getting to know my family better with each passing hour.

Eventually my sister Caroline brings out a guitar and begins to play.

My mom stands next to her and puts a hand on her shoulder, their voices mingling in two-part harmony, the only other accompaniment the sound of the fire crackling a few feet away.

Under the table Jo takes my hand and squeezes. She leans against my arm and I kiss the side of her temple. Everyone grows quiet, listening as the women finish out a popular hymn.

Jack brings out his banjo when they're done and West grabs his drum. I blush when Jo looks over and raises an eyebrow.

"Is it always like this?" she asks.

"On birthdays and special occasions? Yes," I say. "Should we just go?"

"Don't be ridiculous," she says. She snuggles closer, wrapping her arm in mine. "I like it."

We sit together, swaying to the music as my family sings

SARRA CANNON

all our classic songs. It's a mix of church music, country, and a few classic oldies like The Beatles and Bob Dylan. I realize how eclectic and strange my family must seem to her, but Jo is happy and smiling, her cheeks pink from the cool night air.

There's a lull in the music and my sister Cammie begins singing an old gospel hymn.

"Just as I am without one plea, but that thy blood was shed for me, and that thou bidst me come to thee, Oh Lamb of God, I come. I come."

To my surprise, Jo joins in, her voice quiet and soft, like an angel.

"Just as I am and waiting not, to rid my soul of one dark blot, to thee whose blood can cleanse each spot, Oh Lamb of God, I come. I come."

When I glance over, there are tears in her eyes, as if the words mean more to her than I can comprehend. My mother joins in harmony, walking over to where we sit. She places her hand on Jo's shoulder and together, all the women sing the song that reminds me of years gone by, hours spent out here by the fire with family.

I think of my grandfather and how I wish he could be here with me this year on my birthday. How I wish I could tell him one last time just how much I love him. How much he did for me growing up.

I don't feel worthy of this moment. This happiness. What have I ever done to deserve such a good life?

Later, when the singing is done and Jo has once again disappeared inside to help clean away the plates and say goodnight to my sisters, I sit staring at the fire, wondering what my future holds. How long can I really keep this up?

This role of the perfect boyfriend, always supportive and loyal and committed?

I want to be my best self, but there's a part of me that suddenly feels anxious and scared.

Jo fit right in with my family, and they've all been so eager to pair me off. To figure me out. They all want me to settle down, and I could see it in their eyes tonight. They believe that's where I'm headed with Jo.

Only, I'm not sure I'm ready to settle down. I'm not sure I've lived my life to the fullest and become everything I was meant to be. How can I commit my life to just one woman when I'm not even sure of who I am or what I want from my life? If I'm not sure I deserve someone like her?

Which is when my dad finally decides to sit down beside me. He's had a lot to drink and he sort of stumbles to the picnic table, holding himself upright as he clasps the edge of the wood.

"Well, son, another year gone by," he says. "Happy birthday."

"Thanks, Dad," I say, but my jaw tenses. I know he hasn't come to say nice things. I know he's going to push me, and I'm not sure I'm in the mood for it.

"That's one heck of a girl you've got there," he says. "Don't screw it up."

"Come on, Dad, don't do this."

"Do what?" he asks, rearing back like he can't imagine what I'm talking about. "Colton, you know as well as I do that nothing that good stays in your life for very long. I'm just saying you might want to be careful. You've got someone really special, and I'd hate to see you mess things up with her. She seems to truly care about you."

"I care about her, too," I say.

"I'm sure you do. But we both know that you have a tendency to sabotage anything that seems too good," he says. "That's why you keep working at jobs like you do, moving from bar to bar without thought about what it means to have a real career. If you really want to hold onto a girl like that, you've got to start thinking about your future."

"I like my job, Dad. How many times do I have to tell you that?"

"Of course you like your job," he says. "You get to stay up late, sleep in every day, be your normal irresponsible self every day of your life. Who wouldn't like that? But what happens when you've got more mouths to feed? When you've got to worry about putting a roof over your head? You can't count on tips your whole life, Colton. It's time to grow up."

I bristle, my hands tightening around the empty bottle in my hand. Why does he always have to do this? Make me feel like I'm nothing. Like nothing I do is ever good enough.

And maybe it isn't. Maybe I'm no good for Jo or Rob. Maybe I'll never be good enough.

When the door to the trailer opens and Jo steps out, I stand up, ready to go and be done with this evening. I want to get off this property and be as far away from my father as I can right now.

And the thing is, I know he means well. He truly thinks he's giving me an inspirational talk about what it means to be a man. But what he never realizes is that I'm doing the best I can. I'm just being me, and for once, I'd love for that to be enough.

"You ready?" I ask as Jo walks over.

She nods. "Sure," she says. "Goodnight, Mr. Tucker."

"Goodnight, beautiful girl," Dad says, kissing her on the cheek. "You come by and visit us again, now, you hear?"

"I will," she says with a laugh.

I take her hand in mine and wave goodbye to my family not feeling like sticking around to give everyone hugs. Most of my sisters and their husbands are carrying sleepy children back home, anyway, their hands and bellies full.

We get in the truck, and Jo slides up next to me, smiling. But my earlier happiness is gone, clouded by my father's words. His doubts.

"Where to next?" she asks.

"I thought we'd just go home," I say. "I'm kind of tired, to be honest."

"Oh," she says, her lips turning downward in disappointment. "I have a gift for you in the back. Can we stop somewhere for just a minute? Maybe the beach? It won't take long."

"Sure," I say.

I drive us to a spot overlooking the water and back up so that we can sit on the tailgate and stare out at the ocean. We both get out, and I pull the tailgate down.

Jo pulls a blanket off the hidden package in the back, but it's not a wrapped gift like I expected. It's a guitar case.

Tears spring to my eyes. What has she done?

She smiles and brings it over to me. "I hope you don't mind, but I snuck out to your grandfather's cabin and got this a few weeks ago," she says. "I found a place downtown that restores old instruments. They put brand new strings on, polished up the wood, made it look brand new."

I draw the case up beside me and flip up the latches that

hold it closed. Inside, the guitar looks pristine and shiny. Probably better than the day my grandfather brought it home from some thrift store in Alabama.

"I can't believe this," I say, trying to hold back my tears.

I run my hand along the grain of the wood, up and down the brand new strings. My grandfather would have been so happy to see his favorite instrument all cleaned up and ready to play like this. How did she know just how much this would mean to me?

"Do you like it?" she asks.

"I love it," I say, pulling her into my arms. "Thank you."

"I know you haven't played in a long time, and you may not be ready to play now, but I thought this way whenever you're ready, so is this guitar," she says. "I thought maybe it could kind of be a fresh start for you, letting go of what happened and understanding that your grandfather loved you no matter what."

I take the guitar from its case and pull the strap over my head. Even after three years, the instrument feels like home. I place my fingers on the strings and strum a chord, half expecting it to be out of tune. But it's not. It's perfect. As if it's just waiting for me to start making music again.

Jo smiles, standing in front of me, watching.

"I'm so happy you like it," she says. "You look so natural like that."

"I do?" I ask, finding my smile for the first time in the past hour since I talked to my father. "It feels good to hold it again."

"Want to play something for me?" she asks.

It's been so long, but my fingers are itching to play. Something I haven't felt in years. I try to think of what I might possibly remember well enough to play without practicing.

I smile, thinking of a Beatles song that was grandfather's favorite. He always used to say this was the best song ever written. I play the song, "Something", for Jo, accompanied by the incoming tide and the blowing of the wind.

My voice is dry and cracked at first, unpracticed at singing solos, but Jo sits next to me, her smile never dropping from her face. I watch her as I sing, realizing suddenly that my father is right.

I don't deserve her. I'm going to mess this up, just like I mess everything up eventually.

I stop the song part-way through. I'm suddenly freezing cold, my hands numb on the guitar. I'm terrified. It's as if my whole life has come down to this one relationship and everything hangs on me being the perfect guy that she needs for me to be.

"What's wrong?" she asks, placing her hand on my leg.

I pull away, quickly lifting the guitar strap over my head and placing it back in the case.

"I don't know, I guess I just don't feel up to it yet," I say. "Come on, let's go home. It's getting cold out here."

"Okay," she says, but I can hear the disappointment in her voice.

I'm a disappointment. I have been to everyone who ever mattered to me, and I don't want to watch this whole thing go up in flames right before my eyes. I can't handle it.

We get back in the truck and hardly say two words to each other on the way home, the air between us tense. And I know it's my fault. I know I should say something to make her feel better, but I can't force the words.

It's ironic, really. I'm the one they call the life of the party. The fun one. But I can't find any joy in this moment. It's all gotten too heavy, too fast. Too serious. What am I doing?

When we pull up behind the bar, my heart is tight in my chest, choking me.

"Should we watch or movie or something?" she asks. "Or do you want to come over to my place for a while?"

I shake my head, unable to find my voice.

"Colton, what's going on?" she asks. "Is it the guitar? Did I do something wrong?"

"No," I say finally. "It's nothing you did. The guitar is beautiful. I'm just tired is all. I think I may call it an early night."

"I don't understand," she says, following me back toward my garage apartment.

"It's fine," I say. "I think tonight was just a little overwhelming. I'll see you tomorrow, okay?"

"Wait," she says, her voice almost more of a cry. "I had one other present for you."

She stands with me under the light of the garage, waiting.

I have the guitar case in one hand, and I shove my other hand deep into my pockets. I know I'm acting weird, and I want to stop and just smile and be my normal fun self, but I can't even find that part of myself right now. The whole world just feels heavy.

She pulls a card from her pocket and runs her fingers over the top, taking a deep breath.

"Okay, so remember when that guy Owen came in the bar to talk to you?" she asks.

My eyebrows draw together. "Yeah?"

"Well, I didn't tell you then, but I pulled that card he gave you out of the trash," she says. "I know you said you didn't want to audition, but I couldn't let you throw away an opportunity like that."

"Jo—"

"You don't have to go if you don't want to, but I called the station and they said they're still really interested in having you come down," she says. "Owen heard about you co-writing that song with Long Road Ahead, and he says that they think you're really special, Colton. They opened a slot for you to audition, if you want to."

"What? When?" My body tenses. I didn't ask her to do that.

"Two weeks," she says. "From tomorrow. Eight in the morning. You'd go in for the last hour or so of Owen's morning show and just be yourself on air. Give it a try and see how it feels. I thought it might be fun. What do you think?"

I clear my throat. "Jo, you shouldn't have done that," I say. "I threw that card away for a reason. I don't need you to go setting things up for me like that without even asking me."

Her eyes grow wide and she looks like I slapped her across the face, she's so disappointed.

"I'm sorry," she says. "I thought you would be excited."

"What on earth made you think I would be excited?" I say, an edge of anger to my tone that I can't get control of.

"You're such a natural up on stage," she says. "You have the kind of personality that draws people to you so easily. You always make people happy. You'd be perfect for this kind of thing, Colton, I know it."

SARRA CANNON

"I like my job at the bar," I say. "You know I couldn't do a daily morning show and still keep working with you. So is that what this is about? You don't want me working at the bar anymore?"

"Don't be like that," she says, crossing her arms. "You know that's not what I meant. This is a good opportunity for you is all. If you don't want to do it, then don't. But I think you'd be great at it."

I hear my father in her words. A good opportunity. Stop being an irresponsible bartender and get a real job. The bar is fine for her because she's part owner, but me? I'm just the loser who works for her, right?

"Just think about it," she says. "If you really don't care about doing it, no big deal."

"Right," I say, taking the card from her hand. "If I don't go, then what am I really doing with my life, am I right? You can't sling drinks forever and expect to be a real man. Is that not good enough for you?"

She steps back. "Colton, I never said that."

"Not in so many words," I say. But I understand the gesture.

"All I want is for you to be happy," she says. "If you can't see that, then you're blind."

"Well, maybe I'm blind then," I say. "Look, I'm going to bed. I'll see you tomorrow, okay?"

"Don't leave like this," she says. "Angry. I didn't mean to upset you, Colton, I swear."

"It's fine," I say, even though it's not fine at all. Maybe she wants me to be something I'm not. Something I'm not capable of being. "I'll see you tomorrow at work."

She shakes her head, tears glistening in her eyes.

I hate myself for arguing with her, but I can't find it in myself to comfort her, either. Can't she see that I'm no good for her? That I'll never really be the kind of guy she needs in her life? Someone stable and good and responsible?

"Goodnight," I say, turning to open the door.

I pause, part of me hoping that she'll wrap her arms around me and tell me that everything is going to be okay. Part of me wanting her to stop me from going inside.

But she simply says, "Goodnight."

I go inside, slamming the door at the top of the garage stairs. I set the guitar case down on the couch and go to the fridge to grab another beer.

I was a fool to think life was perfect and good. Nothing that good ever lasts. Not in my life. Jo would be better off without me, anyway. I'm no good. A loser who never had a real job or a real relationship in his life.

I sit down on the couch, knowing I'm not going to be able to sleep. Not with my mind racing the way it is.

Which is when my phone rings. The caller ID says it's Willow.

I take another drink of my beer, my stomach rolling. I probably shouldn't answer, but this somehow feels like a sign. A way out of all the stress that's just been piled on my shoulders.

"Hello?"

"Happy birthday, birthday boy," she shouts. There are voices in the background singing happy birthday, and I recognize the band members. "What are you up to?"

"I'm actually sitting at home alone drinking a beer," I say.

"You've got to be kidding me," she says, laughing. "What happened to the Colton I used to love?"

"I guess I got boring," I say, laughing, but feeling no joy in the sound.

"Bullshit," she says. "We've got a party roaring out here at the beach house just for you. Why don't you come on out here and hang out for a bit? Just like old times?"

"I don't know," I say, thinking of Jo and how I left things with her.

"It'll be fun, I promise," Willow says. "Besides, we got a call from our manager that there's another band who just lost their opening act. I'm talking a huge country band, Colton. They want us to come play with them for their last few concerts. It's a big opportunity for us."

"So you're leaving town?" I ask.

"Tomorrow night," she says. "Come party with us, for old time's sake. You can't let us leave without giving us one good night. Besides, it's your birthday. Let loose and live a little."

I bite my lip and look around my lonely apartment. I know I shouldn't go, not with Jo already mad at me and things so weird between us. But damn, I could really use a good time right now. The kind of good time where everything else fades into the background for a little while.

I pull Owen's card out of my pocket and turn it over in my hands, the audition date written on the back in Jo's handwriting.

Maybe I'm really not good enough for her. Maybe she wants me to be more, just like my dad does. And maybe he's right, I'm going to be nothing but a disappointment to her anyway.

If I'm going to sabotage this relationship, I may as well have fun doing it.

"What the hell," I say. "I'll be there in half an hour."

Willow screams and tells the band. Everyone in the background is cheering as I hang up the phone and go to grab my keys. I dump the rest of my beer down the sink and stand there for just a minute, knowing I'm making the wrong decision. Knowing I might be throwing it all away.

But wondering if that's just the kind of guy I am. The kind of guy I was always meant to be.

CHAPTER 36
JO

Daddy takes my hand when the doctor finally comes in. We both know this is the appointment we've been waiting for. Finally, we're going to have some answers, and I just pray it's the kind of answers we need. I pray the neurologist is going to give us an easy treatment plan that will get my dad back on the road to being healthy again and feeling like his old self.

"Good morning, Mr. Warner. Miss Warner," Dr. Walsh says. He sits down at his desk and places a folder in front of him. He sighs, and the weary sound reaches into me, breaking my heart before he even says a word. "I'm afraid I have some tough news for you both today."

My hold on Daddy's hand tightens, and I hold back tears, waiting. I can hardly breathe.

"Mr. Warner, after looking over all your tests and consulting with a few colleagues in my field, I have come to a diagnosis," he says.

"Okay," Daddy says. "What's the verdict?"

He says it with a nervous laugh, but I can feel his hand sweating against mine.

"You have a disease called Amyotrophic Lateral Sclerosis," he says. "Also known as ALS."

Daddy's hand goes limp in mine, and when I turn to look at him, his lips are parted and trembling. "ALS?" he asks.

"What is that?" I ask. I know I've heard of ALS before, but I don't know much about it. "What are the treatments?"

My heart is racing with fear.

"It's a progressive neurodegenerative disease that affects the brain and spinal cord," Dr. Walsh says. "There are some effective therapies and a new drug that has recently come on the market that can slow the progression of the disease."

"What about a cure?" I ask. "What can we do?"

"There is no cure," my father says solemnly.

"What?" I don't want to hear his words. I don't want to believe him. No cure? What does this even mean?

"Your father is right. While there have been many scientific advances in recent years, there is still no cure for ALS," Dr. Walsh says.

"How long do I have?" Daddy asks.

Tears spring into my eyes. Wait a minute. He can't be asking how long he has to live, right? Because that's not something I can handle right now. I look from my father to the doctor, hardly able to see clearly through my tears.

"Most patients live between three and five years after their initial symptoms appear," Dr. Walsh says. "But many patients go on to live full lives for five or even as many as ten years or more. Every patient's progression is unique and difficult to predict. What we can do is start therapy right away, get you started on a drug called Rilutek that's been proven to slow the progression of the disease in some patients."

"Three to five years?" I ask. I shake my head. "I don't understand. There has to be something more we can do. Studies, more tests, some kind of treatment that's out there for this."

"We are going to do everything we can to try to slow down the progression of the disease," the doctor says. "I already have a team of doctors in the area working on putting together a comprehensive treatment plan."

"That's not good enough," I say. "Daddy?"

He takes my hand, his face calmer than I expect. "Where do we start?" he asks. His voice is so peaceful and resolved. Almost as if he was expecting this. As if he knew. "I'm ready to start treatment as soon as possible. Let's do what we can."

Dr. Walsh nods and refers to the folder on his desk. "I've already put in a prescription for Rilutek for you, so we'll get you started on that today. See how your body tolerates it and make sure there are no adverse side effects," he says. "I've also set up some appointments with the hospital's physical therapy department. They'll expect to see you on Friday."

As they discuss the plan for therapy and medication, I sit back in my chair, trying to force air into my lungs. I stare at my father, wanting to be strong for him, but not knowing how to deal with this.

ALS? I don't know what I was expecting to hear from the doctor, but I never imagined it would turn out to be something without a cure. Sure, something he might need chemotherapy for or some other rigorous drug therapy that would take time, but this? I feel powerless. Helpless.

No cure? How can that be? How can a doctor just sit there and tell us there's basically nothing we can do?

I don't want to believe it, but what choice do I have?

I take my father's hand again, and his eyes meet mine. He smiles and squeezes as he listens to the doctor's advice, but in that moment there are only the two of us in the whole world. My father is the person who has meant the most to me in my life. He's the one who has always been there for me, taken care of me, loved me unconditionally.

The news begins to truly sink in as I sit there, watching him take this diagnosis the way he's taken everything in life. With courage and determination, never giving up.

My father is the greatest man I've ever known. The bravest and most selfless. He is my rock and my anchor.

And he's dying.

CHAPTER 37
JO

After the appointment, we don't talk much about the diagnosis. I think we both just need a little more time to think about what this means for us. How it's going to change things.

"I'm tired, Jojo," Daddy says, kissing the top of my head. "I didn't get much rest last night thinking about this appointment, so I think I'm going to go lay down for a little while."

"Okay, Daddy," I say, wrapping him in a big bear hug. "Get some rest. Want me to wake you up for lunch?"

"Sure," he says with a fading smile.

I know he's trying to be strong and positive, but like me, he needs time alone to process the news. I want to give him the space he needs, but after an hour alone at the kitchen table googling everything I can find on ALS, I'm about to lose my mind.

I grab my coat and walk over to the garage, hoping

Colton's awake. I know we didn't end things on the best of terms last night, but I really need him right now.

I'm still not even sure what all that was about last night. One minute everything was going great, and the next he was acting strange. As if I'd offended him somehow. Or upset him. I'm hoping we can put it all behind us now and talk through what's going on with my dad.

But when I knock on his door, there's no answer. I take out my cell and call him, but it goes straight to voicemail. When I turn around, I realize his truck is gone. I don't know how I missed that on the way over, except that I'm not thinking clearly right now.

He must have gone out for breakfast or something. I quickly text him, asking him to call me as soon as he can. He knew we were going in for this appointment this morning, so I'm surprised he isn't picking up. Where is he?

I hope he isn't still angry with me about the guitar. Or the radio appointment. I wasn't trying to push him into anything, but he was acting like I'd made a mistake or judged him in some way. Saying that I didn't want him to keep working at the bar? That was ridiculous. I cherish all our time together, but I do think he'd be great on the radio. All I want is for him to be happy. I never meant for it to upset him.

I sigh and head back to the house. Half an hour later I try calling him again, but again I just get his voicemail. I can't imagine where he must be. Even if he is upset about last night, he still should be picking up the phone since he knows about the appointment. We'd talked about it a dozen times, and he knows I was hoping we'd get a diagnosis today.

I sit down at the table and cradle my face in my hands.

All these weeks, I've been dying for a diagnosis so that we could finally fix whatever it was that was going on. I guess in the back of my mind, I knew it might be something that didn't have a cure. Arthritis or some kind of muscular disease. But I always had faith there would be an effective treatment. Something that would help him manage the symptoms and get back to a new normal.

Only in my worst nightmares did I think he would be diagnosed with a disease that might take his life.

Online, there are stories of survivors who have lived more than five or ten years with ALS, but most of the stories I find in my search are not as positive. Over the course of the morning, I learn that ALS is a cruel disease, slowly taking away most patients' ability to talk, walk, even eat or breathe on their own. The disease does not affect the mind, though, which in some ways is a silver lining.

On the other hand, it means that the person diagnosed knows exactly what's happening to them. My father will have to watch his own body slowly fail him, and there will be almost nothing he can do about it.

Reading through the material online, my heart breaks over and over again for my father.

He has been nothing but a good man. The best man. He has spent his whole life doing so much for others, giving back to his community, raising a small child on his own without ever complaining. He deserves to live a long, full life. He deserves to someday meet his grandchildren and run and play with them in the backyard or at the lake.

But ALS doesn't care what a person deserves. It destroys, regardless of how good a man you are. It's the most unfair thing I can think of, and I would give my life not to see him go through this.

When my father comes out of his room, his hair all wild from his nap, I shut down my laptop and smile up at him, wiping tears from my cheeks.

"Hey, Daddy," I say.

"Hi, Jojo," he says. "What's for lunch?"

His words slur slightly, and I realize it's been getting worse. And that this is just the beginning.

"I thought I would make sandwiches with that home-made bread I baked yesterday," I say. "Sound good?"

"Sounds delicious," he says. "I'm starving."

I stand and start preparing the meal, not noticing that he's taken my place at the table and opened my laptop until it's too late.

"Oh, Daddy, don't," I say. I don't want him to see, which I realize is silly because of course he will want to understand. I just wish I could protect him from this. I wish I could heal him and take this all away.

"It's okay," he says, taking my hand when I place it on his shoulder. "I guess I better find out what I'm up against here."

We spend the afternoon reading through websites, looking for stories online about anyone successfully fighting the disease. We search for specialists within a hundred miles that we might be able to see.

There are a lot of tears that afternoon. A lot of frustrations. But there is also laughter and love.

Together, we search for a plan and a way to make it through the storm ahead.

CHAPTER 38
COLTON

I wake up to pain. I open my eyes to tiny slits and close them again, the light too bright and painful to face.

What the hell happened last night?

I try to sit up, but my whole body aches.

"He lives," Willow says with a laugh.

I raise my head and look around. The entire band is gathered in the kitchen of the beach house and the entire room smells like pancakes and bacon.

I groan. "What time is it?"

"After four," Willow says. She comes over to where I'm sitting on the couch and ruffles my hair. "You were out, man. Haven't seen you like that in years."

I shake my head. "Shit, four?"

I'm supposed to work tonight, and man is Jo going to be pissed. I go to check my phone, but the battery is dead.

"What exactly did we do last night?" I ask.

Greg brings over his special hangover concoction, and I down it, holding my nose against the stench. The taste brings back memories of high school hangovers and drunken nights. What the heck was I thinking, coming over here?

I instantly regret it.

I vaguely remember doing shots out on the back porch, dancing and listening to music so loud it made my teeth rattle.

"You feeling okay?" Greg asks, patting my arm.

"I feel like I've been hit by a damn truck," I say. "I can't keep up with you guys. How are y'all even up and smiling right now? Or was I the only one who got wasted last night?"

"Shit, we've been professional party hosts for years now," Greg says with a laugh. "You're just out of practice."

I try to stand, but my head is pounding.

"Whoa there, cowboy," Willow says, helping me sit back down. "Take it easy. What's the rush?"

"I'm supposed to work tonight," I say. "My shift started twenty minutes ago."

"Uh oh, someone's going to be in trouble with the boss's daughter," Greg says with a laugh.

But it's not funny at all. I think about the argument I had with Jo last night and groan. I was so stupid, getting upset with her about the guitar and the radio show. It wasn't her fault. It was just my dad's words getting all mixed up in my head. I need to get myself right so I can go and apologize. If she isn't so angry she won't talk to me.

If she is, I deserve it.

I really messed up this time, and it sucks.

"You want some breakfast?" Willow says. "We made bacon and eggs and waffles."

"I need to get in the shower and head out," I say. "I'm late."

"Aww, don't rush away like that," she says, grabbing my hand as I start up the stairs. "And don't forget to think about what we discussed last night."

I squint at her. "I have no earthly idea what you're talking about," I say. "Refresh my memory, please."

"Coming along on this leg of the tour with us," she says. "Don't tell me you forgot our entire conversation about that? You said it sounded fun."

"I did?" My brain is a fog, all of last night's memories jumbled together.

"Six weeks on the road," she says. "That's all I'm asking. I'm begging you, Colton. Help us write some good songs. We need you."

"It really would be fun," Greg says. "Just like old times, man. Playing good music. Seeing the country. Touring with some of the big names in country. It's the chance of a lifetime."

I shake my head. I can't even believe I told them I'd think about it. I can't leave Jo and the bar. Not now.

"I'll let you know," I say, not wanting to get into it right now. Right now I just want to shower and get home before Jo kills me.

"We'll swing by your place when you get off work tonight," Willow says. "We have to head out of town around two this morning, so you need to make a decision."

"Two?"

"Yeah, we have to be in Birmingham by noon," Greg says. "But we'll stop at your place to say goodbye either way."

I nod. "Okay, I'll see you guys then."

Upstairs, I strip down and step into a scalding hot shower, trying to wake myself up and get my bearings.

It was stupid to come here last night, but for some reason, I just needed to let loose. I needed to let go of responsibility and figure out what I really want. But now I know. Being in a relationship is scary, but it's worth it. I need to let Jo know how I'm feeling.

I just pray I haven't already messed things up beyond repair.

CHAPTER 39
JO

At four I head over to the bar to get things ready for the night. Knox is working with me so that I can go back to check on Daddy whenever I want, but it was Colton who was supposed to be on tonight.

I've tried to call him several times, but he isn't picking up and I'm starting to get worried about him. I really needed him this afternoon, and it isn't like him to just disappear like this. Is he still upset about last night?

His truck is still missing from the drive, and I wonder if something happened with his family. But he would have called me, right?

I don't get it, but I've got so much on my mind right now, I can't even think about it. Hopefully he's okay, but then again, if he is, why isn't he here?

"How is he holding up?" Knox asks when I walk in the door. He pulls me into a hug, and I have to fight back fresh tears.

"He's doing well, all things considered," I say. "You know

Daddy, he's always trying to find the bright side, even in this. He's determined to fight as hard as he can for as long as he can. He's found a lot of stories online and already reached out to a few people who have blogs and websites dedicated to their fight against ALS. People who have been battling it and surviving it for years."

Knox nods. "That sounds like the Rob I know," he says with a smile. "How about you? You doing okay?"

"I'm feeling a bit numb," I say. "Angry, I guess. I don't want this to be real."

"I understand," he says. "We're going to make it through this together, okay? I've still got that appointment with the specialist in Atlanta in a few weeks. Maybe he'll have some answers your local doctor doesn't have."

"I hope so," I say.

"You know Leigh Anne and I will do everything we can to help out, no matter what," he says.

"Thanks, Knox," I say. "I don't know what we'd do without you."

"Where's Colton tonight," he says. "I don't mind coming in to help, but it's weird for him to call out like this."

"He didn't even call out," I say. "He just up and disappeared. I don't know where he is."

Knox frowns. "That's strange."

I shrug. I've gone through so many emotions over the course of the past several hours that I don't even know what to feel. Disappointment. Worry. Anger. I'm praying for a really slow night at the bar so we can close up early. Heck, I considered closing down completely, but Daddy said we have to keep living and we can't let this stop us from having a normal life for as long as we can.

I know he's right, but it's hard. It feels like the whole world should have stopped this morning, at least for a little while.

An hour later our first customers arrive. I try Colton one more time, but when he doesn't pick up, I decide not to call him anymore. He'll call whenever he's ready, I guess, but I can't dedicate any more of my worrying to him right now.

Throughout the evening, I make my way out back to check on Daddy a few times, make sure he eats dinner and isn't obsessing too much over the internet.

"I'm fine, really," he says. "I'll probably watch some TV and then call it an early night. Tomorrow I want to make some calls to a few specialists I found online. See if we can get in for an appointment and a second opinion."

"Sounds good," I say, kissing his cheek. "Get some rest. I'll see you in the morning."

It's dark out, the weather turning colder. I pull my jacket closer as I walk the few feet back to the bar.

Footsteps shuffle on the pavement, and I pause, peering into the dark shadows near the back door. There are lights shining from the garage, but I forgot to turn on the light by the back door of the bar. I squint, trying to see if someone is back there.

"Hello?" I say, my feet glued to the pavement beneath them.

Someone laughs, and my heart tightens in my chest. I recognize that laugh.

I glance back toward the house, wondering if it's better to make a run for the bar or the house, but I don't move fast enough.

Bryan steps into the light, blocking my path. "Well, well,

if it isn't Josephine," he says. "All alone in the cold, dark night."

"What are you doing here?"

There is a brown bag in his hand, wrapped around a glass bottle. Liquor. I can smell it from here.

He stumbles toward me, and I take a step back.

"I was just walking by, minding my own business, when I saw you scurry back to your house for a few minutes like a little scared mouse," he says. "I came over to see if you would come back out. I've been meaning to talk to you."

My throat is dry, and I wrap my arms tightly around myself. "I have nothing to say to you."

"Now, see, why do you have to be like that?" he asks, throwing his arms to the side. Some of the liquor sloshes from the top of the bottle and lands on the ground at his feet. "An old flame comes back to town and you don't even have two nice words to say to me? Like there was never nothing between us that mattered? How do you think that makes me feel?"

Anger reaches up through my throat, burning. I force it back down, knowing that I can't push him. Nothing I say to him is going to make him realize why I want nothing to do with him. I need to say whatever it takes to get him to let me pass.

"You're right. I'm sorry," I say, hating the words as they leave my lips. "We should talk sometime, really. Catch up on old times. But right now, I've got to get back to work. Maybe some other time, though, okay?"

I step toward the back door of the bar, but he moves to counter me.

"Uh, uh, uh," he says, wiggling a finger back and forth. "You're not getting away that easily, Joey. "You owe me."

"I'm sorry?"

"That's right. You owe me. You embarrassed me both times I came in with my buddies, just trying to have a good time," he says. "You made me look like a fool, and you know how much I hate that."

You didn't need any help from me, I want to say. But I keep my lips shut. I back away two steps, ready to make a run for the house since he's blocked my way to the bar. I slowly reach for my phone in my pocket, realizing too late that I left it in the office inside the bar. Dammit.

"Don't you remember when we used to have some good times together, baby?" he asks, stepping toward me.

I back away again, but he just follows me. I'm afraid that if I run, he'll grab me. He's too close.

Inside the bar, the music's up too loud for Knox to hear me scream, and Daddy has his TV on in the back bedroom. What if no one hears me?

I shiver and take another step backward.

"We used to be real good together," he says, stepping closer. "All I want is for things to be that way again. You owe me that much after everything you put me through."

He reaches for me, and I turn and run. My boot catches on a stone, and before I can catch myself, I fall to the ground. Scrambling, I try to stand, but it's too late. Bryan wraps one strong hand around my forearm and yanks me to my feet.

"Let go," I say through clenched teeth. I try to pull away, but he has me tight.

"See that's what I never understood about you," he says,

pulling me against him, his breath stinking of booze. He leans down, his prickly beard scratching my face. "You used to be all over me with those deep brown eyes, looking at me like you wanted me to teach you how to be a woman. Remember that?"

I close my eyes, struggling against him. This can't be happening. I won't let this happen.

"All I want is for you to look at me like that again, Joey," he says. "There's no one back here but us. Come on, be a good girl."

I lift my boot and stomp on his foot as hard as I can. When he jerks, I yank my arm away and start to run, but he's faster than I expect him to be. He grabs my arm and twists me around, slamming his glass bottle against the side of my head.

Pain explodes behind my eye, and I fall to the ground. Warm blood trickles down my face, and I push against the pavement with my feet, scurrying backward.

Bryan lunges toward me, but headlights pull into the driveway, catching him off guard.

He turns to stare into the light, and I hear the truck skid to a halt. The door to the truck slams closed and Colton appears, hands drawn into fists.

"What the hell do you think you're doing?" he asks.

"None of your—" Bryan starts, but before he can say anything else, Colton's fist pounds into the side of his jaw.

Bryan stumbles back, then pushes forward, pushing Colton back to the truck. He has at least two inches of height on Colton and about sixty pounds, if I had to guess.

Fear and anger and confusion rush through me. I scramble to my feet.

Bryan takes a shot at Colton, but he ducks the throw and Bryan loses his balance. When Colton comes back around, he gets a few good punches into Bryan's gut and face, sending him back onto his ass on the ground.

I run around behind Colton, but he motions to the house. "Get inside, I'll handle this," he says.

I grab his shoulders. "Don't," I say. "Just come with me to the bar. We'll call the police."

Bryan tries to stand, his nose bleeding down his chin and onto his shirt. The bottle he was carrying is smashed on the ground beside him.

"You asshole. I think you broke my nose," he says.

"I'll break a whole lot more than that if you don't get the hell out of here," Colton says.

"Come on," I tell him, not wanting this to get any worse than it already is.

I tug on Colton's arm, pulling him back toward the door. My hands are trembling, but I manage to find the right key and unlock the back door, pushing him inside. Bryan is still sitting on the pavement, cursing and holding his nose.

"Are you okay?" he asks, reaching for the wound on my forehead.

"I'm fine," I say, pushing him away and walking into the main part of the bar.

Knox's eyes grow wide, and for an instant, he looks from me to Colton and back again. Anger flashes in his eyes. "What happened? Did he hurt you?"

"Oh great, you really think I'd do something like that?" Colton asks. "That's just great."

"No, Bryan attacked me out back," I say. "Call the police. Tell them what happened. Colton beat the crap out of him and he's still out there, but I don't want him causing more trouble."

Knox nods and disappears into the back room. There are only a handful of customers in the bar, but they are all watching us, whispering to each other and trying to figure out what happened.

I steady myself against the bar, grabbing a few cocktail napkins and filling them with ice. I press the napkins against my pulsing head, so ready for this cursed day to be over.

"Let me look at that," Colton says, touching my arm.

I pull away, so angry I can hardly see straight. "Where were you?" I ask. "I've been trying to call you all day, Colton."

He shakes his head and runs a hand through his hair. "I'm sorry," he says. "I know I was supposed to work tonight, but Willow and the band called me late last night and asked me to come out. They're leaving town early in the morning tomorrow and I didn't want them to go without saying goodbye."

"So you were out partying with the band all day and night?" I ask. "Why didn't you answer my calls?"

He almost laughs, and the sight of that smile I normally love just fuels my rage. "I guess I got a little too crazy," he says. "I totally passed out and didn't wake up until a little while ago. I drove home as soon as I could."

"Nice," I say, shaking my head. He's been passed out drunk all day while my whole world was falling apart. Some boyfriend.

"What the big deal?" he asks, following me into the store room. "I mess up one time. I'm late for one freaking shift, and you're this angry? I'm sorry, Jo, I really am. I got here as fast as I could, and I don't know what else to say. And thank god I got here when I did."

"Yes, thank you for being my knight in shining armor," I say, turning to face him. "I'm glad you were there when I needed you tonight, because if you hadn't pulled up, God knows what might have happened. But I needed you earlier today, too, and where were you? Passed out in Willow's bed? Drop dead drunk, not even thinking about the fact that my father's big appointment was this morning?"

"Oh shit," he says under his breath, running his hand through his hair again and adjusting his weight from one foot to the other. He reaches for me, but I step back. "I'm so sorry. I completely forgot. How did it go?"

Hot tears streak down my face like lava, burning me up from the inside. "Not good, okay?" I say, choking on sobs. "He's dying, if you must know. And there's not a damn thing any of us can do about it."

"What?" he asks. He grips my shoulders to steady me. "Jo, what happened? What did the doctor say?"

My face crumples and I look away, not wanting to say it out loud again. Wanting to just go to sleep and wake up to find that this whole day was just a nightmare.

"Jo, oh God, I'm so sorry," he says. "Talk to me."

"He has ALS," I say. "There's no cure. The doctor says he likely has between three and five years to live, and that's if we're lucky. So that's what I've been dealing with all day while you were out partying."

He closes his eyes, and I suddenly feel guilty for yelling at him. It isn't his fault Daddy is sick, but I'm so mad I can't think clearly. Everything has started falling apart, and I can feel my whole world spinning out of control. I don't know what to do or how to deal with it all.

"I'm sorry," he says. "I fucked up."

"Yes, you did," I say. "Which, as it turns out, is not all that rare for you, is it?"

"What?" he says.

I regret my angry words immediately. I don't mean them, but I don't know how to take them back. I don't know how to stop it. I just want someone to take all this out on, and he's the one standing here.

"I knew I never should have gotten involved with another bartender," I say, pulling away from his grip and pacing in the storeroom. "You guys with your flirty ways and your one-night-stands. You're all the same, and I knew it right from the start. How could I be so stupid?"

"Jo—"

"No, just stop it," I say. "You said you wanted to know what happened that made me so guarded all these years? That asshole out there? He used to work here, just like you. He used to flirt with all the girls and flash his pretty smile. I know he doesn't look like much now, but he used to be so handsome and charming, and when I was a teenager, I thought he was the greatest thing that ever happened to me."

I can't stop myself now, tears flowing freely down my face as I walk back and forth.

"I was only fifteen years old, but because this was a family business I was allowed to come in to the bar and do my homework, help out sweeping the floors, stuff like that," I say. "Bryan worked the bar most nights, and even though he was twenty-five and much older than I was, he started paying attention to me in a way no guy ever had before. I was young and stupid, thinking that I was falling in love and that it would be so romantic to have an older boyfriend who worked at my daddy's bar. I used to come in and flirt with him and he'd come sit at the back booth with me when my daddy wasn't working, telling me all about his life, making it sound so dangerous and fun."

Colton just stands there, listening, his arms at his side.

"Then one day he asks me to come to a party with him. A grownup kind of party," I say. Shame flares up my spine thinking about how stupid I was back then. "I lied to my dad and told him I was spending the night with a friend. I went to that party, and Bryan got me drunk. Told me he wanted me to be his girlfriend but that we'd have to keep anything that happened between us secret. He told me that he'd had dreams about us running away together, and that he was falling in love with me. And I was so stupid. I believed every word. He told me that if I'd sleep with him, it would truly make me his and would show that we were in love."

"Oh, God, Jo," Colton says.

But I keep going before he can judge me or say another word.

"So I did it," I say. "And not just once. I started going to his parties, hanging out with the older crowd, getting drunk and high on the weekends while my dad thought I was at a sleepover. I thought I was so grown up and special."

I shake my head, a bitter taste of regret in my mouth.

"I got pregnant," I say. "I'll never forget that day. I'd missed at least two periods already, but I didn't really think about it, I guess. Not until a friend said something about hers. So I stole a test from the drug store and brought it home while my dad was at work. And you know the worst part? I was actually dumb enough to be excited when those two pink lines showed up."

"I had no idea," Colton says. He steps toward me, but I lift my hands up to stop him. I don't want him to come any closer.

"I thought that with a baby on the way, Bryan would ask me to marry him," I say. "We could really run away together. I had something like five hundred dollars saved from birthday money and Christmas, and I thought that was a lot back then."

I laugh and wipe the tears from my cheek. I can't even look at Colton. I haven't told anyone about this, ever. My father and the sheriff and Bryan are the only ones who know. It's difficult to talk about, but I need Colton to understand. I need him to know why I'm so broken and messed up.

"I waited a few weeks to tell Bryan about the baby. I think part of me was scared, even then. He'd been spending less time with me, always putting me off when I asked about parties. He said he had to work late or was too tired, but I refused to see the truth," I say. "I used to daydream about how things might be. Our little family. I was so stupid."

I pause, catching my breath.

"One night when he wasn't working, I walked ten blocks to his apartment, smiling the whole way, the test tucked into a plastic bag in my backpack. He'd been drinking, hanging out with some friends. He looked angry when he opened the door, and it scared me, but I thought the baby would make everything alright."

I reach out to grab the silver bar of one of the racks in the storeroom, needing something to keep me standing so my knees didn't give out from under me. These are my most painful memories, and they are pouring out of me like ghosts that have haunted my life for years.

"He wouldn't let me come into his place," I say. "He said his friends didn't need to see me. To be honest, I think now that he must have had another girl over. So I stood out on the porch of his third-story apartment and showed him the test. I wanted him to be happy, but he got so mad. He called me a whore and told me there was no way the baby could be his. I tried to tell him that I'd never been with anyone else, but he just got so angry. I told him I needed his help, that I didn't know what to do. He started yelling at me, and I started crying. Then he hit me."

I lift my hand to my cheek, still able to remember the way the back of his hand felt against my bones.

"I fell down the metal steps outside his apartment," I say softly.

Colton moves toward me, and before I can stop him, he puts his arms around me. I feel his tears fall against my hair and onto my cheek.

"I tried to make it home, but I started bleeding and it just wouldn't stop," I say. "The sheriff found me passed out on the sidewalk about two blocks from the bar. It was late and Dad had called them in, saying I never made it home from school. They took me to the hospital, but I'd already lost the baby."

I don't have the energy to push Colton away. I sink into him, letting my tears flow. Tears for my lost youth. My own naive stupidity back then. Tears for my father and how much hell I put him through all those years ago. How much he's done to get my life back on track since.

None of it is fair, and my heart is breaking all over again.

I pull away after a while, sniffling and trying to catch my breath.

"Daddy wanted to press charges, of course," I say. "But I begged him not to. If he did that, the whole town would know what happened to me, and I just couldn't face it. So he fired Bryan and threatened to turn him in if he didn't get the hell out of town. So he left, and I spent the next few years just trying to be whole again. That's why I've never dated anyone else or opened my heart to any other man. It's too scary, Colton. It's too dangerous."

"I'm sorry," he says again. "I had no idea that's what happened, and I'm sorry you went through all that. I can't even imagine how tough it is to see him in town again. What are we going to do? Are you going to tell the cops?"

I shake my head. "I don't want to dredge all that up again," I say. "Not with everything that's going on with Dad right now."

"I understand, but you can't have him attacking you, either," he says. "He should be in jail."

"It's too late to bring charges for what happened back then, but I can press charges for the attack," I say. "I'll figure it out tomorrow. Right now, I just want to go home and crawl into bed. It's been a long day."

"I'll walk you home," he says. "Do you want me to stay with you for a while?"

I look up at him, tears clouding my vision. I realize I simply can't do this. I'm too tired. Too scared.

"Colton, I think it's better if we cooled things off for a while, okay?"

"What?" he asks.

I shake my head, fresh tears falling down my cheeks. "Right now I need to be focused on my dad," I say. "You're just a distraction right now. And to be honest, I'm not sure I can depend on you after today."

"What are you saying?"

"I'm saying it's over." I look away, unable to face him. I don't want it to end this way, but I don't know how it can continue. My heart is already so broken and raw, and I need to be strong for my father. I can't keep my heart open to Colton, too. I just can't do it.

"You don't really mean that," he says, taking my hand.

I pull away, sobs choking me. "I do," I say. "I don't have room for this in my life right now. I need people I can depend on. Not another bartender boyfriend who's just going to hurt me all over again."

He steps back, as if I've just punched him in the gut.

"Is that really what you think of me? You think I'm like him?" He points toward the door.

I shake my head, not knowing what to say. I don't know how to do this.

"If that's what you think of me, then you don't have to say anything else," he says. "I love you, Jo, but what I need in my life is someone who believes in me. I thought you were that person, but now I see you're not. You never were."

He walks away, slamming the store room door behind him. I lean against the wall, sliding down until my butt hits the floor. I cradle my face in my hands, letting all the tears I've held back for years flow out of me like a river of sorrow. A river of regret.

CHAPTER 40
COLTON

My heart is breaking as I step out into the night. The cops are out back with Bryan in cuffs. He's leaning against the side of the police car, his shirt stained with blood.

I really don't want to deal with this right now, but the officer on duty wants to talk to me about what happened. Jo's dad comes out of the house, but I don't have a chance to talk to him. He rushes inside to find Jo.

I tell the officer everything that happened, scared that they might try to charge me with assault.

Jo comes out, though, her face streaked red with tears. Seeing her out here like this, dealing once again with a man who broke her heart into pieces when she was just a child, makes me so angry and sad I don't know what to do.

I love her with all of my heart, and all I want is for her to be happy and to feel safe.

I want to talk to her when the cops are done questioning

SARRA CANNON

me, but she's already gone inside with her dad when they drive away, Bryan in the back.

I walk alone to my apartment, feeling empty.

Maybe she's right. Maybe she would be better off without me in her life right now. She doesn't need me to screw things up, not when her father's life is on the line.

Without even thinking about it, I get my bag from the closet and begin filling it with my clothes. I pack up everything I own into a single duffel and a box, realizing that this is what my life amounts to right now. I've disappointed everyone I love in one way or another.

Jo needed me to be there for her today more than anything, and just like I did with my grandfather, I missed it. I forgot about the most important appointment they've had so far, and I wasn't there when she needed a shoulder to cry on or someone to share her fears.

She's better off without me.

They all are.

At two, when I hear the band's bus pull up, my mind is made. I'm going with them.

I set the note I've written on the counter in the kitchen and take one last look around the apartment.

Maybe it was stupid to hope that I could make something of my life. That I could be someone important. I know now that being a man has nothing to do with what kind of job you have or how much money you make. It means being there for the people who depend on you. The people who love you.

I couldn't do that for her, so instead, I'll give her this last gift. If I'm nothing more than a distraction, I'll take myself

292

out of the equation and get out of her life. It's the best thing I know to do for both her and her father.

I grab my bags and my guitar and head out to the curb where the bus is waiting. Willow and the guys cheer as I step onto the bus, but I feel numb. Hollowed out.

I swipe at a tear on my cheek as I look back at Jo's house and the bar that's come to be my home, not sure that anything in my life will ever matter as much as these past few months with her.

CHAPTER 41
JO

olton is gone. I woke up this morning to go apologize, realizing that I'd made a huge mistake yelling at him the way I did. I want to explain to him that it had just been a hard day and that I wasn't thinking straight.

But the apartment is empty. I find a note on the kitchen counter, written sometime in the middle of the night.

DEAREST JO,

WORDS CANNOT EXPRESS JUST HOW MUCH THESE PAST FEW months together have meant to me. I have never known a woman with such fire and determination and loyalty. I can honestly say that I'm a better man for having loved you.

The last thing I would ever want is to hurt you. I'm so sorry I wasn't there when you needed me most. You see, I realize now that I'm not good enough for a woman like you. You deserve so much more, and I hope with all my heart that you find that someday.

Long Road Ahead asked me to go back on tour with them, and it seemed like the perfect opportunity to give you the space that you want and need.

Please give your father my love and tell him I said to keep fighting. If anyone can beat this, it's Rob.

And please know that no matter how many miles there are between us over the next few months, I will never stop thinking of you.

I will never stop loving you.

YOURS,
Colton

PART OF ME WANTS TO RIP IT INTO SHREDS AND STOMP THE pieces into the ground. Losing him has ripped my heart from my chest, and I don't know how I'll ever get over him.

But part of me knows it's my own fault. I asked him to open up to me, but I never was able to do the same for him. Not really. Somewhere deep inside, my walls were still up, just waiting for a chance to break things off before I let him hurt me. So instead, I ended up hurting myself. Pushing away the one man I ever truly loved.

Over the next few weeks, I throw myself into researching ALS. I study everything I can find in the library on campus and on the internet. I talk to specialists and with Knox's help and money, arrange appointments from Atlanta to New York.

I hire a few new bartenders to help out so that I can spend more time with my father, and Knox is sweet enough to help manage the place in our absence. I miss Colton every single day, wondering what he's up to out on the road and if he's happier there. Every time one of the band's songs plays on the radio, I have to turn it off for fear of my heart breaking all over again.

Bryan spent a few nights in jail and then left town. I hope he never comes back, and I will never forgive him for hurting me again. Not once, but twice. And the second time, he played a part in me losing the best thing that ever happened to me.

I regret my words to Colton that night. Telling him that he was nothing more than a bartender. He's so much more than that. He didn't deserve that from me, and I hope that someday I get the chance to tell him that.

Time passes faster than I want it to, and I do everything I can to spend as much of it with my daddy now when he's still walking and talking and smiling. He's in such good spirits, determined to live life to the fullest. He talks about taking a trip to see the Grand Canyon, something he's wanted to do his whole life and just never took the time to do.

"No regrets, Jojo," he says with a smile. "I have no idea how much time I have left on this earth, but I'm going to make the most of it."

I love that man more than words can say, and I try not to think too much about what the coming months or years may bring. I try to stay in the moment and live each day as it comes. Some are harder than others.

But without Colton, it's hard to have no regrets. I've lost him, and I will never forgive myself for that.

CHAPTER 42
COLTON

A chance of a lifetime. That's what the band keeps saying about this opportunity to tour with one of the biggest country bands. We've been traveling all over the south for the past couple weeks, the band opening almost every night to a sold out crowd.

I know it's a great opportunity for them, and I should be grateful to be here sharing it with them. This is a part of life that most people never get to see. A true behind-the-scenes look at fame in the making.

But it's hollow for me. Empty without her.

I stand in the wings watching the band as they finish up their set, but all I can think about is home. What is she up to tonight? How is her dad doing these days? Have they gotten any answers?

I spent some time online looking up ALS, and it broke my heart. I want nothing more than to be there for her now. I know that her father is everything to her, and the news that she's going to lose him someday to this terrible disease has to be tearing her apart.

I know that Rob is a fighter, though, and he'll never give up. He'll never stop looking for a cure or a way to live life to the fullest. I just wish I could be there to witness his strength. His journey. I wish I could be a part of their lives, no matter how tough the days ahead might be.

There are days I think about going home. Telling her I'm sorry and that I want to make things right between us. That I want a chance to prove to her that I could be the man she needs.

But I'm scared.

I don't want to hurt her any more than I already have, and if she doesn't want me in her life, I don't want to push her. I just want her to be happy and safe.

I step away from the stage and walk back to the bus. It's quiet in here with the band gone, and I sit down at a small booth and table toward the front. I pull out my guitar and strum a few chords, wondering what my grandfather would have to say about all of this. Would he tell me to go home and fight for the girl?

God, I wish he was here right now to tell me what to do.

I wish he could tell me whether he forgives me for not being there that day in the hospital. I miss him so much, even now.

I cradle the guitar close, letting my fingers work the strings, finding a melody that feels right. Making music is such a holy thing. Like praying and getting an unexpected answer inside the music. There's always something to learn inside the notes of a good song, and every good songwriter has to dig deep down inside themselves to find the tune that's really going to mean something. It's like stripping yourself bare in front of everyone, showing them all the ugly things you've done and felt.

I realize in this moment that this is why I stopped playing after my grandfather died. I didn't want anyone else to see my shame, but without being true to my own emotions, no music could push through. Nothing true, anyway.

So here alone in the bus, I test it out for the first time in years. I pour myself into the instrument and the sound of the chords, searching for something that strikes a match in my soul.

And when I find the right combination, tears spring to my eyes.

My heart opens, bleeding onto the strings with every note I play. And in return, the music teaches me something I never knew about myself.

I've spent my entire life trying to be people's sunshine. My mother has called me that since the day I was born, saying that her precious baby boy—a true gift after so many girls—was there to bring her joy. She said that I smiled the day I was born and every single day after, and that my gift was to make people happy.

So I hung my own worth on that idea. Making other people happy. I learned how to make them smile when they were feeling down. I learned just the right thing to say when someone needed a laugh or a bright spot in their day. I focused on having fun and being the life of the party.

But I never have truly thought about what I want in this world. About what makes me happy.

The truth of it hits me straight in the chest like a bullet.

This is the reason I've struggled with long-term relationships. The reason my relationship with my father has always been so strained. I was so focused on trying to make sure people were having fun that I didn't really open up to them. I never truly became vulnerable to show them who I am. I never really stood up for what I want or fought for what would make me happy.

With my father, I've never felt good enough, because nothing I ever did seemed to make him happy. With my girlfriends, the minute things got rough and I didn't know how to fix it, I bailed or wasn't there the way they needed me to be. The extent of my joy-bringing had come to an end, because cracking jokes or throwing a party can only take you so far.

Real relationships are made in the moments of nakedness, when your soul is laid bare. And when Jo finally opened her past up to me, I left, thinking that was what she wanted from me. Thinking that would be best for her.

But I realize in this moment, as I play a new song, that I did exactly the opposite of what she truly needed. I left because I thought I couldn't make her happy.

But happiness is not what she needs. She needs love, and if I simply had the courage to follow my own heart and love her, then I would be exactly the man she always needed me to be.

The doors to the bus swing open and Willow climbs on, giggling, still high from the performance, but I'm not here anymore. I'm already miles away in my mind.

"Colton, did you hear us out there?" Willow says. "Did we nail it or what? I swear, that crowd was magic."

I look up from the guitar and the small slip of paper on

the table where I've scribbled a few lyrics.

She eyes me. "Why do you have that goofy, distant look on your face?" she asks. "What are you up to?"

She walks over and snatched the paper off the table, reading.

"Holy shit, this is good," she says. "Are you writing again?"

Her hand is trembling. I know that handing this song over to her would make her day. Hell, maybe it would make her whole career.

"Can I ask you a question?" I say.

"Sure, whatever," she says, still reading and nodding her head. "I want to hear this. Do you have a melody in mind yet?"

"When you guys recorded Picking Up The Pieces, how come you never listed me as the co-writer?" I ask.

"Huh?" she asks, not even looking up. As if nothing matters to her but her next hit song.

"Why didn't you share credit with me?" I ask. "On the album, it only lists you as the songwriter. I'm just wondering why you never thought to include me. I mean, most song-writers get royalties for their work, right?"

She looks up, jerking her head back, as if this is some-thing she's never considered.

"Is this about money?" she asks. Her mouth twists and she shakes her head. "If you want some money for the songs, you know I'm happy to talk about it. I never figured that mattered to you."

"It's not really about the money," I say, pulling the guitar strap over my head and placing the instrument in its case. "It's about the fact that you never thought about it."

"Colton, what are you getting at? Why are you asking me about that? It's been years since we recorded that song."

"You know that I didn't even know you guys were going to record it until I heard it on the radio?" I ask. "Imagine that. Writing a song and not even knowing it was going to be on the radio, as if I had nothing to do with it."

"You gave me that song," she says. "You wrote it for me."

"I wrote it with you," I say. "There's a difference."

"So, what? You want credit for it now, after all this time?" she asks. "I'm not even sure how to do that, but I guess I could call the record company if you want me to."

I shake my head and stand. She doesn't even understand why this matters to me. Have I failed to stand up for what I want so often that people think I'll be happy even when they're walking right over me?

How have I been so blind?

"Where are you going?" she asks when I grab my duffel bag from the back. "Colton, come on, if this is about money or something, I told you. I can write you a check. Just name a number."

I take the slip of paper from her hand and stuff it in my pocket.

She frowns and stares up at me. "What's going on?"

"I'm sorry, Willow," I say. "I appreciate the chance to tour with you guys for a while, but I've got someplace I need to be. I'll see you around, okay?"

I step past her in the narrow hall, but she places her hand on my arm.

"Don't go," she says. "I need you."

I smile. "Someone else needs me more," I say. "Tell the

guys I said goodbye. I'll catch up with y'all next time you're back home. Goodbye, Willow."

She stares, mouth open, as I walk down the steps and out into the night, finally ready to follow my heart.

CHAPTER 43
JO

I awake to another day, the sun streaming in through the curtains. I take a deep breath and close my eyes, not ready to get out of bed.

Like most mornings, my first thought is of my father. How will be feeling today?

There is a part of me that hopes to see some kind of improvement. A better day or a step in the right direction, but Dr. Walsh has told us that with ALS, there may be good days and bad days, but there is never significant improvement. The best we can hope for is a slow progression. More time on the clock.

I swipe at a tear, determined that I will not break down today. Today I will be strong for my daddy. And for myself.

Today will be a good day, because we're together.

I wrap the blankets tighter around my arms and an image of Colton flashes through my mind. I close my eyes and imagine that first night together in the cabin, and what it felt like to lie next to him until dawn, tangled up together.

I miss him more than I ever could have imagined.

I want to call him and tell him to come home, but I'm scared. What if he is having the time of his life? What if he's realized that we were a burden to him?

I pull his letter from the drawer of my bedside table and read it for the hundredth time.

Does he still think of me?

It feels like he's been gone forever.

I fold the note and put it back in the drawer. I shower and dress for the day in jeans and a long-sleeved t-shirt that's soft and comfy. I put on my favorite fuzzy socks and pad out to the kitchen where my father is already awake and having his first cup of coffee.

He has been having more trouble with his hands lately. Grasping things, especially when they are small. We've switched to mostly plastic in the house, paper cups with no handle and a wide base. He's doing great, and I'm so proud of him for not giving up.

"Good morning, Jojo bear," he says. "How's my beautiful girl?"

"Good morning, Daddy," I say, kissing his temple and giving him a hug. "How's the coffee?"

"Strong," he says. "Grab a cup and sit down."

"I was thinking about making muffins," I say.

He laughs and shakes his head, but when I turn to question him, he looks down at his tablet and continues to swipe through news articles. He used to read the newspaper every morning, but now that it's harder to hold onto and turn the pages, he decided it was time to make the switch to new technology. We bought him a cutting-edge new tablet, and believe it or not, he loves it.

"What are you laughing at?" I ask, taking my favorite mixing bowl down from the cabinet.

"Jo, sweetheart, look around," he says. "What do you see in this kitchen?"

I frown and look around. Okay, so the counters are covered in baked goods. Homemade bread. Muffins. Cakes. Pies. Cookies. Most of them are wrapped, though, with name tags attached. This afternoon, I plan to play the baked-goods-fairy in town and deliver them all over town.

"Do you not see the humor in the fact that your first thought this morning is to make more muffins?" he asks, his shoulders shaking from laughter.

I purse my lips, trying not to smile, but I can't help myself. "Maybe you're right," I say. "I may have gotten a little bit out of hand."

"A little?" he asks. "Try crazypants."

"Daddy," I say, smacking him on the shoulder. "Baking is how I cope with stress."

"Oh, I remember," he says. "When you were fifteen I thought I was going to have to buy a whole new house just to store all the bowls and pans and things you kept buying online. I think I gained twelve pounds that year off cookies alone."

I smile and shake my head. "I can't help it," I say. "Let me have this one thing."

"Bake away, my dear," he says. "But first, grab some coffee and a muffin and sit down with your old man for a minute."

I humor him, pouring myself half a cup of coffee and filling the rest with cream and sugar. I choose a cranberry muffin from one of the many overflowing baskets on the counter and sit down across from him.

"What's up?" I ask. I can tell he has something specific he wants to talk about.

"How are you holding up, kiddo?" he asks.

I shake my head. "I'm fine, Daddy," I say. "We're going to get through this."

He raises an eyebrow. "Oh, I wasn't talking about the diagnosis," he says. "I'm talking about your breakup. And don't pretend you haven't been thinking about him. As much as I'd love to believe those frequent tears are all about me, I know I can't take all the credit. So spill it. How are you really doing?"

I lower my head and try to hide fresh tears. I blink and cut my eyes at him. "You know me too well," I say.

"You're my Jojo bear," he says. "It's just been the two of us for a long time. I might even know you better than you know yourself."

I nod. "You might," I say. I take a deep breath. "I miss him, Daddy. More than I thought I would."

"Of course you do," he says. "You love him. Anyone can see that."

"So why did I tell him I wanted to break up?" I ask. "I don't even know anymore. After he disappeared all day and then seeing Bryan again, I don't know. I just snapped. I was so scared that I was messing up all over again, choosing someone that would only hurt me. But it wasn't really him I was afraid of. I think I was afraid of myself."

"What do you mean?"

"I've been thinking about it a lot lately," I say. "I worked so hard to learn how to protect my heart and shut people out. Before Colton came along, I'd gotten pretty damn good at it."

"You're telling me," he mumbles.

"I'm not even sure I realized I was doing it. All I kept thinking anytime a guy would hit on me or someone would try to get close to me was that opening myself up in any way was just asking for pain and regret," I say. "As long as I kept my world small, I thought I'd be able to control it. I thought I'd be safe, and that nothing could touch me like that ever again."

"Life doesn't work like that," he says.

"No," I say, wiping away a tear. "It doesn't."

My father takes my hand across the table, leaning in. "Pain comes to us no matter how hard we try to shut it out," he says. "What you were really shutting out was the chance at happiness."

His words hit me so hard, they nearly knock the breath from my lungs.

He's right. I denied myself happiness and love for so long, thinking that safe and alone was better than risking it all for something more. If I kept my life on an even keel, I could never fall very far.

"I don't know what to do," I say, meeting his eyes. "I don't know how to fix this, and I'm terrified I'm going to spend the rest of my life regretting the fact that I pushed him away. That I didn't open up to him until it was too late."

My dad takes in a breath and squeezes my hand. "Here's the thing about regret," he says. "We all make mistakes. We all experience disappointment and pain. But it's the things we let slip through our fingers because we were too afraid to go after them that we regret the most."

I look at him, unable to stop the flood of tears.

"I'm so sorry that you were hurt so badly when you were

so young, but that's on me," he says, his bottom lip trembling. "I was so wrapped up in my own sorrow, still mourning the loss of your mother and throwing myself into my work that I wasn't paying attention to the one person who mattered most to me in the world. That's why after it happened, I broke things off with Kelly. I cut back on my hours and hired more help. I made you my sole priority, Jojo. Because when you realize that someone is the most valuable person in your life, you do whatever it takes to make them feel loved. To make them feel safe and important."

I scoot closer to him until our arms are touching.

"I realized a long time ago that the only way to live a life without regret is to give all of yourself to everything that matters," he says. "If it makes you happy or makes your heart sing, if it seems worthwhile or touches your heart in the deepest places, then you open yourself up and you give. You risk everything, even your own heart, to follow your dreams and your passions. Yes, you're going to fall along the way. Some people that you trust will hurt you or fail you, but I'm telling you Jo, the rewards and the love you receive, the lessons you learn and the person you become, will make it worth any pain that you feel. That's why I've always encouraged you to go out and spend time with friends, put yourself out there, follow your dreams of cooking or starting a catering business. Whatever you want to do, you should do it.

"None of us are guaranteed tomorrow, and that has never felt more real to me than it does right now. You made some mistakes, but you cannot continue to punish yourself for that your entire life. You deserve to be loved, Jojo. You deserve to follow your dreams, but none of that will be possible if you aren't willing to risk getting hurt. Being vulnerable. Letting go of that fear that holds you back time and time again. You can't hide from life, Jo. Not anymore."

I stand and collapse into my father's lap, letting him rock me like he did when I was just a little girl. I cry until there are no more tears, the truth of his words hitting home in a way I never expected.

"You're right," I say, laughing through the tears. "I know you're right. But it's too late, Daddy. I already messed things up between us."

He raises an eyebrow and points to an article on his tablet. "According to the internet, Long Road Ahead is playing in Atlanta tonight. That's only a few hours from here, so if you get on the road now, you might even beat them there."

I feel a million years lighter. I'm scared and nervous and trembling, but I know with a sudden fierceness exactly what I have to do. Even if he tells me he doesn't want to be with me. I have to tell him how I feel.

I kiss my father's cheek and stand up, wiping the tears from my cheeks.

"Daddy, I have to go," I say. I kiss him again and run back to my bedroom, giddy and terrified at the same time.

I throw on my boots and leather jacket, grab my purse and run for the door.

My dad is laughing and crying at the same time. He pulls me into a hug.

"Go get him, Jojo," he says. He throws a fist into the air and lets out a loud whoop.

I roll my eyes and laugh through my own tears. My dad is crazy, but he's mine, and I love him more right now than my heart can contain.

Trembling, I get into my car and drive, wiping tears from my eyes so that I can see the road. I haven't even had time to set my GPS yet, but I just start driving, wanting to get to Atlanta as fast as I can.

The radio is tuned to the local country station, and as the current song winds down, a familiar voice comes on. I slam on my breaks and stare at the radio. How is this possible? Am I dreaming?

I turn up the volume and pull over to the side of the road.

With trembling hands, I pull my phone from my purse and look at the date. I laugh and bring a hand to my mouth, hardly able to believe it. Today is the day I had set up the radio interview with Owen in the Morning.

Colton's voice comes through loud and clear. "Well, I'll tell you, Owen, it was quite the adventure," he says. "You wouldn't believe how crazy it gets out there on the road."

"Is it really all booze and women like they show in the movies?" Owen asks. "I've always wanted to know what that would be like, touring with a famous country music band."

"There are definitely a lot of fans who will do just about anything to get an autograph, and some of them, as you can imagine, are ladies," Colton says. "But it's the weirdest thing. The minute I got on the road, there was only one woman I could think about, and no one else in the world mattered."

"Oh, really?" Owen says. "Folks, I think we have a little romance brewing here on our morning show. Care to fill us in on who the lucky lady is?"

My phone dings and I see it's a text from Penny. All in caps.

TURN ON YOUR RADIO, NOW!!!!

I laugh and text her back.

I'm listening.

I'm sure I look like a fool parked on the side of the road, radio blasting, tears streaming down my face, but I don't care. My heart is open and the whole world is brand new.

"I believe you may have met her," Colton says. "She's just about the most gorgeous woman in the state of Georgia, if I may be so bold. Heck, maybe even the world."

"You wouldn't happen to be talking about that cute little bartender I saw you cozying up to over at Rob's, now would you?" Owen teases.

"Now, I'm not the kind of guy to kiss and tell, but if that bartender happens to be listening right now, there's something I'd like to share with her right now, if you'll let me."

"Oh, please," Owen says. "I'm absolutely captivated by this story, Colton. Tell us what you have for us."

"Before I left to go on the road, she and I had some harsh words," Colton says. "We said some things we didn't mean, and before we could clear the air, I left. But I'm telling you—and if any of you out there have ever been in love, you'll understand me here—I could not get her out of my mind. Not even touring with a famous band could distract me from her. I missed her like crazy."

"Gosh, that sounds like the perfect story for a country song," Owen says with a laugh.

"And that's exactly what I wanted to share with you all today," Colton says. He clears his throat, and I hear his fingers tap the strings of his guitar.

My hand goes to my mouth. I'm breathless, not believing this is real. Wanting to remember this moment for the rest of my life, I close my eyes and listen. I open my heart and am present in the moment in a way that I have never been before. I release all my fears about what might happen or where things will end up between us. Instead, I just think about now, and how lucky I am to have this right here and now.

"Last night while the band was onstage, I picked up this guitar for the first time in years," Colton says. "It used to belong to my grandfather, and after he passed away, I had a hard time playing. But this woman, she encouraged me to pick it up again. For my birthday this year, she surprised me with this guitar, all cleaned up with new strings and everything."

"She definitely sounds like a special woman, Colton, I'll tell ya," Owen says.

"She is. She's the best, really, and I hope she's listening right now," Colton says.

"And if she is, what do you want to say to her?" Owen asks.

"If you're listening, Boss, I just want you to know I wrote this song for you," he says. "And that it comes from the heart."

I press my lips together to keep from crying out. He remembered our conversation on the beach road when I asked him to write a song for me. He still loves me. He has to.

The music begins coming through clear and simple. It's all Colton. His voice. His fingers on the guitar. And I know that this is the greatest gift he could have given me. Even before he begins to sing, I can feel the love inside the music, and I know that he has missed me just as much as I have missed him.

"There's never been another woman who has turned my head like you do," he sings. "There's never been another lover who has touched my heart like you do. And if you're listening to my heart true, I hope you know how much I miss you."

Hands trembling, I put my car in gear and pull a U-turn, heading back toward town. The radio station is just on the edge near the beach, and I listen as I drive, wanting to get there to be with him.

"Because there's nothing in this world that means so much to me. And there's no one in this universe that I'd rather be, waking up next to."

His voice is shaky, but clear, and the music is beautiful and heartfelt.

"So baby please tell me you're out there, thinking about how we almost lost something that's just too good to lose. Darlin', please tell me you're willing to give me another chance to show you what I'd rather choose," he sings. "Because we were meant to be. Don't let the past take that away from me."

I pull up at the station and slam the car into park. I leave my keys in the ignition and run straight for the door. The receptionist stands, mouth open.

"Can I help you?" she asks.

"You hear that?" I ask, pointing to the speakers playing our song. "He's singing that for me."

The woman puts her hand over her heart. "Oh my goodness, darlin', you better get your pretty self in there," she says. "Second door on the left and down the hall."

"Thank you," I say.

I take off through the hallway, down to the second door on the left, pushing through and running full speed down to the studio.

A few people wandering the halls stop to question me, but I don't pay any attention to them. All I care about is finding those deep green eyes, and showing him that I'm here.

At the end of the hallway, Colton sits behind a large window that takes up half the wall. His guitar is cradled against him, looking so natural, like he was always meant to play music. Like he's finally truly come home to who he was meant to be.

Owen tilts his head in my direction and raises and eyebrow. Colton's eyebrows come together, questioning, but the moment he looks up, his hands freeze on the guitar and the music is silent.

Our eyes meet across the distance, and I lift a hand in a small wave, tears streaming down my face.

He smiles, his eyes filling with tears. "If you'll excuse me for a second, Owen, I believe I've got something I need to take care of real quick," he says.

"For you folks that aren't here in the studio, the woman in question has just driven up and run into the studio," Owen says. "I'm going to tell you guys, this is the single most romantic moment in WKTX Fairhope history. I'm not much of an emotional kind of guy most of the time, but watching these two young folks, I have to be honest.

I've got a little tear in my eye. I wish you all could see this."

Colton sets his guitar down on the floor and steps out of the studio. He crosses to me and in one swift motion, lifts me into his arms.

"I'm so sorry," he says, his breath warm against my cheek. "I never should have left. I thought maybe you'd be better off without someone like me to screw up your life, but I realized something when I was out on the road."

"What was that?" I ask, holding onto him so tightly I never want to let go.

He pulls away and looks into my eyes. "I realized that I wasn't me without you anymore. That I had found the one person in the world who completes me, and if that was true, then you couldn't possibly be better off without me. That we belong to each other, Jo, and that we should never be apart again."

His words settle into my heart, healing so much of my past. Making me whole again.

"I'm so sorry that I said all those things to you," I say. "I was so scared of getting hurt again, Colton, that I thought it would be better to push you away than to risk my heart. But the thing is that being without you hurt more than anything. I love you."

"I love you, too," he says.

He kisses me then, all of his love poured into that one moment.

Around us, everyone begins to applaud, and I pull away, burying my face in his chest so that no one can see how red my cheeks are.

"So you're home to stay?" I ask, finally.

"Home is wherever you are," he says. "For the rest of my life."

He lifts me into his arms again and swings me around. I lean my head back and laugh, the sound true and free and, for the first time in my life, completely fearless.

EPILOGUE

JO

I t's a gorgeous spring day. The morning sun is shining, its warmth like a promise against my skin.

I reach for my father's hand. He holds them in a curled position most of the time these days, but I place my hand over his and squeeze. Kelly is on his other side and she holds onto his arm.

Daddy smiles, a single tear sliding down his cheek as he stares out across the large expanse of the Grand Canyon.

"I have dreamed of this moment," he says. "But never in all my dreams did I imagine it to be this beautiful. This much of a miracle."

Colton puts his arm around my shoulders and we share a glance. I know that there will not be many more moments like this for my father. The medicine has not slowed the progression of the disease, and over the past few months, his health has declined so much faster than any of us expected. But we take each day as it comes, making the most of the time we have together.

My father is an angel, never complaining about his struggles. I know that more than anything, he worries about me. He is almost more upset about the thought of me having to watch him decline than he is about actually going through it himself, and if that doesn't speak to the kind of man he is, nothing else will.

He is selfless and brave and stronger than any one person should ever have to be. I am blessed to have him as my father.

The doctors say he will not be walking much longer, so Knox has already filed for the necessary permits to build special accommodations in the house and the bar for a wheelchair.

Some days, I still cry. I cry for all of those who have been touched by such a cruel disease. I cry for those who have had even less time than what we have had. I cry for myself and the fact that my father may never meet my children.

But most days, I am happy. I am grateful for every moment we are able to spend together.

"Woohooo," my father shouts, his voice echoing across the canyon, along with his laughter.

Beside Colton, Knox joins in, calling out so loud that his voice is returned to us a dozen times over. Leigh Anne laughs and bumps his shoulder, her eyes bright and filled with joy. I went with him last week to pick out her engagement ring, and I can't wait to see it on her finger soon.

Colton can't resist joining in, and soon our entire group is sending our voices out into the great expanse. If anyone else is nearby, they probably think we've lost our minds, but I don't care. Times of love and laughter are more precious than anything, and life is too short to worry about what other people think.

I lean into Colton, resting my head against his chest. Ever since he came home, we have been closer than ever, sharing more than I ever thought I would share with a man. He pushes me and encourages me and, best of all, loves me no matter what.

We often spend our Sundays at his grandfather's cabin. The roof is fixed and most of the dust and cobwebs have been cleaned out. We spend lazy days playing checkers or hanging our feet off the end of the dock, talking about our dreams and what we want most out of life.

He will soon be starting his job with the morning show in Fairhope, and even though I'll miss him working at the bar with me, I'm so proud of him for finding something he truly loves. Owen thought he was a natural and hired him practically on the spot.

When Colton told his father about the job, the man embraced him and told him he was proud of him, and I know that moment meant the world to Colton, even if he won't admit it.

And my dreams?

I finally decided to take the leap. The bar closed down two days ago so that the contractor could break ground on a new addition. All of the proper permits and loans are in place, thanks to some help from Penny. We'll reopen in six weeks if all goes well. Instead of Rob's Bar, we'll now become Rob's Bar and Grille. A subtle but important change.

I'm nervous and scared, but I'm learning to embrace the fear. I'm learning to take risks when it matters. To follow my heart where it leads. To be vulnerable so that I can truly experience all that life has to offer, both good and bad.

To give all of myself to the things and the people that matter most.

No regrets.

ABOUT THE AUTHOR

Sarra Cannon is the author of several series featuring young adult and college-aged characters, including the bestselling Shadow Demons Saga. Her novels often stem from her own experiences growing up in the small town of Hawkinsville, Georgia, where she learned that being popular always comes at a price and relationships are rarely as simple as they seem.

Sarra owns her own publishing company and has sold three-quarters of a million copies of her books. She currently lives in Charleston, South Carolina with her programmer husband, her adorable redheaded son, and her beautiful daughter.

Love Sarra's books? Join Sarra's Mailing List to be notified of new releases and giveaways!

Also, please come hang out with me in my Facebook Fan Group: Sarra Cannon's Coven. We have a lot of fun in there, and I often share exclusive short stories and teasers in the group.

Want more? Come join us LIVE three times a week on my YouTube channel.

Connect With Sarra Online:
www.sarracannon.com

www.ingramcontent.com/pod-product-compliance
Lightning Source LLC
Chambersburg PA
CBHW051954240626
47153CB00005B/1755